Brenna Lyons

BRIDE BALL

FIREBORN
PUBLISHING

FIREBORN PUBLISHING COPYRIGHT

STATEMENT

This book is written in US English.

PUBLISHER

FIREBORN
PUBLISHING

**PO Box 5216
Haverhill, MA 01835**

DEDICATED TO...

Grimm, the first love of my fantasy life, as it is for so many fantasy authors.

Tamer, the love that was meant to be.

PROLOGUE

"It really is time, Edward," King Benjamin decreed with some measure of finality. "You've put this off long enough."

Edward sighed, staring out through the windows that overlooked the royal gardens. He'd suspected this was coming when his father had sent for him. "Perhaps, if I went abroad—"

"Rulers of Lenvia have always wed our own."

Again, it was absolute. Twenty-five was an unseemly age to be a royal bachelor, and his bride must be Lenvian by birth. If only the whole thing wasn't so tedious.

"Come now. She needn't be nobility or royalty. Your own mother wasn't, when I met her."

Edward winced, biting back the completely uncharitable observation that his mother was precisely the type of woman he didn't want.

Alana was pretty enough, but as far as Edward could tell, she'd never loved King Benjamin, even when he was Prince Benjamin. She was little better than a long-term prostitute and surrogate, highly paid to be sexually inventive and receptive...and to provide at least one heir to the throne. She had produced only Edward, by her choice, and so he was in the hot seat.

"If you went out among the people," his father suggested, setting off the horror show in Edward's mind.

"I'm always too visible. The moment someone spies me, I am swarmed with women."

"Eager women," Benjamin noted.

"Shameless wantons," he corrected.

"And the problem with that is what? I rather enjoyed the game."

You never grew beyond the game. "So, did I, when I was twenty. I find it tedious now."

For a moment, they seemed to arrive at an impasse.

His father broke the silence. "You will marry in the next year, Edward."

"And if I don't marry? What will you do? Disinherit me?" From the standpoint of his sexual exploits, that might be a blessing. "There's still Uncle Matthew and Darren," he pointed out.

"Lenvian law allows me to arrange a marriage for you, if you refuse to wed. Like her or not, you choose someone...or I do it for you."

His heart stuttered at the idea of an arranged marriage. His mind raced, searching for some way to find what he sought. "A series of Grande Balls," Edward suggested. "Bride Balls."

Benjamin raised an eyebrow in surprise. "You're saying?"

"It will be done my way," he insisted.

"If it results in a bride, your search can be conducted in any manner you wish, Edward."

"I have your word on that?" he asked.

"You have it."

SECTION I:

CINDER

CHAPTER ONE

Amber turned from the table, wiping flour dust from her hands onto her apron as she marched smartly to the door. The knock came again, just as she reached for the handle, an impatient demand for attention. She opened it, staring at the man standing outside.

He was impeccably presented, a dark suit that suggested a professional man or a mid-level noble. He offered a slight bow of his dark head to her. "Lady Reanne of Oakmarch?" he asked.

"My grandmother," she offered with a similar bow for courtesy.

"Is she about? I must speak with her."

"Mr...?" Did he honestly believe she would admit him that simply, without even a name to explain himself?

"Lewis Elmstead." He pulled a fold of parchment from his inner coat pocket, bearing the prince's seal. "If you please?"

Amber nodded, all but stumbling out of his way and waving him inside. It wasn't often that someone bearing a royal seal graced their home; for her Nana's sake, Amber had to be perfect in her service. She closed the door behind him, then led the way up the stairs and toward her grandmother's rooms with a whispered word of welcome for him.

Nana's parlor was open, as it nearly always was. Amber motioned to the prince's emissary to wait and strode inside.

"Nana? Have you time for company?" she inquired, hoping it was appropriate to ask such a thing when it was a guest of this importance.

Nana's beautiful blue eyes met hers, her smile making the creases in her ancient face deeper. "Ah, my Amber. Is it time for tea already?"

"Not quite, Nana. A royal representative needs to see you." Her mind spun. How did one see to the comforts of someone of this status? It had been so long, and Mora had been hovering the last time... *Tea! Of course.* "But I will bring tea and fresh bread with jam."

Nana looked up at last, glanced toward the open doorway, then nodded with a grim smile. "Show him in on your way, dear."

"Yes, Nana. As you wish." It was a relief to know she'd offered the right response.

She went back to the hall, offering a smile that felt strained to the emissary. "Lemon or milk, sir?" she asked.

"Milk." He motioned to the parlor. "If I may," he hinted.

Her face burned in embarrassment. "Of course." Amber stepped back into the room. "Nana, may I present Mr. Lewis Elmstead?" She hurried away to the kitchen before further pleasantries were exchanged.

Heating the water and steeping the tea didn't take long. In short order, she had Nana's finest stoneware set on a tray and headed up the stairs with it.

The murmur of voices announced that the two were in earnest discussion about something. Amber breezed into the room and set the tray on the serving table as quietly as she could. A servant should always be inconspicuous.

"So, there are three young ladies in the household?" Elmstead asked, making note of it in a small leather-bound book.

"Indeed, there are," Nana replied.

"Sugar, sir?" Amber asked, seizing what seemed the ideal moment to interrupt.

He didn't look up from his work, ignoring her as most of the higher classes would. "No, thank you. Just milk, if you please."

"Marmalade or elderberry?"

His pen stopped moving. "Pardon?"

"On your bread, sir? Do you prefer marmalade or elderberry?"

"Elderberry, thank you." He went back to his work, addressing Nana. "And all three will attend?"

Amber spread elderberry jam on two thick slices of warm bread and mixed sugar into Nana's cup of tea.

"I should say so," Nana replied, as if it was an offense that the man had asked her such a question.

That voice nearly stopped Amber cold. It was haughty, something Nana was not known to be. It was as if she'd suddenly taken lessons from Mora.

She moved on, delivering the cups and plates wordlessly. Not wanting to intrude further, Amber headed for the door.

"Amber, dear," Nana called out. "Sit. This concerns you."

She came to stand before them.

"Sit," Nana ordered again.

"But my dress is covered in flour."

"And it will brush off. Sit."

Amber nodded, settling in her father's old chair.

"Their names?" Elmstead requested.

"This is my granddaughter, Amber of Oakmarch. The others are Ladies Marquita and Kambry Montberry."

"Daughters of the Duke, I presume," he intoned.

"On his first wife, Lady Mora. My son married her shortly after the Duke's mistress presented him with his son, and he took her to wife to secure the child."

"Your son was Lady Amber's father?" he pressed.

Amber darkened. She wasn't a titled lady, a fact that Mora never let her forget. Still, it would be rude to correct the gentleman.

"He was. My late husband was of the old leanings, though."

Elmstead scratched at something in the book, most likely the title he'd assigned her in error. She knew her face was crimson and she ached to escape the conversation before the emissary announced she wasn't welcome at whatever function they were discussing. But Nana had ordered her to stay. She had to sit quietly and hear his condemnation, no matter how much it galled her to do so.

"Your son had no heirs?"

"No. Xandra, Amber's mother, died trying to bring forth his son. It is a shame that my husband still lived, then."

He looked up, his expression curious. "You would have sanctioned the match?"

"Of course. Xandra was a lovely and gracious woman. She and Marcus were quite in love. But she was lowborn, and Nathaniel wouldn't allow Marcus to marry her, unless Xandra produced a son for him."

"But he did allow his son's illegitimate child to stay," he noted.

Amber bristled at that, clenching her teeth to silence her protest that a mistress's child is not illegitimate. She wasn't heir, but no woman truly was. She had no title, nor did she want one. She was hardly the result of some tavern fling. Her father had always declared her openly and with pride.

"Marcus had the right to any offspring he'd openly claimed. Even Nathaniel couldn't argue that."

"Of course." Elmstead dismissed the discussion that quickly.

He's dismissed me.

He continued, oblivious to her anger. "The three, then. They must bring an escort, as you know."

Nana sighed. "I fear I am far too old for such amusements. I imagine Lady Mora will accompany them."

He added a note to the book and snapped it shut. "Very well, Lady Reanne. I should be on my way."

Almost as a matter of form, the emissary took a sip of the tea, then lifted the bread and took a dainty bite. His chewing slowed, and he took a second...a larger one. When he'd swallowed it, he smiled.

"This jam is excellent, Lady Reanne."

"My granddaughter makes it," she offered, puffing up in pride that he took notice.

Elmstead focused on Amber fully, and she fought the urge to wiggle in embarrassment. His gaze panned from her face to her chest, and Amber wished, not for the first time, that she had something less revealing than Kambry's reworked, discarded dresses to wear.

They were well within the laws for modesty, but those were lax.

"Does she?" he asked, his smile widening.

Amber cleared her throat. "I would be happy to gift you an assortment from the pantry," she offered, peeking at Nana out of the corner of her eye, relaxing at the old woman's nod of encouragement.

"I would like that."

"Very well," Nana said brusquely. "You can take care of that while you show Lord Elmstead out. Have a good day, sir."

Elmstead took her hand without looking away from Amber. "A pleasure, Lady Reanne. Thank you for your hospitality."

"Always offered," Nana replied.

He rose, and Amber did likewise. She hurried ahead of him, wanting to be rid of him though she wasn't certain why that was.

At the pantry, Elmstead crowded close to her, fingering Amber's hair. Warning bells went off at that, and she turned, jams in hand.

"Elderberry, marmalade, blackberry, and currant," she informed him.

"And are you as sweet?"

"P-pardon?"

His hand settled at her hip. "I could use another mistress."

Her breathing went ragged in panic. What was the proper way to rebuff him without causing offense? "My grandmother expects—"

"She offered hospitality."

Surely, that didn't mean Amber was required to bed with him. Nana wouldn't do such a thing to her.

Elmstead smiled, but the smile made her heart pound in fear.

"We could have a taste. If I am pleased, the opening—"

"I have a lot of work," she offered, realizing how lame it sounded, even as the words issued forth.

"I take it you're not willing?" he asked. To her relief, there was no snap of annoyance.

"I'm afraid not. It's not that you are displeasing, sir," she hastened to add.

"But you are not of the heart to be my mistress." He didn't question it.

"I'm afraid not."

He nodded. "Very well, but keep me in mind. When Lady Reanne passes, Lady Mora is not likely to tolerate your presence."

She nodded, her heart aching. Elmstead knew her greatest fear; she only wished his mention of it didn't sound so much like a threat.

"I am kind to my mistresses," he assured her.

"I will bear it in mind." But selling herself into such a situation with a man she found no attraction to wasn't to Amber's tastes. She'd rather live in squalor with someone that made her heart pound in excitement than in luxury with one that made it pound in fear.

Elmstead smiled in a way that Amber was sure some women would find devastating. "Another time, then." He collected the jars and turned toward the door.

Amber hurried ahead of him again, opening the door and bidding him a polite "good day." He stepped through and made for his vehicle without a backward glance. She forced herself to shut the door slowly, then rushed to the window to make certain that he left promptly.

Elmstead handed the jars to a guard, who stored them in a large pack on the front seat of the vehicle. Then the lord slid into the rear seat and smoothed his suit jacket.

"That was an extended stay," the guard noted. "Did you find a diversion inside?" It was obvious that he was teasing the lord.

Elmstead glanced toward the house, his eyes locking on the window she was peeking through. She shut the drape with a gasp, hoping she hadn't encouraged him.

"Nearly, William. Nearly."

Doors closed; the vehicle roared to life and then rumbled away toward town.

Amber took a calming breath. She looked toward the floor above, seething at her grandmother's plans for her. Without a thought to the dinner that needed roasting, she launched up the stairs, taking them two at a time.

"Nana!" Amber burst through the doorway into the parlor, stopping in military form as her father often had, planting her fists on her hips. "How could you?" she demanded.

Nana sipped her tea, unperturbed by the show of temper. "He offered you a place. Didn't he?"

"As his mistress." She swallowed a wave of disgust.

"I was Nathaniel's mistress."

How many times had she repeated that? *As if her positive experience negates all other possible outcomes.*

"He's twice my age, at least. And my mother was a mistress, if you care to recall. Had she lived, all would be well, but she didn't." And where had that left Amber?

"Yours was an extreme case. Your father trusted too much. He left too much in Mora's control, believing she would be good to you."

Amber snorted in an unladylike manner.

For once, Nana didn't offer correction. "Why did you turn him down?" she asked, jumping topic to topic as she always did when they came to this impasse.

"Why should I accept him?" Amber countered.

"Lord Elmstead did nothing for you, then?"

"No," she admitted. "He was nice enough, in his own way, but..." How did one qualify what she wanted? A man that made her heart sing?

Nana considered that. "You need a younger man, one that excites you."

Amber pressed the heel of her hand to her forehead, feeling the first twinges of pain that would soon be pounding. "Nana," she began patiently. "I do not *need* a man, at all."

"Yet, but someday soon, you will."

She nodded miserably. Nana wouldn't live forever. When she died, "Lady" Mora would set Amber out, even if a blizzard blew.

"A young man then." She waved a folded piece of parchment with a broken seal. "And this is the perfect place to find one."

Amber groaned, plodding to the chair she'd used earlier and dropping into it, her head aching. At the very least, it already needed dusting. She couldn't do much more damage, could she? She consigned herself to some torture of the old woman's devious mind. "What now?"

"The prince is throwing a ball."

"I don't know how to dance, Nana. What would I do at a ball?" She'd be hopeless, a laughingstock. A ball would hurt her chances, not help them. Besides that, she wasn't a noble. Last she checked, balls were for the nobility and royalty.

"How convenient that it is not that sort of ball."

Amber screwed up her face in confusion. "What other sort of ball is there?"

Nana handed the parchment over, and Amber spread it flat on her lap.

To the ladies of Lenvia, I send greetings,

Be it known that His Highness, Prince Edward, seeks consorts, mistresses, and/or a bride. To that end, there will be a series of evening events in the four quarters of the Kingdom. The next Bride Ball will be held the 20th of Lunn at the estate of Lord Lewis Elmstead, to begin at dusk. All ladies, high and low, are urged to attend. In addition to His Highness, all noblemen of a want will be welcome to...

Amber scanned the rest, including the rather extensive list of rules for the event. "All young ladies must have a female escort, who will be responsible for their actions. No weapons or aphrodisiacs are permitted on the premises, under the harshest penalties allowed by law. Aphrodi... A *sexual* ball?" she asked.

"There is dancing there," Nana mused, "but not those tiresome court dances. A woman need merely be swept away at a Bride Ball."

"I have heard they are—"

"Delicious."

Hardly the word Amber would have used for it.

"Oh, I wish I was young enough to escort you," Nana sighed, her eyes glittering at some far-off memory.

"You cannot be serious. Being pawed by noblemen?" The thought sickened her.

"Only if you invite it. A simple refusal will end any unwanted attention."

Amber picked that apart, looking for something to attack. Nana was making that difficult.

Not to mention, Lord Elmstead had taken her refusal well enough. Of course, he believed she'd be forced to call on him someday; he'd made that clear enough.

But she'd heard about Bride Balls. Women did the most shocking things there: sexual displays with men and other women, bared bodies for sale...

"What would I wear?" Amber asked, seizing at one thing Nana couldn't have an answer to. Nothing she owned was appropriate for a Bride Ball. *Thank the Goddess Mother!* She couldn't go in her work dresses, and it was a safe wager that Marquita and Kambry were not going to lend her something suitable.

Nana chuckled. "I have the very thing. It may not be the height of fashion, but it will showcase your attributes nicely." Her gaze fell, rather pointedly, on Amber's chest.

Amber felt her face burn, and she found it hard to breathe, let alone speak. "Showcase? You don't mean..." She crossed her arms over her chest at that thought.

"You won't be walking around with your wares on display...unless you wish to."

"That's quite all right, thank you."

"Then, it's decided," Nana stated.

"What?" Amber hadn't decided anything. "I don't know what to do."

"It's simple. Meet the noblemen. If any among them stokes the flame within you, give him leave to seduce you. If anything disturbs you, refuse. If not, pursue pleasure. If it pleases you both enough, accept a position...or a trial position."

"And...if it doesn't please us both enough?"

Nana raked her gaze up and down Amber's body. "Your first time may not be, though it is for some. We could..."

"Nana! You are joking, I hope." Amber forced her legs to relax, abruptly aware that she was clenching her thighs together in rebellion at the suggestion.

"A sensible choice. The nobles like educating a virgin. You are more likely to make a coveted arrangement, if they know you've never experienced—"

"I may have a headache coming on," Amber moaned. *May?* It was pounding behind her eyes with sickening intensity.

"If you do, have it now. On the night of the Bride Ball, you will want to enjoy yourself fully."

"Nana," she pleaded.

"Trust me. If some young buck makes you hunger, be willing to play."

CHAPTER TWO

"You had no right to," Mora fumed.

Amber paused outside the parlor door, rolling her eyes. It always came to this. Nana owned the estate until her death. Any choice dealing with the house, grounds, or the bulk of the wealth was hers. Yet, Mora complained at every turn that Nana wasn't frugal enough, that Mora's stipend had to be increased, that one of Nana's changes would reflect badly on Mora and her daughters socially.

So, it had come to this again. Amber knocked, wondering what they were arguing about this time.

"Come in," Nana called before addressing Mora again. "You have a duty to the estate and to Marcus."

Amber entered and set down the tray of tea and cookies, pouring and preparing without question of what they wanted. She'd served them often enough to do so in her sleep.

"*Cinder* is not of this estate, and Marcus is dead. I owe him nothing. I owe his bastard even less, no matter your allowances for her. If anything, the girl is your responsibility."

Amber's hand faltered at the venom in Mora's voice. Mora spat untruths on a daily basis, and as far as Amber could tell, she'd never cared for Marcus and Amber as Nana had...as Xandra reportedly had.

Keeping a straight face, Amber put a second spoon of sugar in Mora's tea. It was certain to infuriate her, since Mora was positively obsessive about her weight.

"You know I'm too old to attend a Bride Ball," Nana reasoned, taking the tea and cookies Amber offered her with a slight nod of thanks.

"Then she won't go. I won't be responsible for a backward little snip that isn't mine. I'll carry her regrets," she offered in stomach-churning false graciousness.

"I seem to recall that your own early Bride Balls were not always a stunning showing," Nana replied.

Amber paused, halfway to Mora, shooting a look of surprise at Nana as the tension in the room rose. Nana wasn't typically so circumspect; there was a story behind that simple statement, a story she would likely never know.

Mora's expression eased from fury to feigned disinterest that proved Nana had struck some sort of blow. "I will not take her. That is final."

Nana smiled sweetly, though her eyes hardened in rebuke. "Then I'm afraid you'll have to prepare your daughters out of your usual monthly stipend, Mora. After all, Marquita and Kambry aren't of the estate, either. Perhaps, the Duke might wish to offer aid to their cause?"

Amber bit the inside of her cheek, swallowing down a hoot of laughter. The Duke of Montberry aid his daughters? That one was beyond amusing. As far as she could tell, the man had washed his hands of his daughters, the very day he'd turned Mora out in favor of his mistress, a fine testament to how he felt about the lot of them.

Mora stared at Nana, her fury at the edges of control. Her stepmother ignored Amber's offer of tea, so she sat it on the low table and headed for the door.

"You can't," Mora protested.

"Oh, but I can. Amber, take this, please."

She turned back, taking the half-empty teacup and depositing it on the tray again. It was obvious that Nana wanted her to stay in the room, so she took up a serving position at the tray.

Nana continued. "Come now, Mora. You don't wear *much* to a Bride Ball. Surely, your purse will support that well enough...unless you wish to—"

"It will support," Mora snapped. She scooped up the teacup and drank down a healthy mouthful, coughing and sputtering on it, her face going crimson beneath her powder.

Amber bit back another smile. "Is there a problem, Lady Mora?" she inquired, feigning concern.

"You put extra sugar in my tea," she raged.

Amber furrowed her brow, adopting a look of confused innocence that no one in the room would buy as sincere. "One spoon only...though perhaps a bit too rounded?" she suggested.

"Much, and you know it."

"My apologies, stepmother. I will try harder." Mora hated to be reminded that she was Amber's stepmother, and Amber loved reminding her, because of it.

"Leave us, you unruly little beast."

Amber looked to Nana. "Do you require anything more, Nana?" she asked, making it clear that she was Nana's servant and not Mora's. It was a prod, a snub that she would surely pay for later, but for now, it was precisely what she wanted to impress.

Nana smiled. "No, dear. I will manage. I'll send Mora to let you know when to remove the tray."

Amber escaped without laughing, though the chickens were treated to the full explosion of her mirth.

* * * *

"That was a horrible thing to do," Nana admonished, but she did so with glee in her expression.

"She deserved it." Amber waved it off with a flour dusted hand and went back to the rolling of the pie crust.

"I thought you didn't want to go."

"I don't, but I dislike Mora's posturing more than that. She has no right to speak to...or about any of us that way, least of all Father and Mother."

Nana shook her head but didn't offer correction. She'd long since abandoned trying to force Amber to call her stepmother "Lady Mora" in private. Since Mora and the hens were out clucking about some clothier for "appropriate attire" for the Bride Ball, there was no one who cared to overhear her being so disrespectful.

Nana shifted on the cushioned chair Amber had drawn into the kitchen for her. "You've decided to attend, then?"

Amber halted in her work, her hands fisted on the ends of the rolling pin. She went back to it...slowly, weighing her options. "I can't. You heard Mora." Though she hated allowing Mora any victory over her, she was relieved she wouldn't have to endure the Bride Ball.

"Whether she transports you or not, I have named Mora as your escort."

She considered it, working the dough with half a mind to the task. "Then how would I get to the ball? How would I get inside?"

"I can hire Keane to take you, and if you're on the list, you have only to announce yourself to the manservant coordinating. Since your proclaimed escort will be inside, you'll be admitted. They only turn away women who arrive without benefit of an escort."

Amber wondered why that was. Why would they want an older woman watching over the younger, if the men were not permitted trickery or force in bedding them?

"Well?" Nana pressed her.

"I have nothing to wear, and Mora will... Well, you know what she'll be like, if you—"

"I'm certain one of my old outfits would do nicely."

"Mora would still—"

"Cause a scene? Highly unlikely."

Amber set the rolling pin aside, staring intently at it to avoid meeting Nana's eyes.

"It's settled, then," Nana decreed. "You're going."

Amber groaned. "There's no talking you out of this, is there?"

"You're going, Amber. You must. If not for me, then go for yourself."

"I fail to see how this travesty would be that much better for me." Amber peeked up at Nana's expression.

As she feared, the old woman wasn't ordering her; Nana's dark eyes pleaded with her, and Amber had never been able to stand up to that.

She sighed. "As you wish, Nana. I'll go...but I cannot promise that I'll meet someone."

"Good. I'll find just *the* thing for you to wear."

"That's what I'm afraid of," she muttered in return.

* * * *

"This isn't one of those horrid drugs that makes one gain weight, is it?" Marquita questioned, staring at the small pink capsule in distaste.

Amber rolled her eyes and went back to the dishes.

"Goddess, no," Mora replied. "But it will make sure you are fertile at the ball."

"What if the prince demands contraception of his own?" she continued.

Amber grimaced, paying special attention to the dish in her hand, though it was no dirtier than any of the others. She did so more for a way to hide her disgust than any urge to see that one cleaner than the others.

This entire thing was distasteful. It had been more than a week of plans to seduce the prince, of plans to conceive a son by him if possible.

Amber was starting to hope the prince had adequate guards, since they'd even discussed the possibility of drugging him with an aphrodisiac. Surprisingly, Mora seemed adverse to the idea. That was a first for her.

Mora sighed. "It can't be helped. Most men don't, but he may. If you do seduce him, you're nearly guaranteed to catch."

A clink of stoneware announced Marquita taking the pill down. "Awful," she complained. "I loathe pills."

"Get used to them," her mother advised. "You'll be taking one every day for the next month. Longer, if he makes an offer. I purchased a two-month supply, to start, and we can procure more. You must produce a son, before he tires of you. He can take mistresses, but the princess who presents his heir is nearly guaranteed to be his queen for life. Few kings dismiss a wife that has given them an heir. Worst case, he chooses to leave her to her amusements and takes mistresses to his bed."

"I won't have to, will I?" Kambry asked, seemingly concerned.

"Thanks to *Her Ladyship*, no. Once I purchased your costumes and jewelry, there was only enough left in my stipend to supply the drug to Marquita."

That was typical. Though the drug would supply both daughters for a month, and Mora could buy one or both more with her stipend the following, she focused on Marquita alone.

Her snub of Nana was even more expected.

Amber rinsed the scrubbed plates, her jaw tight in fury, hoping the water would drown out Mora's voice.

There was a moment of silence, no doubt Mora waiting for a reaction from Amber. She could keep waiting, keep staring at Amber's offered back. If there was one thing twelve years with Mora had taught Amber, it was that nothing annoyed her stepmother more than being ignored. She wondered how many times the Duke had ignored her and wagered with herself that it was a high number.

Kambry fiddled with her teacup. Amber didn't have to look at her to know it was Kambry. It was a nervous habit of hers, one that usually ended in censure. Today was no different.

"If your hands cannot be still, Kambry," her mother snapped, "clasp them in your lap."

The cup settled. "Yes, Mother," she answered dutifully.

"Better."

"Mother?"

"Yes, Kambry?" It was obvious that Mora's patience was quickly wearing thin.

"What if one of us does catch, but His Highness doesn't offer a contract?"

Kambry always was the smartest of the three.

Mora didn't agree. "Don't be daft! Once the doctors establish paternity, you'd have an estate and a sizable stipend to live on. After all, producing a lawful heir to the throne, bastard or not, carries reward. If the prince were to die without producing heirs, the bastard would inherit all. That's how Hein Matthew and Hein Darren evolved."

It was true, for the royalty. Only the fact that King Benjamin and Prince Edward had been only-children kept the Willowmarshes in the running for the throne. If the king had a second son or the prince had two, Hein Matthew and his son, Hein Darren, would revert to lesser nobles, Dukes most probably.

"If the child is male," Kambry pressed, her voice tentative.

"Of course, if it's male. Even if the child is female, you could still make a coveted position, though you'd have to dispose of the bastard first, preferably before you ruined your body with producing it...but afterward, if testing is inconclusive."

Amber deposited the last plate in the drainer a little more forcefully than the others she'd washed, turning abruptly and taking to the stairs.

Mora and Marquita wore twin looks of dark satisfaction. To Amber's surprise, Kambry seemed discomfited.

She always was the smartest of the three.

Perhaps she was the most empathetic, as well. Looking back at her life, Amber had to admit that it was nearly always Marquita and her mother needling her. Kambry hadn't done so, since they'd been children, well over a decade earlier...and always following Marquita's lead.

CHAPTER THREE

"Let me off here," Amber requested.

Keane shot her a look of disbelief. "Why would you do that?"

"You know my stepmother. If I'm announced, she will make every effort to embarrass me."

He winced. "She would, but how will you get in without being announced?"

"I have a plan for that, but you need to let me off here." Ahead, she could see the curve that would lead them to the front entrance.

"As you wish." He pulled the vehicle to the side of the road to let Amber out. It was his father's vehicle, an older model that had seen better days, but it was quiet and well-maintained.

She pulled her mask on, held her cloak tight around her body and bolted into the gardens. The cool, night air teased at her uncovered skin and the satin cups of the bustier caressed her, bringing her nipples to hard points.

"Oh, yes. Like that," a male voice panted out.

Amber paused, waiting for some sign of what direction it had come from, hoping not to stumble over someone's sexual play. A series of moans from her right sent her forward and to the left. Luckily, there wasn't another couple that direction, and she made the patio without incident.

At least that far... She almost turned back at the patio.

The women gathered there were in the most outrageous outfits she'd ever seen. One was in sheer lace that revealed her entire body. Another was in a weave of leather straps that left her augmented breasts bare and would bare her probably-shaven mound with a single buckle. Still another wore a short skirt with no panties beneath, a fact that was impossible to miss when she leaned forward; she did that often.

Amber tried not to stare at the half-nude women with their padded or surgically-enhanced breasts. In their quest for a choice position, it seemed no expense had been spared.

The talk was even more disconcerting. Some named which nobles had already sampled their wares that evening and boasted of expected offers. Some talked about the prince, postulating on who he might choose. By the last of it, Amber wanted nothing more than to escape into the depths of the ball, and she did so, pushing her hood and cloak to her back to bare her modest outfit.

Slipping into the ballroom was akin to slipping into the depths of the unholy underworld. Everywhere, couples and more gyrated against each other in what she presumed was dancing. Others were engaged in heated kisses or blatant touching.

She picked a route toward a seemingly sedate round of conversing lords and ladies, only to find herself passing peek windows into a walled area that contained a veritable orgy of sex partners that obviously enjoyed their audience. From the reactions of those at the windows, they enjoyed watching nearly as much as those inside enjoyed being watched.

Her face burning, Amber bolted for the punch bowl, passing by two soldiers who seemed to be stationed at the table. It was spiked, of course, and there was no sign of an alternative, so she sipped at it.

The conversation she'd sought proved even more blatant than what she'd heard on the patio. Amber made for a deserted stretch of wall, nearly hopping in place, staring at her drink for lack of anywhere safer to paste her gaze.

Why did Nana insist on this?

A few nobles wandered her way, invariably older men...and drunken. The younger wanted something more impressive, more engaging. She turned them down politely, and they left with nods and offers to seek them out later.

Amber groaned. How was she supposed to find a noble when she choked at the sight of them?

A familiar laugh caught her attention, and she looked toward the head of the room, coughing on a mouthful of punch. Marquita and Kambry were performing a sex show for a well-dressed, masked gentleman that she assumed was the prince. They turned in unison and draped themselves over him, stroking his body and whispering in his ear. He kissed Kambry and then Marquita, tangling his hands in their hair.

She looked away, taking a deeper drink of the punch. They were shameless, and perhaps a drink would calm her nerves, so she could last another hour of this and satisfy Nana's insistence that she try.

Tears stung at her eyes. She'd be better off marrying some land-owner's foreman than attempting this. She shouldn't have come. She didn't belong—

"Care for a dance or a moment of conversation?" a rich, male timbre inquired.

Amber turned to dismiss him...and the words stuck in her throat. He was young, and he was beautiful. He was dressed simply, in loose, tied trousers of suede. His bare chest was tanned and ridged in muscles. His lips were full and dark, and though a brown, suede mask that matched his trousers concealed most of his face, his deep blue eyes and the fluff of blonde hair drew her eyes.

Her heart pounded in excitement. *A younger man... Oh, but Nana was right about that.*

"Pardon?" she managed.

"A dance or a bit of conversation?"

* * * *

Edward had all but given up. The women of the southern reaches were even worse than the north and east. He knew his willing stand-in, his cousin Darren, was getting his fill of both promises and payments on them.

He was a stone's throw from admitting defeat and moving on to another idea. It had been folly to try this. Edward had been hoping a family in dire straits would force a daughter out, but apparently that wasn't going to happen. The type of woman he *wanted* to meet would never come to this travesty.

What caught his attention first was an uncertain thing. Perhaps it was her wild-eyed look at the voyeurs' row, how she bolted for the punchbowl, her breasts bouncing in the bodice of the modest bustier.

Yes, that caught his attention. Without a doubt, it had. Her breasts had bounced as implants never would.

She'd shaken her head in misery at her first taste of the punch, and she'd sipped at it afterward, wandering from one group of revelers to another, choosing red-faced solitude, in the end.

Edward vowed to approach her before she had a second cup...if he approached her. He wanted her honest reactions, not ones fueled by Elmstead's finest stores.

She seemed discomfited, avoiding eye contact, turning away the nobles who approached her, even those Edward knew to be among the wealthiest here. She made no move toward Darren, believing—as all save Darren, Elmstead, Edward's parents, and the royal guards would—that his cousin was the prince.

Edward was halfway across the floor to her, when she looked toward Darren. He paused, gauging her expressions...and started moving again a moment later.

She was clearly disgusted. Her crimson cheeks went pale, and she winced. She looked away, raised the cup to her lips with a shaking hand, and drank deeply. Still, she didn't look back to Darren or try to approach him.

It was the moment of truth. "Care for a dance or a moment of conversation?" he offered.

She turned to him in apparent misery and went still, her color returning in a rush, her eyes scaling his body, from bottom to top. She stopped at his face, her breathing ragged.

His heart stuttered at the sight of her tear-heavy lashes. She was so decidedly out of her element, it tore at his heart. Edward wanted to smooth the riot of dark ringlets, kiss away the tears, hold her in a place far from this insanity.

"P-pardon?" she whispered.

"A dance or a bit of conversation?" he offered again.

She looked toward the groping throng and swallowed hard. "Conversation, thank you."

It was matter-of-fact, sensible, completely endearing. "Very well." He fished for an opening that would be non-threatening and nonsexual. "It's a lovely outfit," he offered. "I've not seen its like in many years."

She smiled weakly. "My grandmother's," she admitted, "but I'd rather wear it than..." Her eyes locked on something behind him, widened, and shifted away.

"It is all a bit much," he agreed. "I believe Bride Balls were much more civilized in your grandmother's day."

"Were they ever civilized?" She clapped a hand over her mouth, shooting a look of panic at Edward.

He laughed until he felt his ribs would surely fracture and tears welled in his eyes. "Perhaps not," he conceded.

Her hand retreated slowly. "You're not insulted, then?"

"Why should I be?" he asked, perplexed by her assumption.

"I thought..." She waved her hand as if at a loss for words.

"Thought?" he prompted her.

"You were looking for a mistress, like the rest. I mean...why else would you be here?"

Why else, indeed? Edward hadn't considered what the type of woman he wanted would think of him being here. "I think a man with a wife he loves has no use for mistresses. That is what I really want. As for the rest... No. This is not my idea of how to find that wife."

"Then why are you here?"

"My father," he answered in half-truth. With such a finite timeline to find a bride, extreme measures had to be taken.

"Oh." That one word conveyed a wealth of disgust.

Edward forced his voice to remain neutral. "Meaning what?"

She sighed. "Only that he is of the old leanings, I suppose? Some women are worthy to marry. Others are only worthy to be mistresses, unless they bear sons for you."

Her heartfelt assessment stunned him. She couldn't be a scorned mistress. She was too young, too uneducated in the games of society.

Edward realized she was waiting for a response. "Actually, not. My father would allow me any woman I wish as wife. He simply..." He looked around at the decadence of the Bride Ball. "foolishly, I think, believes this is the way to find one."

She nodded, glancing around the room as he just had, sighing. Her gaze returned to his face. "I must agree."

He smiled. "And why are you here?" He didn't doubt the answer would be of the type he'd been searching for.

She laughed lightly, her color high and dark eyes glittering. "My grandmother is very like your father. Try as I might to encounter some mishap, there was no escaping coming here."

"Then we are both cursed," he quipped.

"I am afraid so."

His heart was light, his head spinning. "Would you care for that dance now?"

Her smile disappeared, and she peeked around his shoulder like a stag caught in torchlight.

"A simple dance," he offered. "Not what they are doing." Edward didn't have to look at the dancers to know what she feared.

"I don't know how to dance."

"Would you like to learn?"

She blushed, nodded, and offered her hand. She let him lead her to the edge of the dance floor.

He wrapped his hands around her waist, guiding her movements gently, a swaying motion that fired his cock to aching readiness. She gasped, searching out his eyes.

The tension left her body, and she went fluid in his hands, a warm wave teasing him with the promise of more. Her arms circled his neck, and her hands tangled in the back of his hair.

The spectacle around them ceased to exist. There was only the raven-haired temptress in his arms, her eyes sliding shut, her lips parting slightly.

It was too much. Edward leaned his head toward her, tilting it to one side, letting her breath warm his mouth. If it wouldn't spook her, he'd kiss her, long and hard.

"I want to kiss you," he whispered, seeking her agreement.

Her face closed on his, her lips brushing across his, sending sweet sparks down his body to settle in his groin.

"More." How he managed to form the word was a mystery to Edward, but he did it.

She nodded, kissing sweetly at his lower lip, then his upper.

Edward moved one hand to her face, playing his thumb between her soft lips. She licked at it, tasted it in seemingly innocent mimic of oral sex.

"Wider," he urged her.

Her lips parted further, far enough for Edward to ease his thumb out and tease his tongue inside. She gave a demure little shiver at the contact, her scent teasing at his nose.

By the Goddess, she was driving him mad, and she'd done nothing more than allow Edward the most basic of liberties.

Allow. That was the difference, as he'd known it would be. He could wager on going no further with confidence. There was a sense of anticipation with this woman, the thrill of acceptance.

"I want to lick every finger-width of your body," he whispered.

She gasped, but she didn't draw away.

"We can stop whenever you wish."

Her eyes opened, and she looked at the far end of the room, shaking her head, retreating slightly, real fear making her shake.

Edward followed her line of sight, his jaw tightening at the view he had of the voyeurs' row. "It's horrid," he voiced, though he'd stood both sides of such walls, in his younger days.

She shifted abruptly, her head turning back to him. He looked down at her, noting her confusion in a rush of happiness.

He spoke, before she could find the words to question him. "One treats a consort that way...perhaps a mistress. I seek a wife or nothing at all."

"Is there so much a difference?" she asked.

"I believe so."

She seemed confused by that.

"I have rooms upstairs," he offered. "Just the two of us, and I will stop...any time you wish it."

She seemed to ponder it, as if the safety of the kingdom itself depended on it. Edward held his breath, aware that his heart was pounding hard at his ribs.

"And you wish to..."

"Lick you. Kiss you." *Perhaps more than that, depending on your responses.* The fact that there was no guarantee he'd bed her was both an agony and exciting.

"And...if I say 'no' to more?" She wasn't teasing him. She honestly wanted to know his mind.

I may fall in love, that quickly. "I would ask permission to see you again, but I would escort you safely here...or wherever you wished to go."

She kissed at his lower lip again. "Yes."

CHAPTER FOUR

Amber gasped at the moan emerging from deep in his throat. Was he really so affected? She couldn't believe that a man like this was pursuing her, considering the other wares for rent or sale that night. And...a wife or nothing?

He turned, wrapping an arm around her waist, guiding her silently from the ballroom and into nearly-deserted corridors. She tried not to watch the couples they passed, though it was hard not to contemplate what might happen next between herself and the noble escorting her to his rooms.

One woman stroked her hand up and down a man's member, and Amber wondered if her escort was so large. A glance at his soft trousers hinted that he was, which sent a rumble of delight through her thighs and womb.

A man suckled at his topless partner's nipples, and Amber's head swirled. Would *he* do that to her? What would it feel like? If he meant to lick her all over, would he do it on his own or would she have to ask him to do it? Could she do something so wanton?

Another woman suckled at a man's cock, on her knees before him, his hand tangled in her hair.

His whispered entreaty to the Goddess brought Amber's eyes up. She knew that voice.

She knew the face as well. Lord Elmstead's eyes opened, then locked on Amber. A smile curved his lips up, and she looked away, mortified to be sighted going to a nobleman's rooms in the lord's house less than a month after refusing the lord himself.

Warm breath fanned her neck a moment before a soft tongue bathed her exposed throat. Amber's knees went weak, and she stumbled, grasping at his body for balance.

A moment later—or what felt like a moment, they stood, his arm supporting her against his chest. The firm meat of his buttock was under her hand. Amber pulled back, fisting her hand against her squirming stomach. Good Goddess, he would think her a wanton like the rest.

"Are you well?" he asked.

"Yes." But she trembled and could not say why she did. "I—I tripped," she lied. In truth, Amber had no idea what had befallen her. It had been akin to a faint, but she was certain it was altogether different than that.

"I startled you," he decided. "I will take care not to do so again."

A low chuckle came from Lord Elmstead's direction, deepening what she was certain was already a crimson blush.

He didn't look around at his host, though his jaw tightened slightly. "Can you walk now? Or should I—"

"No!" Amber calmed herself. "I am capable, thank you." And Elmstead would have no reason to laugh at her naivety again.

She allowed her gaze to trail to his arms, wondering at what being carried by him would feel like. Amber had a vague memory of what she believed was her father carrying her mother to their bedchamber.

The thought of her escort doing the same was sexually arousing.

As if I am not already aroused?

He turned, holding her flush to his body. Amber's knees quaked lightly, and his hand slid just under the lower edge of her Nana's bustier. The shock of his fingers on her flesh was electric, though she'd never thought the soft meat of her abdomen an erogenous zone.

They stopped, and her escort opened a door, guiding her inside a dimly-lit room that was almost too warm, even in the chill spring night. Or perhaps it was she that was hot.

The door closed, and an irrational fear gripped her. What was she doing? Was she mad? She didn't know this man.

As if he could hear the pounding of her heart, he turned to her, stroking his fingertips up the line of her jaw until he cupped her face. "Calm," he soothed her. "Say the word, and I will see you home this instant."

Home. Not to the ballroom? Amber wondered at that. Did he think her ill? Or, was there some other reason for it? She dared not ask.

All the same, her heart rate slowed, and her breathing smoothed. Even when she didn't ask for assurances from him, he gave them. She knew that about him. She trusted that he meant every word he spoke to her. "No. No, that won't be necessary."

Her voice was calm in comparison to her rioting senses. Everything around her was *him*: his body, the cadence of his breathing, his eyes softly assessing, his scent enticing her to taste.

His lips closed to within millimeters of hers, until the radiant heat of his face and breath seeped into her mouth. She let her eyes slide shut, wanting to focus on that one sensation and nothing more. What had Nana called this? It was something about sharing the very air that sustained the lovers.

He nuzzled her lips wider, tilting his face to one side to fit his lips to hers. His tongue caressed at hers, sending a pleasant shock through her. He did it again...and again.

Amber found herself pressed to his body, with no memory of closing the distance between them, her cloak pooled around her ankles. Her hands tangled in the back of his hair, and her tongue thrust against his. It was a hard kiss but not brutal, not forceful.

He eased his mouth away, his breathing ragged, his arms flexing against her ribs. Without a word, he eased his chin under hers and urged hers up, baring her neck.

His breath taunted her, and she knew what he intended next. The stroke of his tongue against the sensitive flesh at the join of neck and chin nearly folded her knees a second time. It was slow, silken, warm even in the warmth of his rooms.

He didn't hesitate, moving on minutely to stroke again. The overlapping touches moved steadily downward, wrenching sighs and sounds that should have been pleas for more from her.

The first lick at her collarbone succeeded in weakening her knees. Amber crumpled, and his hands tightened at her waist to stop her slide. One retreated. She was abruptly in his arms, vaguely noting movement as she laid her cheek to his chest. Her hands slipped from his neck to his shoulders, and the delicious feel of his muscles undulating beneath her fingertips forced a moan from her.

Amber didn't question that the piece of furniture beneath her was a bed. She didn't care that it was, either.

His body eased away from hers, and the bed shifted. She opened her eyes, noting his concern with a twisting in her gut.

"Water?" he offered.

She shook her head.

"Are you well?"

Well? Her body sang in pleasure. She nodded.

His smile made her stomach flutter, and the pulse beat of need picked up tempo.

The smile faded into an expression Amber didn't recognize but her body did. It was something potent that stepped up the tension between them.

He lowered his head, nearly retracing the last lick he'd laid, stroking the suede of his mask against her as he turned his head and suckled lightly at her skin. She arched up off the bed in the intensity of sensation, slight pain mixed with pleasure. It seemed she'd urged him on; he suckled harder, until the area numbed in a disconcerting series of bursts and points.

His mouth retreated, fanning warmth over the spot as sensation returned. It throbbed with the same rhythm as her sheath, a primitive cadence that seemed to drive her every move.

His movements became more feverish, less meticulous, as if he knew they didn't have to be now. Every stroke of his tongue echoed over her body.

Amber fisted her hands in his hair, squeezing her eyes shut, moaning her protest as he paused.

He turned slightly, snaking his tongue inside one satin cup of her bustier, missing the nipple but finding the circle of darkened flesh that surrounded it. Just that teasing touch had her panting, shaking, needing more.

Her sopping panties rubbed uncomfortably against her. Her skirts felt heavy and hot, and the damned bustier was in the way of what she wanted from him.

He straightened. His hands circled her, lifting Amber slightly. His fingers teased at the top hook and eye at the back, silently asking permission to open them.

"Yes," she gasped. "Oh, yes."

Each movement was painstakingly slow, a hook or two at a time, until half the row was undone. Then he pushed the bustier down, uncovering her breasts.

"Oh, Goddess," he breathed.

His tongue traced the edge of the nipple bed. He moved inward, spiraling slowly, finally reaching the nipple at the center.

There was a moment of stillness, an unbearable taunting. Amber arched her back, crying out sharply as she forced her nipple to his upper lip.

His tongue retreated, rasping against it. His lips parted, and he suckled at her. Just when Amber thought she could feel no better, he took more of her, all of the nipple bed and a portion of her breast, as well.

She barely noted the hooks and eyes sliding open, as he sucked at her breasts in turn. He followed her down to the bed, sliding the bustier from her body and tossing it away.

His head came up slowly. Amber opened her eyes, curious to see what he was doing. He surveyed her half-nude body, his expression hungry.

"All of me," she breathed.

He nodded, starting at the lower swell of her breasts. It was sublime, yet it was torturously slow. Amber wanted to hurry him along; she wanted it to last all night, at the same time.

No. Not all night. She had to be home before Mora and the cackling hens, or there would be more than animosity to deal with, and Amber didn't care to put up with that sort of hostility and abuse.

He paused. "I did something wrong? Something you didn't care for?"

"No." How could he think such a thing? She'd never felt so wonderful.

"You tensed."

Her face radiated heat. She couldn't admit why she'd really tensed. Confessing that she was planning to leave while he was... Well, it just wasn't right.

"We can stop," he offered. "If anything I do—"

"No. Don't."

He seemed to consider that. "A suggestion?"

Her heart pounded in her throat. Had he already found her lacking? "Yes?"

"Don't think." It was a whispered seduction in itself. "Just feel."

Yet, being told not to think made her do precisely that. She was inviting this man to do the most intimate things with her, and she knew nothing about him. "What is your name?" That would be enough for her.

"My name?" The question seemed to confuse him...or to put him on edge.

"It hardly seems right..." But how best to phrase it?

"Go on," he urged her.

"To be so...intimate with a complete stranger. I would never suggest we stop long enough to become fully acqua..." She grimaced. "I suppose we are becoming rather fully—"

"Not remotely." There was no teasing in that. He hesitated for a moment. "Christopher," he offered with a bow of his head. His eyes locked with hers. "And yours?"

The truth stuck in her throat. Why, she couldn't say. She trusted him. And yet, the thought of giving Christopher her given name terrified her. Amber was an unusual name in Lenvia. Kambry and Mora were much more common.

What a thought that was! Amber, common by birth, had a unique name, while—

"Mi'lady?"

"My apologies, Christopher." She managed a tense smile. *I definitely think too much.*

He waited patiently for an answer.

"Cinder." If it became something more, she could admit it was a pet name her father had given her and not her true name, the one he'd chosen at her birth.

His most devastating smile returned. "It's beautiful...unusual, like you."

Her heart skipped at that. "You think I'm beautiful?" Unusual was probably true enough.

Christopher lowered his head, pressing his lips to the soft meat of her belly. "Stunning," he breathed.

Amber tried to be still, but the solid touch of his lips had her moving beneath him, urging him on, eagerly seeking more.

His fingers pulled at the tie on her skirt, undoing the double, then sliding the bow open a millimeter at a time. Her breathing hitched at that. Christopher loosened the waistline and eased it down to her hipbones.

He moaned, running a finger under the waistband of her plain panties, tangling the tip in her woman's curls. Amber thrust her hips up, certain she'd never felt something so enticing and even more certain that his finger circling her clit, as she sometimes did, would be enough to send her over.

"Goddess! You are so perfect."

Christopher hooked the fingers of both hands into the waistbands of skirts and panties together. The stroke of fabric down her body was accented by the warmth of his breath following in its wake.

It buffeted her tender center, and Amber spread her legs as far as the panties allowed, drinking in the sensation greedily. Her entire body vibrated in anticipation.

Would he lick there, as well? Would he circle her nub with that silken tongue instead of her slightly-roughened fingers?

Every finger-width on your body...

Goddess! He was going to. Amber whimpered at the thought of it, tipping her hips up to capture more of his breath.

"Are you asking?" His voice was rough, breathless, as if he'd taken a gut shot in a fight.

I suppose I am asking. "Oh, yes." Amber couldn't seem to catch her breath, either.

Christopher turned his head, playing his tongue along the inner line of her thigh. She cried out in surprise and delight. Surely, he was teasing her.

"You make me crazy." His voice rumbled against her thigh. "I can barely contain myself."

She wondered if he meant that figuratively or literally. The idea of watching his cum shoot was oddly enticing. Would he want her to help stroke him off? She would do it, just to see his enjoyment, to know she'd managed to make it happen.

"Then don't contain yourself."

His head turned, and his tongue stroked up her seam, causing her to spasm in the depth of sensation.

"You're going to come for me, aren't you?" he teased.

"Yes." Amber didn't question it. He'd had her at the edges since the corridor. She licked her lips, her mouth abruptly dry.

Christopher knelt up, removing the rest of her clothes and her shoes in a few efficient movements. His gaze roamed her body, and he grumbled what was probably a curse under his breath.

His hands circled her ankles and slid upward, cupping her calf muscles...then her knees. He lifted the backs of her knees, guiding them up and out, until she was open to his heated gaze.

His cock pressed out against his trousers, wetting them with further evidence of his arousal. Amber swallowed hard, her thighs trembling at the thought of his powerful body thrusting between them, at that hard shaft filling the aching void within her.

But Christopher was in no rush to get there. His mouth pressed to the inside of one knee, his breath firing her skin in a manner not unlike warm water in a bath might. His tongue flicked out, tasting her as he'd promised he would. He turned, repeating the exercise on the opposite knee. Back and forth, he traveled, closer to her clit with each pass, driving her crazy for the two experiences she wanted most from him.

His hair brushed over her center, and Amber went rigid, the first whispers of coming orgasm stealing her breath. Her hand fisted against his shoulder.

One more move... Touch me once more, and I'll come for you.

As if he heard her, Christopher's mouth was suddenly there, wrapped round her clit, his tongue flicking lightly, faint sucking motions between.

She screamed, arching up, colors swirling before her eyes, warm shocks dancing over her extremities. Christopher compensated for her movements, ruthless in his attentions now.

Wave after wave of orgasm had her alternately begging him to stop and cycling her hips against his insistent, exploring mouth. Who was she kidding? The last thing she wanted was an end to this.

Amber came to consciousness slowly, splayed out under Christopher, bathed by his still-stroking tongue, panting in the pulse beat of need, the space so close to his tongue conspicuously empty.

"More," she breathed.

He sucked at her clit again, setting off another wave of pure delight.

"No, no, no," she gasped out. "More." *All of you! Goddess, I'll go mad, if I don't get filled soon.*

45

Christopher knelt up between her thighs, his eyes questioning. Amber reached out, playing her fingertips along the growing wet spot at the tip of his cock. His jaw tightened.

"More," she repeated, wishing she knew the proper words to ask for what she wanted without offending him, in the process. Did a woman call his member "cock" or was there a gentler word used with a nobleman? What did he expect her to call her own body? The act?

Why had she never asked Nana? Because she'd never believed such a moment was possible?

* * * *

Edward's head spun with the combination of her taste and the knowledge that she wanted all of him. Or, did she? Cinder wasn't being clear.

He unfastened his trousers, and her hands slid inside, stroking him with fingers that held just the edge of roughness, attesting that she was lowborn. One hand wrenched the fabric away while the other pushed him toward shooting on her smooth belly. Goddess! He'd give her every drop.

The grip on his cock changed, and Cinder laid back, her eyes pleading. He had to know what she sought.

Edward leaned forward, planting his hands above her shoulders, caging her upper body with his. "Is this what you want?" he asked. "Do you want me to come to your hand?"

She shook her head, though she continued stroking.

"Do you want me inside you?" He prayed that she did.

Cinder bit her lower lip in a show of nerves, nodding.

His muscles tensed in anticipation, and he lowered himself, letting Cinder guide him to her ready body. The air vibrated in ragged breathing, his and hers alike.

"Move your hand," he instructed. Goddess, but this was going to feel good.

She complied, took a deep breath, and nodded her readiness.

Edward argued that he should go slowly. Something about Cinder demanded it, despite her expertise with driving him sexually mad for her.

Another part of him demanded a show of possession. That voice won out, and he thrust up hard, groaning at the tight channel engulfing him.

Her cry wasn't one of pleasure, as he'd expected...as she'd gifted him thus far. One small hand braced against his chest. The other pressed to her belly, trembling lightly.

Edward forced his eyes up to her face, biting back a curse at her pained expression, certain now that he'd rammed hard at a virgin.

"Stop," she panted out. "Please, stop."

"Of course." He'd promised to, but even if he hadn't... "Why didn't you tell me?" he demanded, heartsick at causing her such pain.

Her voice was abruptly strong, though a touch off of hysterical. "You're the experienced one," she snapped. "You couldn't tell I wasn't?"

"You're right," he conceded. "You have my apologies. I should have seen it." He had known, on some level. That nagging voice, the one that demanded a slow approach, had warned him off. Edward had chosen to ignore it. This was his fault.

He started to ease out of her, but her hands grasped hard at his hips.

"I don't want apologies. I want you to be still for a moment." While she'd had difficulty telling Edward what she wanted in pleasure, she was clear enough in pain.

He nodded his agreement, at a loss for the first time in years. He'd bungled this precious moment.

Oh, but he paid the price for his folly, holding rigidly still while Cinder's body taunted him with whispers of movement. At one instant, he swore he was about to go off from that little stimulation, but he regained control.

"Don't you ever go flaccid?" she asked wearily.

"If you were still as well, I might," he offered cordially. *Unlikely, but I'll say it anyway.*

Her hands loosened. "Then perhaps you should..."

Edward eased back, and she whimpered, squeezing her eyes shut. He slid free of her body, and she drew her legs up, turning to her side to curl in on herself.

He lowered himself to the bed behind her, gathering Cinder into his arms. There were no words between them. Those would come later, when she was calm.

Instead, Edward left her long enough to pull the quilt over them both. In moments, she was asleep in his arms, her trembling easing and then stopping altogether.

CHAPTER FIVE

Amber woke with a start. Where was she? This wasn't her bed in her little room, across from Nana's.

A sigh beside her brought her head around...and the rest came back in a flash. She was still in Christopher's bed, with the man in question beside her, nude save for his mask, the quilt drawn up to a hand's-width below his nipples.

He'd allowed her to stay, probably out of a sense of responsibility for her. He expected to see her home; he'd promised to do so, and he was a man of honor.

Surely, he hadn't let her stay out of a wish for her company. Christopher hadn't climaxed, also out of a duty to her. He'd felt it right to care for her, in her discomfort, and so he'd foregone his own wants.

But like a man who has had his advance rebuffed, grace in defeat does not indicate joy in the outcome. Amber didn't know much about the sexual games of the nobility, but she knew this much: men didn't want women that failed them, sexually or in producing sons.

She eased out from beneath the quilts, wincing at the aches and pains in her abdomen and thighs. Her hands shook, but she managed to pull on her skirt and cinch the knot. Her low shoes came next. Finding her panties and bustier took longer, and she realized the futility of trying to work the tiny hooks. In the end, she pulled on her cloak and carried the rest of her clothing.

Amber paused, taking one last look at Christopher. A mad urge to lift his mask and take in his face pulled at her. She halted a step closer to him, coming to her senses, at last. If she did that, he'd wake. The last thing she wanted was for him to wake.

No doubt, he'd be relieved to find her gone. It would save him the posturing and gallantry and save her the discomfort of knowing it was a duty to him to see her home.

Moreover, she didn't have the time to wait for him to wake...or even for him to dress and primp, if he were awake. Already, the sky was lightening. If the Goddess was kind, Mora hadn't realized Amber was gone yet, and she'd be able to take her place without incident.

That was assuming Keane was still there, as promised. If not...

She couldn't worry about that now.

There was a balcony with stairs down to the lawn just beyond the dual glass doors. Since she couldn't remember the way out of the wing Christopher had taken her to, she had no time to waste, and she didn't want to chance running afoul of Lord Elmstead again, the balcony route seemed the best option.

Amber eased the door open and slid into the chill beyond, closing it with nothing more than a faint click. She hurried down the stairs, turning toward the far end of the drive at a trot, her breath making thick clouds in the coming-morn air.

"Halt," a gruff voice ordered. "What are you doing here?"

She faltered, looking back at the soldier in shock, half turning toward him. His uniform was unlike any she'd seen before. The insignia of a captain was easy enough to pick out, but there were other symbols, ones she couldn't identify.

Amber moved a step away, as he started to advance, trying to understand his challenge of her. The morning after such an affair, people would be stumbling and sauntering away in trickles. What was it that made him challenge her?

"I told you to halt, girl."

He drew his sword, and Amber's heart stuttered in fear. Though it was ceremonial, she knew it was functional as well...lethal, if needs be. Words deserted her.

"You'll have to come with me." The sword moved in a menacing arc, down to a fighting position instead of a warning one.

Amber stumbled a few steps further, all but tripping over her skirt and landing in a heap. Why was he taking a fighting stance? She hadn't threatened him. She hadn't shown a weapon. This was all wrong. His reactions weren't protocol, as she knew it from her father.

His expression hardened. "I gave you an order, girl." His grip changed, a clear sign that he was readying the sword for use.

She was certain this spelled disaster. Even if the threat of Mora wasn't hanging over her head, the soldier was treating her as a criminal, an enemy of some sort, someone that posed a danger. Goddess only knew why or what he'd consider his duty in such a situation.

Her logic extended that far and no further. Only one thought was clear to her. *Going with the soldier is not an option.* She turned and bolted away.

"Halt! I said— Goddess take it!"

Heavy footsteps pounded after her. They weren't gaining, but Amber laid on speed all the same. The bustier slipped, the satin trailing off of her arm. She didn't stop for it, didn't even slow. If she did, the soldier would catch her, and it was a given that he wouldn't be pleased that she'd run from him.

The footsteps stopped, and she chanced a look back, wincing at the sight of the soldier scooping up the bustier from the dew-coated grass. He turned and ran for the house with the costume in his hand.

Though she didn't understand the sudden change, Amber didn't question it. The soldier wasn't chasing her, and she had a solid chance of making it off the grounds before he managed to raise the alarm.

The sight of Keane's battered vehicle wrenched a sob from her. She launched into it and slammed the door behind her, holding the cloak shut with one hand.

Keane startled awake. "Was that necessary?" he snapped.

"Yes. We have to hurry, Keane. It's nearly sunrise."

"Why should we hurry? Mora and the beasts are still inside."

Amber searched the remaining vehicles, staring at Nana's car in relief. "We still have to hurry," she managed woodenly.

"As you wish," he replied, starting the engine.

She didn't breathe easily, until they'd passed the gates without incident.

* * * *

"Highness!"

Edward groaned, burying his face in the pillow, his brow furrowing. What was on his face? A mask?

"Thank the Goddess." The voice sounded of relief.

"I would thank Her for more sleep," he grumbled, still working at the mask problem. He was nude, which was normal, but what was the mask about?

A blast of cold air shocked Edward awake, and he reached for the quilt pooled low on his chest. Other hands were there first, dragging the cover the wrong direction, exposing more of Edward to the frosty air. A curse followed, and someone started shouting for a doctor.

Edward grasped the quilt and yanked it over himself, shivering. He opened his eyes to the sight of the frantic captain leaning over him.

"A doctor should be here soon, Highness," he rattled on.

"Doctor? I don't need a—"

The captain reached for the quilt again. "Let me see where you're bleeding from."

"Bleeding? I'm not bleeding." None of this made sense. "Did you leave a door open somewhere? Close it," he ordered. Maybe then, this insanity would end and he could get back to sleep.

"Highness, please..."

Edward grimaced at the sticky feeling along his thighs and abdomen, the sensation of matted pubic hairs...and it all came together. *Blood! Her maiden's blood. Cinder.*

He turned to the empty side of the bed, his heart pounding. "Cinder? Where is she?" Edward whipped off the suede mask and looked to the captain for an answer.

"The girl?" he asked dumbly.

"Of course, the woman." A flutter of movement drew Edward's eyes down to the bustier in the captain's hand. His stomach rebelled. Edward grasped at it, extracting it from the other man's grip. He shook it at the captain in warning. "Where is she?" *Goddess help me, if they've harmed her, I will—*

"You were my first concern," the captain replied.

"Meaning?" Was it impossible to get a speedy, coherent answer from the fool?

"I stopped pursuing her to return to you."

"You let her leave?" he demanded.

"My first—"

"Find her! I want Cinder delivered to me within the hour, unharmed and unmolested, not so much as a hair disturbed." How he retained the presence of mind to make that last part clear was beyond him, but he knew he had to. "Tell one of the other men to wake Hein Darren and Jason. I'll need Lord Elmstead and the guest list immediately...in his study."

The guard hesitated, seemingly dumbfounded by this turn of events.

"Now, Captain," he roared. "If I do not have her within the hour, you will pay the price of failure, personally."

"Yes, Highness." The guard bolted away, shouting more orders.

Edward pushed from the bed, seeking out a pair of lounging pants to start the day. It wasn't the way he'd wanted to start it, that much was certain.

In the main room, he stared at the open door to the balcony, his heart aching. Why did she leave him?

* * * *

Amber crept into the house, shivering. Her shoes and the lower reaches of the skirt were soaked in dew, and without a layer beneath, her cloak wasn't sufficient.

She toed off her shoes, leaving them near the heater to dry. Though they lit fires for ambiance and the mental equivalent of warmth, the heat came from more conventional means.

That accomplished, she hiked the skirt and sprinted for the bath she shared with Nana, still aching lightly. There was little chance Amber had time for leisure, but she had to wash. She stripped her few remaining clothes onto the floor while the tub ran, then sank into the water, wincing at the heat against her chilled and newly-used body.

A moment of peace was all she allowed herself. Then she scrubbed herself clean, let out the water, and dried off. The towel wrapped around her and the clothing held to her chest, she headed for her room, padding down the corridor.

Safety was almost her own.

"Amber?" Nana called.

She sighed. "Can we not tonight?" she inquired, letting her exhaustion show.

"But we must."

She nodded, trudging into Nana's room. The sooner they got past this, the sooner Amber could get back to her own miserable existence. She settled on the edge of Nana's bed gingerly, crowding next to her grandmother's frail, old legs.

"I see you met someone," Nana stated confidently.

Amber looked up at her, horror dawning. Would everyone know? That would complicate things with Mora and the hens.

"The love bite," Nana continued, motioning to Amber's shoulder.

She nodded, touching the mark. At least her dresses would hide it.

"And how did it go?"

"The first time is not enjoyable." *Liar! Save that fateful thrust, it had been immensely enjoyable.*

Nana smiled an all-too-knowing smile.

"For either of us," Amber qualified, blinking back the tears burning at her eyes.

Her smile faded. "He didn't make an offer?" She sounded as if the idea was incomprehensible to her.

"I didn't satisfy him," she admitted miserably. "Why would he?"

"But...what went wrong? A man—"

"I'd rather not," Amber pleaded. Wasn't living it bad enough? Now, Nana wanted to pick apart how she'd failed so miserably?

"Another time," Nana conceded. "When it's not so fresh in your mind and heart."

Amber was certain that this sense of loss would never fade, but she nodded her agreement. Anything that ended this discussion and let Amber retreat to ease her wounds—literally—was fair game.

Nana plucked the skirt from her hand, her brow furrowing. "Where is the bustier?"

"I...lost it." *The other conversation I do not wish to have.* But the costume was Nana's, and she deserved an accounting of how it came to be lost.

"Lost? How could you lose such a thing?"

Amber groaned. "Must we, tonight?" She hardly understood it herself. Explaining it was going to be torture.

"Tell me," she ordered.

"A soldier chased me from the grounds. I don't know why he did, so please don't ask it."

Nana scrunched her nose in distaste. "What did he say?"

"Only that he meant to arrest me, and his sword was drawn. I panicked and ran...and lost the bustier I was carrying."

"I don't understand any of this," Nana complained. "Why did your young man not return you to your escort? Or home?"

Her face heated. "He fell asleep after the disaster...and I—"

"You left without waking him?"

Amber nodded.

"Then how could you know his intentions? Really, Amber."

She sighed. Nana was rarely this exasperated with her. "He... He was angry at the way... Oh, what does it matter? I never got his title, so even if I wanted to apologize for the way I left him, it's impossible. The only name I know him by is Christopher, his given name."

Nana's brow creased, as if she half-remembered something, which wasn't uncommon. "I don't think I know a Christopher, but I haven't been socially active in more than a decade."

"What difference does it make?" Amber repeated miserably. "I didn't make a decent impression. Did I?"

"Leaving as you did? Probably not, but don't worry. Young men are single-minded creatures. If he is of a mind to find you, he will."

Amber's stomach dropped out suddenly, but whether it was in excitement or dread, she couldn't say.

Be realistic! There's no chance he wants to find me.

* * * *

"How?" Edward growled, face to face with the captain who'd woken him. "How could you let her slip away?"

His expression showed discomfort at Edward's anger, but he held himself at rigid attention. "You were my primary concern, Highness."

"I was fine."

"How could I know that?"

He couldn't, and Edward couldn't argue that. Still, the delay had cost them catching Cinder before she could make her escape. For that alone, Edward wanted the guard to pay dearly.

"Dear Goddess, Edward," his father exploded, striding through the door in a dressing gown, no sign of lounging pants beneath. "What is this? A search of the grounds? People rousted out of bed? Talk of you coated in blood?"

"It wasn't *my* blood," Edward countered, letting his irritation show.

Darren strode in, clothed much as Edward was himself, soft lounging pants and nothing more. Elmstead was at his heels, dressed in a warm sweater and trousers, being one of the first woken and in charge of overseeing the search of the grounds in Edward's stead.

"I never thought blood play was to your tastes," his father offered, seemingly bewildered at the statement.

Edward speared him with a quelling look. "It's not."

Darren howled in laughter, planting his hand on the stone fireplace, newly lit for the day by sleep-deprived servants. He took a cup of coffee from the tray headed for the table, still chuckling as he raised it for a sip.

Benjamin turned on his nephew. "And *what* is so amusing about this?"

Darren motioned to Edward with the cup. "Only he could go to a Bride Ball teaming with willing wantons and find the only unwilling virgin in the room."

Edward felt his face heat. "She was willing. By the Goddess, she was willing." Just the memory of how willing she'd been had him semi-erect again.

"Then where is she, cousin?" Darren mocked him.

He shrugged. It was one of the things he wished he knew. Why had she left him before daybreak and without waking him? How did she escape trained royal guards? Why did she—

Well, he knew why she ran from the guards. They'd likely frightened her to death.

His father took Edward by the shoulders, his expression grim. "You had her and then lost her?"

"I had her, but I think it more accurate to say that your guards lost her."

The captain sighed. "My first duty—"

"Enough," Edward roared at him. "I am sick of that excuse."

And his head ached; the captain's voice grated at it. Edward considered dismissing him, just to silence the fool. Then again, standing at attention for long periods of time was damned uncomfortable; the captain deserved a little discomfort in return for Edward's. "Do not speak to me again, unless I address you directly. You should not acknowledge that order aloud."

Blessed silence met him, thank the Goddess.

Benjamin shot a look of surprise at Edward, a look that pointed out his son was not acting at all like himself. "Would you recognize her?" he questioned, releasing Edward's shoulders.

Edward scowled at him. "Since I'd intended to make her my wife, I should hope I would." Reining in his sarcasm was poorly executed.

Elmstead cleared his throat. "If I may be so bold?"

"Be," Edward barked. "Since there was no 'Cinder' on the guest list, you can hardly do worse than I have."

Darren snickered into his coffee cup. "She used a false name? With you?"

"She..." He sighed. "She didn't know who I was...precisely," he admitted.

His father stared at him, working his jaw as if half-forming words.

"I want a woman that wants *me*, not my crown."

"Your crown is part of who you are," Benjamin insisted.

"My way. Remember?"

His father nodded his agreement, though he was clearly unhappy at giving it.

"Lord Elmstead," Edward called out, without taking his eyes off of his father. He plucked a slice of bread with jam off an offered tray and bit into it, groaning at the burst of flavor washing over his tongue. He hadn't realized how famished he was. He took another bite, a larger one, narrowly restraining himself from wolfing it down and grasping another.

"Yes," Elmstead managed. "While it is impossible to say for certain, masks and all—"

Edward turned to him. "You know who she is? Why didn't you mention it earlier?"

"I..." He cleared his throat. "I hadn't realized there was some question of *who* she was. I thought the aim was to catch her before she fled the grounds. Admittedly, that did not go well. Still, I believe I can clear up the question of her identity." He looked toward Edward's chest. "In fact, if she is the lady I believe she is, she made that."

He glanced down in confusion, his gaze settling on the slice of bread he'd been savoring. "The bread? Is she a servant in your household? A baker's daughter?" She certainly worked for a living, based on the rough touch of her fingertips.

And if she was hiding within the manor...in servants' quarters that might have been overlooked, her escape had been easily managed. It was enough to make him regret punishing the captain. He glanced at the man in question. *Almost enough.*

"No. She isn't my servant, and it was the jam she made...not the bread, though her bread is— Not that it is of importance." Elmstead shifted nervously.

Edward stared him down. "How do you know her, Elmstead?"

"I met her when I delivered the invitations." But he wouldn't meet Edward's eyes.

"And? You delivered well over a hundred invitations to hundreds of young women, not accounting for those delivered by your guards and servants, of course. Why would you remember this one woman, out of hundreds?"

Elmstead darkened. "I offered her a place as my mistress. You see, when her grandmother—"

"You *what*?" Fury coursed through Edward at the thought of Cinder in the hands of one who played the games as extensively as Elmstead did.

"I didn't touch her, if that's what—"

"Since she was virginal, I imagine whatever did happen—"

"She turned me down, altogether," Elmstead inserted. "I told her to keep me in mind for when her grandmother passes. So...obviously, I kept her in mind, for just such an occasion. How could I know you would take an interest?"

Edward considered that. "When her grandmother... What of her grandmother?" Cinder had spoken several times of a grandmother. The woman had provided Cinder's outfit for the ball. She'd pushed Cinder to attend, to find a husband or lover.

Elmstead's voice broke him out of his train of thought. "She's the daughter of a mistress. When her grandmother passes, she'll likely be turned out of her home."

If there was a chance that her granddaughter would be turned out... It fit nicely.

"Edward?" his father asked.

He ignored Benjamin, meeting Elmstead's gaze instead. "What is her name?"

"Amber. Amber Oakmarch, daughter of the late Lord Marcus Oakmarch and his mistress, Xandra."

Something pressed at his conscious mind, a memory of their brief conversation. "Did Marcus *want* to marry his mistress?"

Elmstead stared at him in shocked silence.

"He did." Edward smiled, knowing now that he'd found her. "Of course, he did." It explained everything.

Well, not everything. I still don't know why she left me.

"How did you know it?" Elmstead asked.

"It doesn't matter."

"Jason?" Benjamin intoned, motioning toward the guest list they'd been poring over.

Elmstead nodded toward the book. "She'll be listed under Lady Mora Oakmarch."

Jason flipped through the alphabetical listing, his finger trailing down the appropriate page. He stopped, staring at the entry. When he didn't immediately offer an answer, Edward's lungs started to ache in the breath he hadn't realized he was holding.

He let it out on an irritated demand of "Well?"

"She didn't attend."

Elmstead groaned. "I thought for certain—"

"Are you sure?" Edward ached at the loss of her again.

Jason turned the book, indicating the pertinent block of names. "Lady Mora and her daughters, Ladies Marquita and Kambry Montberry, attended. Amber Oakmarch sent her regrets. Unless it was entered in error—"

"Do you think it was?" Edward asked, turning to pin Elmstead in his gaze.

The lord darkened. "On any other occasion, I would state that it was impossible for Brand to have made such an error."

"And now?"

His host appeared at a loss for words. Finally, he managed a shaky response. "I was so sure it was her. That was what prompted the laugh in the—"

Edward nodded. "Well, then... I suppose we should go pay a visit to—"

"Now?" Elmstead asked, aghast at the suggestion.

"I doubt she's deeply asleep," Edward offered acidly.

His father scrubbed a hand over his face, looking harried. "Don't you think you ought to dress first?"

Edward looked down at his bare chest, running a hand over it. "Probably." But if it meant finding her, he wasn't sure he cared.

"You might want to consider waiting to pursue her," Darren offered, without a hint of his usual humor. "Just until you're certain she's the right one, of course."

Edward turned to his cousin, his heart pounding, feeling the tension building inside. "Is there a reason I should wait?" *And by the Goddess, it had better be a good reason.*

"Jason said she's related to Marquita and Kambry Montberry?"

Jason replied for him. "Amber Oakmarch's stepsisters of Lady Mora Oakmarch. They were the children of Lady Mora's first marriage to the Duke of Montberry," he prattled on.

Darren winced, and Edward felt his heart stutter.

"And what difference does that make, *cousin*?" Edward inquired, abruptly wishing he'd had more sleep.

"Well, I saw you with your...uh..." He motioned uncertainly, his entire body an alarming shade of scarlet that made his hair seem to glow.

"Bride, I can only hope."

Darren nodded sheepishly. "I thought you were fairly settled."

"You *bedded*—" He hesitated at Darren's flinch. "Which one did you?" He didn't question it.

His cousin didn't reply.

"Both of them?" Edward asked, the sick pounding in his head expanding to include his roiling stomach. He looked at the bread he still held and pitched it at the table. His appetite could be dead for weeks, at this news. "As me." Somehow, he knew the answer.

"I wasn't supposed to be *me*," Darren replied, managing a strained smile.

"Goddess, I could choke you right now," he grumbled.

"I'm only mortal, Edward, and what they offered was enough to tempt a god."

"As me? Couldn't you have restrained yourself for one night? Or...at least changed clothes and—"

"Easy for you to say. You get to fade into the walls at every Bride Ball. I am draped with willing women, making offers—"

"Now you know why I hate it," Edward snapped at him.

"I *don't* hate it. I love it. I just hate not being able to—"

"Well, you did!"

Darren smiled crookedly. "Oh, I did, at that," he drawled.

"This isn't the time," Edward warned him.

His smile faded to a brittle copy. "So... What will you do now?"

Edward took a calming breath. "You didn't make them any promises, did you?"

"Only consideration. You're considering them all...in some manner."

And rejecting them all, save Cinder. "Jason, start at the beginning of the list of attendees. Elmstead, you've met these women. Circle any that could be mistaken for Amber Oakmarch. Cross off any that can't be. If you don't know the lady, leave her. If you know which of your servants issued the invitation in question, ask them about the ones you don't know. Leave any they can't call immediately to mind."

"And Amber Oakmarch?" Jason inquired.

Edward considered Elmstead's certainty. "Circle her. Consider every woman on that list, those that attended, and those that supposedly didn't."

He turned to leave, intent on seeking out a pain pill for his throbbing head. His gaze settled on the captain. "You are dismissed," he granted gruffly. "I suggest you steer clear of me, until this is settled."

To the captain's credit, he didn't open his mouth to acknowledge the order.

CHAPTER SIX

"I hear the prince is searching for his bride," Kambry confided to her older sister, leaning across the table in a manner Mora would censure her for.

Amber rolled her eyes behind the cover of her book. Who cared what the prince did? Let him pick the lucky woman and have a palace full of fat, happy babes.

"He knows who we are, Kambry," Marquita replied irritably, no doubt reasoning that His Highness would have no need to search for them. "And had he wished to find us, it wouldn't have taken him more than a week to do so."

Amber didn't take delight in that, as she usually would. "Marquita the Spoiled" not getting her way was typically fodder for days of giggles, but not today.

At present, that reminder only reinforced that if Christopher had wanted to find Amber, he could have managed it in less time than this. Even with a fake name, there were only so many un-augmented ladies of Amber's description to be found.

"It sounds as if he's making a show of it," Kambry sing-songed. "He's going house to house, searching for the lady. I heard he has something of hers that was left behind."

Marquita moved so abruptly that she rattled the stoneware on the tabletop and sloshed tea. Amber peeked at the mess over the cover, then pretended not to notice. If the tablecloth was ruined, it wasn't her fault. And it wasn't one of Nana's precious lace cloths, either. It was one of the tacky damask monstrosities that Mora favored.

Marquita's excited chatter cut through her preoccupation.

"My garter?"

"No one knows or no one will say. But... I do know that he went to Maplelane and Beechgrove, skipping us completely."

There was a tense moment of silence. "You think he means to come here last and make a grand show of it?"

"It could be. It is worth considering, given the circumstances."

Amber closed her eyes, saying a silent prayer that Kambry was correct. It wasn't that she had some burning urge to see her stepsisters succeed in their quest, but if they did, there was reward to be had of it.

For one thing, at least one of the chattering hens would move to the palace...or some summer home. Even if he only wanted one of the sisters, though he'd reportedly had sex with them both at the Bride Ball, the new "princess" could probably arrange for an advantageous marriage for her sister, removing the second hen from the house, as well. That meant immediate relief to a large portion of Amber's headaches.

Better, Mora would spend much of her time visiting her daughters and playing at court. Amber would have to spend little time with the "lady."

Of course, there was still the problem of Nana dying. Mora wouldn't give the house to Amber; it would be too close to defeat for her. To top it, there was always the chance that "the princess" would be dismissed, as Mora herself had been. Mora was too old to make a coveted position, and there was only so much of each year she could visit a daughter who didn't have a whole palace to let.

"Cinder!"

Marquita's demand cut through the fog of her thoughts. Amber sighed at the fact that her stepmother and stepsisters could make her beloved pet name sound so much a curse. It had always been a happy name, when her father used it.

Her heart quickened at the memory of it on Christopher's lips. It had been pleasant then, as well.

Realizing she still hadn't answered, she lowered her book, spearing Marquita with a bored look. No doubt, she was about to be ordered to clean up Marquita's mess. "Yes?"

"What will you do, if we go away?" It was a cruel question, meant to infer that Amber had nowhere to go and nothing to do, without the duty of serving them.

Rejoice! She feigned indifference. "Care for Nana...and marry a farmer or driver, I suppose. When she passes, I mean. Until, then, she needs me."

"Poor Cinder." Marquita affected a sigh.

Amber felt her temper coming unglued.

She had no opportunity to be pushed to venting. The door opened, and Mora rushed in, hanging her wrap. Kambry and Marquita straightened in their chairs, probably hoping their mother hadn't seen them slouch.

Mora turned, looking harried, though her appearance was impeccable, as always. "Marquita! Kambry! Present yourselves."

They rushed over, and Amber shut her book. She rose with another sigh, as Mora fussed over her daughters' hair and clothing. If they were primping, it meant important guests of Nana's house, whether Mora entertained them or Nana did. For Nana's sake, Amber would make certain Oakmarch left a favorable impression on them.

She tucked the book in her apron pocket and mopped at the spilled tea. "Bread and jam?" she asked, to be certain.

"To your room," Mora snapped.

Amber looked up in surprise. "Pardon?"

Mora leveled a look of cold dislike at her. "To your room...now."

"As you wish." She marched smartly to the stairs, not offering so much as a single backward glance, studiously ignoring their fawning and planning.

It was surprising that Mora wanted her gone. The possession of servants would make the household seem richer. Her stepmother likely didn't want any possible competition for the attention about to be heaped on Marquita and Kambry, not that a plain little servant girl was much competition.

She slowed, considering that. She had felt lovely once, when Christopher had singled her out, when he'd proclaimed her "perfect."

Amber wasn't perfect, of course. She wasn't even especially pretty. She'd never had milk baths and cosmetic surgeries...not that she wanted them. Amber had work-roughened hands that she kept moderately softened with a lotion her grandmother had given her and a pumice stone.

She closed the door to her room behind her, settling on the bed, pulling out the book again. From outside, she heard the approach of several vehicles.

Amber didn't go to the window. What would be the point of it? They weren't her guests; she wasn't even expected to serve them. She would probably not know them, based on the fact that she'd never been banished from the lower reaches when guests arrived before.

What did it matter? They'd think her beneath them, anyway.

Christopher didn't seem to, though it must have been painfully obvious to him that I was lowborn.

It was a maddening thing to be the daughter of a lord and be nothing more than a servant in your own home, but that was the fate the Goddess had served her. It did no good to cry over it or whine as Marquita did when she felt she was hopelessly behind the fashions.

She opened the book to the page she'd abandoned downstairs and started to read. It was a favorite, one her father had read to her many times.

The sound of Nana's cane brought her head around. Amber started to stand, then reconsidered when she realized Nana was headed for the stairs.

Mora didn't want Amber seen. It would serve Mora right if she and her daughters were forced to serve Nana a cup of tea. If the Goddess was just, they might singe a ruffle or a bit of lace. Amber wouldn't wish a burn, even on them.

She settled back into her book, losing herself in the world between the covers as she always had, startling at a new sound.

The footsteps heading back up the stairs were heavier, too heavy to be a woman. They sounded of boots, a man's tread, determined...military? Her heart started to pound, and she fisted her hand around the edge of the book.

The footsteps stopped at her door, and Amber forced herself to continue breathing, however erratically. The knock was quick and hard.

"C-come in," she managed. Whatever this was, it was best to meet it seated. At least, she wouldn't hit her head if she fainted away.

The door opened and a soldier stepped inside. "Amber Oakmarch?" he asked gruffly.

She nodded, feeling lightheaded. Visions of the soldier that had chased her down raced in her mind, and she was suddenly certain she was about to find out what offense she'd committed that night.

Amber prayed it was a minor thing. If they took her away, who would care for Nana?

"Come with me, if you please." It wasn't a question.

Amber rose on quaking legs, dropping the book on her bed. At least, if they arrested her, they wouldn't take the book. She walked to the doorway, and the soldier cleared it for her. He kept pace behind her on the way to the stairs, not touching her but close enough to grab her, if she ran.

Where was there to run? *Nowhere.*

* * * *

"You're really going to do this?" Edward asked. He still couldn't believe Darren was serious.

His cousin smiled. "You didn't experience them."

"I don't *want* to."

William, Elmstead's driver, laughed heartily at that. The guard beside him kept his silence.

The house they stopped at was a well-kept little estate. The "manor" was the size of a large family home, consisting of perhaps eight bedrooms...maybe one more, depending on what common rooms it claimed.

It was a charming place. Early spring flowers pushed through the night-frosted ground. The smells of baking reached them before the door opened to reveal a woman of about his mother's age, her auburn hair pulled into a fall of ringlets cascading over her shoulder.

Edward was glad that he'd brought guards along. Considering Darren's intimacy with the Montberry women, thinking his cousin was Edward, the Goddess only knew what would happen next. The last thing Edward wanted was the two pawing at *him*; the guards were ordered to prevent that.

"Welcome, Your Highness," Lady Mora Oakmarch offered. Her gaze flicked to Darren, started to slide away, then returned, no doubt noting the wealth his clothing attested to. "And... I do not believe we've met, sir." She ignored the guards, as most nobles would.

"I believe you have," Edward quipped.

Darren elbowed him, and Lady Mora's brows rose. "Hein Darren Willowmarsh," his cousin offered with a slight bow of his head.

Her smile returned...then spread. "Oh, my. *Two* young royals, then. Please, do come in." She turned away, motioning to someone behind her, most likely her daughters.

Edward took the lead, wincing at the sight of the younger women. Their bodices were half-unlaced in invitation. Ringlets of copper hair on the shorter and blonde on the taller were strategically let down to infer wanton behavior and arranged to draw the eyes to the nearly-indecent display of breasts.

"How nice to...see you again, Your Highness," the blonde purred.

It was time to shatter her illusions. "I am afraid I've never met you, dear lady."

"Of course. You met so many people at the—"

"It wasn't me," Edward restated.

Darren stepped in. "I apologize for the deception, Marquita." He shifted his eyes to the shorter. "Kambry."

Their smiles faltered. Even Lady Mora seemed somewhat peaked.

Darren cleared his throat. "You see... Edward had asked me to act as his decoy, so he could mingle in secret."

"But you let us think," Kambry began heatedly.

Mora whispered something to her daughters that caused Kambry to choose silence. A moment later, three vibrant, if not sincere, smiles returned.

Lady Mora clapped her hands once. "Now that we've cleared up that misconception, why don't we sit, and you can tell us why you've decided to grace our home."

Edward would rather have stood in his nervous state, but he sat out of courtesy, refusing the offer of bread and jam.

Darren leaned forward in his chair. "I've told my father about your offer, that I wanted to accept it, if you are of a heart to, knowing I'm not Edward."

"And he said?" Lady Mora inquired before her daughters could respond. There was a tension about her that made little sense.

"He has no objection to the pair," he offered tactfully. "However, he doesn't care for the messy complication of marrying one, when it may be the other that bears me an heir first."

Mora stayed silent, letting Darren get to the runner's tape at his own pace.

"He wishes me to take both as mistresses, until one presents me with a son. The one that does first will be my wife and the other my mistress."

There was a moment of silence.

"And what assurances have my daughters?" Mora asked.

"Five years. I am a relatively young man. I won't take any other mistresses or a wife for that long."

"Daughters?" she asked.

Marquita smiled sweetly. "Agreed, as long as we have equal time of you."

Darren nodded. "You may well exhaust me, but I can promise it."

Kambry hesitated only a moment. "Agreed." But she seemed troubled by it.

Mora nodded. "Very well. Shall we—"

"A moment, Lady Mora," Edward interrupted her. "There is one more thing."

In the silence that fell, Edward could hear someone moving on the floor above.

"Yes, Your Highness?"

"I understand there is a third young lady in the household, one by the name of Amber Oakmarch?"

She tensed, and her light blue eyes hardened to slate gray. "There is."

"She has dark hair and eyes and is less...endowed than your own daughters are, Lord Elmstead tells me. About the height of your Kambry."

"She is."

Marquita's jaw tightened, but her tongue remained leashed.

"I should like to...examine her," he offered delicately.

"For what reason?" Mora's voice was deceptively sweet; every pore oozed anger that seemed to taint the air around them.

"I met a woman of that description at the Bride Ball, but she slipped away from me."

Mora laughed lightly. "It couldn't have been Amber. She didn't go to the ball."

"You're refusing to let me see the woman then?" He added a challenge to his tone and expression, annoyed by her impertinence.

Her face paled a shade or two, half-masked by her cosmetics. "Of course not. I only fear you're wasting your time. Amber didn't go to the Bride Ball."

"Of course, she did," a new voice corrected sharply. "She was gone nearly all night."

Edward stood, turning to the stairs, taking stock of the speaker. She was elderly, white hair pulled up in a simple bun, leaning on a cane but with bright dark eyes that belied her age.

He fished for the lady of the house's name. "You were saying, Lady Reanne?"

She took a pained step down the stairs, her gnarled hand gripping hard at the banister. Edward waved his guards to her, and the corporal scrambled up the stairs, offering his arm.

Reanne took it with a smile, then started speaking as she descended. "Mora refused to escort Amber, so I asked my driver's son, Keane, to chauffer for her."

Mora paled a notch more. "She had nothing to wear," she protested. "She has no etiquette. She would have embarrassed the family."

Reanne reached the floor and hobbled toward them, assisted by the attentive corporal. "You are correct that Amber owns nothing appropriate to wear to a Bride Ball, but I had an outfit from my youth that was still serviceable...if somewhat behind the styles."

Edward's heart stuttered in excitement. What had Cinder said?

"My grandmother's, but I'd rather wear it."

"She couldn't have come in without an escort," Mora insisted.

"Her proclaimed escort was already inside." Reanne sank into the chair Edward had vacated. She offered the corporal a smile and nod of thanks.

"She wasn't announced," Mora continued.

Reanne chuckled. "I cannot imagine how she managed that, but Amber is a resourceful one."

Marquita fluffed her hair, seemingly bored with the topic of conversation. "Well, I certainly didn't see Cinder there."

"What did you say?" Edward asked, praying he hadn't misheard her.

"I said that I didn't see her at the ball."

"Not that. What did you call her?" he insisted.

"Oh, *thaaat*. Cinder was a pet name her father gave her when she was a child." She screwed up her face in disgust. "Always playing in—"

"Lady Reanne." Edward forced his voice to remain calm. "Where is your granddaughter?"

She smiled an all-too-knowing smile. "In her room. Reading, I would imagine. Amber is always reading, when she has a moment to. If you wish to summon her, it is the furthest room on the left, upstairs."

He nodded to the same guard that had helped Reanne down the stairs, marking him as gentle enough in his regard to be charged with this task. Edward itched to go himself, but that would be unseemly, until he knew for certain that she was his Cinder.

No. *That* was unseemly. Though his father would try to coerce her to marriage, Edward would respect her choice in the matter.

She had a choice, and she could choose to leave him...again. His heart ached at that. Wasn't losing her once bad enough?

Footsteps returned, and Edward steeled himself, he believed, for every eventuality. Darren appeared at his shoulder, offering comfort silently as she stepped onto the stairs, the guard a step behind.

The body was right. The lush curves filled her dress as they had the costume. Her dark hair was drawn back in a tight braid. She was jittery and pale, even her full lips pink instead of the red he remembered. If only he could see her eyes, he might be sure.

As if she heard his internal musing, Amber looked around and spied him. She stopped short, her eyes widening and flicking back and forth between him and Darren.

Edward groaned inwardly at that. With the masks between them, she had no more clue which man was the one who'd mounted her than Marquita and Kambry had.

Amber's eyes locked solidly on Edward, making him question that belief. Did she know? Was it a lucky guess?

She swallowed hard, backed off a step, and collided with the corporal behind her. The guard's hands clamped down on her shoulders, and Amber gasped.

Edward tensed, preparing to move. The guards knew better than this; they knew Amber wasn't to be harmed.

Darren addressed the situation before Edward could. "Gently. And...she looks faint, don't you think? Lady Mora, could you bring a glass of water for her?"

It wasn't really a question, and though she scowled at being relegated to servant, Mora sauntered off to comply with the order given.

The corporal guided Amber down the stairs, bringing her to Edward. Her eyes never left his, even while Darren was speaking, and her expression was unreadable.

"Cinder," Edward greeted her.

She winced and then nodded. There was no bow, no greeting in return, making Edward wonder what she thought was going on.

"Do you know who I am?" he asked. Did she realize he was the man she'd been intimate with? Or...was it simply the presence of "the prince" in the house that unnerved her?

She darkened, shooting a sidelong look toward her family, a sure sign that she knew precisely who he was. Still, there was no greeting for him. Her eyes met his again, and her head swiveled slowly back and forth in a negative response.

She lied? Edward couldn't believe she had the nerve to lie about it. Did she feel nothing for him?

He reached out and grasped the square neckline of her dress, easing it aside. The corporal moved his hand from that shoulder to her arm, freeing the material to slide away.

Amber didn't fight him. She didn't protest the move, though she trembled lightly.

The incriminating love bite appeared from behind the fabric, the purple and green of healing tissue not quite picking up the crimson of the skin around it, standing out in stark contrast.

Edward ran his fingertips over it, raising a brow in challenge of her claim not to know him. He put out his other hand, and her bustier settled in it, courtesy of one of the other guards.

Darren chuckled darkly. "Perhaps she should try it on for size, cousin," he suggested.

Amber folded her arms over her chest, pulling at the corporal's hold to accomplish it, obviously terrified by the idea that he might demand such a spectacle of her. "Please don't, Christopher. I don't know your family name. I swear it."

He stared at her for a long moment, working that comment through. "That was why you said you didn't know—"

She nodded, shooting a nervous look at the guards.

Edward motioned the corporal to release her, his head spinning. "Dear Goddess..." She had no clue who he was, even now. That much was clear.

Darren laughed as heartily as he had when he'd learned Edward had her virginity. "You used Christopher with her, and she used Cinder with you? It's no wonder you're both confused."

"We need to talk," Edward informed her. How could she not know who he was now? How could anyone mistake it?

"You lied?" she whispered, easing her dress back into place as if feeling exposed. "Your name isn't Christopher?"

A hoot of cruel laughter escaped Marquita's red-painted lips. She stifled it at a sharp look from Edward; he turned back to Amber, noting her misery in confusion.

Mora pushed a mug of water at her stepdaughter, clearing her throat when Amber didn't immediately take it.

Edward grasped the mug and waved her away, then scooped up Amber's hand and placed the mug in it. He hesitated. "It's as much my name as Cinder is yours. It is my second name, and my family used it when I was a child." While his grandfather was king...and also an Edward, it simplified matters to do so.

She nodded grimly. "Do you prefer it?" Amber was blunt. She'd always been honest and straight-forward.

"I do, but my family no longer uses it."

She nodded, taking a sip from the mug of water. "What do they use?" Her voice was reed thin.

He sighed. "Edward."

Amber closed her eyes and laid a hand to her forehead. "The...uh...the prince...Edward?"

Darren snorted in amusement. "Is there another Edward in the four quarters? It is a royal name."

She shook her head, seemingly more upset than she'd been moments earlier. "Then I wish you well, Your Highness." Amber turned from him, running blindly into the guard at her back.

"Amber!" Lady Reanne called out the rebuke, no doubt as shocked as Edward was himself by her reaction.

The corporal held her by the wrists, murmuring an order for Amber to be still, ignoring the water splashing against his jacket, courtesy of her weakly-executed bid for freedom.

"I believe the two of you need to speak in private," Reanne suggested, regaining her composure.

Amber's shoulders slumped in defeat, and she stopped pulling at the corporal's hold. "I will show him to the guest parlor," she agreed. "Or to yours?" There was a hopeful note in her voice.

"The guest master," her grandmother corrected.

Her head swung toward the old woman, wild-eyed, her body stiffening. "Nana," she gasped. "You can't be—"

"You can show Prince Edward to the room or be dragged there by his bodyguard. The choice, ultimately, is your own."

"It's unseemly," Amber protested.

"So is a Bride Ball, but you managed that well enough."

Amber darkened. "If you insist," she countered hotly.

"I do insist."

Edward smiled in spite of himself. It was obvious that the two butted heads often, but Reanne had succeeded in getting Amber's agreement. He wondered if she'd gotten her granddaughter's agreement to attend the Bride Ball in a similar fashion.

At Edward's nod, the corporal released her wrists and took a step back, clearing the way for her. Amber pushed the mug into his hands, leaving the guard to fumble it as she stalked around him, creating even more of a mess of his uniform.

Edward bit back a bark of laughter, smirking at the guards' incompetence in the face of one determined woman. *So, this is how she escaped them.* He didn't question it.

Amber marched around the guard and down the corridor beneath the stairs, her back ramrod straight, never more than two steps ahead of Edward. She led the way to the second door on the right.

There was no play at welcome. She swung the door wide, strode through, and left Edward to close it for himself or not, as he chose.

Closing it was the foregone conclusion. They needed privacy, and though he'd prefer somewhere more private, this would have to do.

CHAPTER SEVEN

She didn't look at him. Amber stood at the far side of the room, her back to him with her arms crossed over her chest, fairly vibrating in anger that Edward was at a loss to comprehend.

"Do you prefer Cinder or Amber?" he asked, as a means of breaking the tension.

It didn't work. "Since only those who don't look down on me call me Amber, I suppose Cinder is appropriate."

That stung. "You think I look down on you?" What had he said or done to give her that impression? Edward seized on the only thing that came immediately to mind. "If this is about letting the corporal restrain you—"

"My thanks for that," she offered in a voice dripping with sarcasm. "After all, striking *you* is treason."

Blow number two. "I don't understand," he admitted. That was unusual for him, but this conversation had stolen his center of balance. What had he done to deserve this cold reception? For that matter, why had she run from him, in the first place? He opened his mouth to ask it, but she spoke first.

"We both know why you're here, so—"

"Somehow, I doubt that," he grumbled.

Amber went rigid. The silence stretched between them. Finally, she sighed. "Say it, then."

"I thought you understood my purpose at the Bride Ball."

"A wife or nothing," she quoted back, but she did so without softening. Considering her background, why would that offend her?

"Yes. Is that so unpal—"

"And obviously, you've found what you want."

Her venom at that stunned him. *What did I do to make her hate me so much? Or...does she hate all nobles and sees me as no different?* No, that made no sense. There would have been no question at the Bride Ball that he wasn't lowborn. "I thought I had." How had he misjudged her this badly? *I don't know that I have...yet.*

Her back jerked, as if she held back a sob. "Then go collect it," she snapped.

"I'm trying to."

Amber turned on him, seemingly shocked beyond words, looking faint again.

She shouldn't be shocked. She shouldn't be confused. What did I do wrong? "Amber—"

"Me?" she squeaked.

"Who else would I be here to—"

Her face hardened into a mask of anger that left no doubt she felt him guilty of some affront against her. Her eyes flashed in fury. "As if I'd want the likes of *you.*"

Blow number three sliced deep. "What? What are you—"

She advanced a step, looking as if she'd pummel him, given the chance to. "Just how many women did you bed at the ball, Your Highness? I know of at least three."

Edward stared at her, dumbstruck. *What in the Goddess's holy name is she—*

Amber continued, without allowing him the chance to question her about it. "You're no different than Lord Elmstead and the Duke of Montberry, are you?"

"You were the only one," he assured her. *Goddess, why would she think that of me?*

She shot him a look of hurt; it wounded him to see it, to know that she believed it of him.

"Reason it, Amber. You came to my bed and left at just before sunup." When would he have had time to bed someone else?

That confused her...for a moment. "I came late. It must have been earlier, then."

Edward tried to piece it together. Was she relying on some idle chatter, some mad— *Goddess! Of course!* "You mean your sisters," he realized. She hadn't been downstairs for the revelation that they'd slept with Darren. It was little wonder that she thought him indiscriminate and indiscreet.

"Oh, yes," she fumed at him. "My *step*sisters are such shrinking violets that you forgot them completely."

"I didn't bed them, so there was nothing to forget."

Her mouth moved, but whatever sounds she meant to make never emerged. Her brow creased in confusion.

"You saw Darren," he began gently, motioning to the corridor.

Amber looked toward the closed door, her teeth working at her lower lip and her color returning in a rush that left her cheeks pink and appealing.

"When I approached you at the Bride Ball, where did you think Prince Edward was?" He kept his voice low and calming, hoping she'd stop and reason it through, given the time and space to do so.

She cleared her throat, darkening, her muscles relaxing slightly. "On the dais..." She paused, peeking up at him, looking sheepish. "With Marquita and Kambry."

"That was what I wished people to believe."

"Why? If you threw the Bride Ball, why hide in the crowd?"

Edward managed a grim smile. "Because, I wasn't searching for a wife like Marquita or Kambry. I didn't want someone selling herself, as they were. I'm sure they're skilled enough, but would there ever be honest enjoyment between us?"

Amber darkened to scarlet. "Oh, I believe they enjoy sex well enough...and their partners are rumored to be satisfied." Blunt, as always.

"If that's what they want," he conceded. "Darren was taken enough that he's made an offer."

She nodded, but she didn't reply.

Edward's nerves jumped in unease at her silence. "Do you understand now?" he asked.

She shook her head slowly, solemnly.

He chanced a few steps toward her, heartened when she didn't back away. "What don't you understand?"

"I'm... Nana said men like teaching a virgin, but is someone who's inexperienced to the point of ineptitude really ap—"

"You think *you're* inept?" Goddess, if she was any better, he'd never have been able to hold off for her.

Her gaze slid away, and she shrugged.

Edward eased his hands around her waist drawing Amber to his body.

Her breathing hitched. "You know who I am. You don't have to..." She jerked her head to the right.

He looked that direction, coming to the realization that she meant the bustier, now pressed to her hip, a moment later. Edward tossed it away, then settled the hand to her lower back.

"Chr...Edw..." Her eyes pleaded with him, at a loss, now that she knew who he really was.

"Christopher." He'd always preferred the pet name, and it might help Amber relax, if she thought of him as Christopher and not Prince Edward.

She nodded, taking a calming breath.

"I want to kiss you," he whispered.

Her eyes slid shut, and she swayed toward him, her lips parted slightly. Edward teased her with caresses of his lips and tongue, letting his eyes drift closed as his cock surged up.

Amber moaned, her hands creeping up his arms to his shoulders, her body nestling closer to his. She became bolder, her tongue venturing past his and into his mouth, her hands tunneling into his hair.

Moments later, they were molded together, their mouths meshed hard and their tongues dancing. Edward removed the barrette from her hair, combing his fingers through it, then cupping the back of her head to deepen the kiss further.

Goddess, but she met him with all she had. It was all he could do to ease away from her and not start taking liberties he wasn't certain she'd offer.

"That," he panted out, "was not inept."

"But you didn't..." Her passionate expression melted into one of misery.

Realization was a moment behind. "You were in pain." And still, he'd nearly come, but now was the wrong time to admit it.

Far from reassuring her, his reply seemed to confuse her further.

Edward berated himself again for his rush with her. "I was the clumsy one. Every shred of common sense told me you were new to the experience, and I didn't listen to it."

She shook her head. "I asked—"

"Yes, but I should have gone slowly."

"But...how can you know I won't...again?" She fidgeted, uncomfortable with something, but whether it was the idea of trying again or simply her inexperience with such discussions was a mystery.

"We could settle that," he suggested, raw in need.

"Here? Now?" Amber whispered hoarsely, looking toward the door, as if the thought scandalized her, as if the fact that her grandmother had sent them to this room held no meaning for her.

"I want you as my wife," he reminded her. *There was a time when it seemed she didn't mind that idea.* "Would you rather my bed than one in your own home?"

"There's been no agreement," she protested weakly.

"Then agree—"

"But you don't know—"

Edward forced a sigh in the place of the growl he wanted to vent. "You think it's unwise to agree before I know we're sexually compatible—which I might note I have no question of—but you think it's unseemly to prove it without an agreement? You try me to no end."

He'd meant it in teasing, but Amber blanched as if he'd struck a blow.

"And I love that you do."

She met his eyes, stunned.

"Agree to this," he cajoled, drawing his lips down the line of her jaw to her chin. "Let me prove we're compatible."

"Yes." Her answer ruffled his hair.

Edward returned to her lips, playing at her in hard, fast kisses while he stroked at her hair and unfastened the back of her dress. He eased her arms from his neck, removing the sleeves so the fabric pooled at her hips.

He went to work on his jacket, jerking it off the ends of his arms and sending it flying in the general direction of her bustier. His shirt went next, leaving them chest-to-chest, their mouths mating, over and over.

The swivel of Amber's hips broke them apart. Edward watched her work the dress and panties down her hips, licking his lips in anticipation. They slipped down to her knees, and she shimmied them off her feet, toeing her shoes off so that she stood naked.

Edward barely breathed. His hands fumbled at the buttons on his trousers; he yanked them open, his urge to be inside her at a fever pitch.

Calm. The last thing you want to do is hurt her again. He didn't, but controlling himself after more than a week without her was going to be difficult.

Amber's hands eased inside the waistline, pushing them away...and his underwear with them. She stared between their bodies, her eyes wide in something resembling wonder.

He raised his hands and raked them through her hair, drawing Amber closer to his body. The feeling of his cock tangling in her feminine curls had him shivering in need.

She hesitated.

"Is there a problem?" he asked.

"I can't..." Amber pushed his trousers another finger-width. "If you're holding me like this, I can't—"

"I don't care." Edward was hard and aching. It would be a sure sign of the Goddess's power, if he restrained himself long enough to get inside her, let alone undressed before it.

Amber looked up at him, questioning that statement. He didn't answer. Edward tilted his head and brought his lips to hers, enticing her open for him.

Her hands trailed up his thighs, paused, then caressed his cock. She learned his dimensions, tested his feel, played in the fluids leaking from him, all the while forcing him closer to the abyss.

Edward had to change what was happening before he spent in her hand. Though it would prove she could pleasure him...and be damned enjoyable at the same time, it wouldn't prove she could take him inside.

He prayed Amber wasn't still tender from their first time. It was unlikely, given the amount of time she'd had to heal. Still, there was no knowing if he'd taken all of her hymen, in his haste.

It was unacceptable that she believe it was insurmountable. Edward had to ease her into the sensation this time, provide adequate pleasure, even if she also felt a bit of pain, so he could convince her that the pain would subside with time.

He guided her toward the bed, leaving her mouth as he eased to the surface. Edward placed his hands on her hips, drawing Amber down over him. He turned, raising his legs to the mattress between hers, nearly groaning at how hot and wet she was.

Amber shifted against his thigh, biting her lower lip as she experimented with the joys of touching. Her hands went to his hips, seeking balance or purchase.

Edward slid his hand between his thigh and her ready body, playing at her clit. Her eyes fluttered shut on a gasp, and his mouth watered to taste her again. She cycled her hips, riding his fingertips, seeking her climax.

Knowing if she'd recovered from their last encounter was imperative. Edward eased one finger inside her, stilling as she did, her hands clasped tight on his waist.

For a moment, her panting was the loudest sound in the room. He didn't advance or retreat, though he teased at her clit with his thumb.

Amber started moving again, more fervently. Edward watched her, greedy, determined to feel and see her shatter on his hand.

She didn't disappoint him. Her head tipped back, until her hair brushed his thighs and knees with every movement. Her sheath jerked, tightened, then started undulating around him.

Edward slid a second finger into her contracting body, and she let out a little mew of want. At the edges of restraint, he added a third, pushing slowly into the crowded channel. Her head came up, her eyes meeting his. Edward stroked the fingers in and out of her slowly, testing her response.

Her gaze trailed down his body, raising goose bumps in her wake. She stopped at his waist, no doubt considering his cock.

"You want to feel it," he whispered, hoping it was true. "Smoother than my fingers, thicker, longer."

Amber nodded, a dreamy look in her eyes, as if imagining what it would feel like. Her body clenched around his fingers in silent demand.

Edward moved his free hand to his cock, stroking it suggestively, then bracing it up from his body for her. He slid his fingers free, making a show of painting her climax on the head of his cock, mixing it with his own fluids.

She watched him hungrily, then shot him a questioning look.

"You control this. Take as much of me as you're comfortable with...as slowly as you wish." *Goddess help me hold off for her,* he begged silently.

"What if I can't take all of you?"

"That will come in time," he soothed her.

"Can you... If I don't, can you..." She darkened.

"It's not going to take much of you." Already, the urge to spend was riding him hard.

Amber eased up high on her knees and shifted further up his body. Edward tipped his hips, stroking the tip of his cock against her clit...then lower, teasing at her slit. A low moan escaped her lips, and Amber eased down over him, going still as the head gave way to shaft.

Edward panted back his body's call to thrust deep and spend, squeezing his eyes shut tight. When he opened them, it was to the sight of Amber's questioning eyes.

"You are so potent," he explained.

She seemed surprised that he found her so, but she took several more finger-widths of him. Perhaps, she was testing his claim. Edward couldn't be certain, but he encouraged her with half-formed pleas for more.

The feeling of her body engulfing more of him stole his sanity. He cried out in pleasure, and she retreated slightly along his length.

"Yes. Like that," he managed. "By the Goddess, yes."

Amber returned, halfway down his length, slid back, then came at him again, nearly reaching his still-circling fingers. Edward moved them, bringing his hands to her hips, riding the wave of his rising body and tightening slightly as she came down deeper.

"Oh, yes," she echoed him. "Like that."

The next downward motion of her hips took Edward nearly to the root. He met her eyes, pushing his hips up to seat the last of himself in her.

Her eyes slid shut, and she stayed there, probably acclimating to the sensation. Edward held his ground, though the need to move was maddening.

Amber rocked lightly, little wisps of motion that rendered his breathing harsh and choppy. He cycled his hips, affecting deeper thrusts.

She murmured something he didn't quite hear. It sounded of a request...perhaps a plea.

"Tell me," he grumbled. "Tell me how it feels. Tell me what you want."

Her eyes remained closed. "The way you took me before," she gasped out. "I want you...above..."

Edward rolled her beneath him with a growl, taking the dominant position. Her legs wrapped around his waist, and she rose against him, drawing Edward further into her body. His patience and control at their breaking points, he started thrusting, half-afraid it would be too much for her.

Far from it, Amber grasped hard at his shoulders, her short nails leaving hot trails. Her legs tightened around him, and she bucked hard against him, her breathing ragged.

"What do you want?" he repeated. By the Goddess, he wanted to hear her say it.

"More."

"You want all of me?" he asked for clarification. "As deep as I can go?"

"Yes," she shouted, her sheath whispering the precursors to another climax. "Yes, Christopher!"

He settled further back on his knees, pulling her legs from his hips and urging them up and out to open her body. Amber stared at him, quaking lightly.

"Without changing positions completely, this is one of the deepest..." he explained hastily. "Do you trust me?"

She nodded, seemingly beyond words, as she'd often been their first night together.

Edward pushed inside her, shuddering as he reached deeper than he had been before. A wild drive to imprint his length on her untried body assaulted him. But would such an aggressive move frighten her?

Amber moaned, arching her back. "Now, Christopher," she begged.

That spelled the end of his control. Edward pistoned his hips, trying to even his breathing and heart rate, to stave off release.

"You're mine," he informed her.

"Yes." Her eyes were heavy in arousal, her hips rising and falling in his rhythm.

By the Goddess, she'd never want another, if he could help it.

That was his last coherent thought. After that, it was only sensation...flesh against flesh, slicked by their body fluids and sweat, their mixed taste and scent, the pounding of the bed and their rising sounds.

Amber shattered around him, screaming in ecstasy, pulling at Edward as if there was any way to draw him further into her. He cried out at the sensation of her body milking him dry, roared in triumph as Amber shouted his name, sank over her in the aftermath of a draining climax.

They lay together, his cock jerking in continuing spasms, releasing the last of his pent-up cum into her. Edward nuzzled at her lips, stroking inside her mouth when they parted, sharing her breath. He pressed his forehead to hers, every finger-width of his body sensitized as a result of their loving.

"Will you agree?" he asked.

There was a moment of disconcerting silence between them.

"Yes. I will."

CHAPTER EIGHT

Amber sighed, burrowing further under the quilt. The house was unnaturally quiet, and for a moment she felt certain it was the middle of the night. The light around her was so brilliant that it illuminated the space behind her eyelids, making her vision rosy, even with her eyes shut, belying the idea that there was darkness beyond the windows.

Her brain worked at that. Her room didn't get direct sunlight, between the angles of the sun and the trees on that side of the house. That was one of the reasons none of the other family members wanted it, the reason Marquita had claimed Amber's old rooms when her father died. The only rooms that got light this bright were Nana's, Mora's and the two hens'.

And the guest rooms. Dear Goddess!

Amber opened her eyes, blinking in the harsh evening light. The dark shape looming over her attained form and detail.

Christopher was watching her, his head cocked up on one bent arm. His expression was unreadable but intense. She drew the quilt up from her belly to her chin, feeling as if she was on display.

Don't be stupid! He's seen me nude. Twice, to date.

He smiled, and her heart rate eased slightly.

"You are unaccustomed to waking with a man," he mused.

Her cheeks burned. "I thought we'd established that the night of the Bride Ball," she quipped in return.

Christopher chuckled darkly. "I meant that I realize I frightened you. You will probably appreciate having your own rooms at the palace."

Her heart ached at that. He wanted to marry her but not to share a bed with her? The thought of cavernous, empty rooms left her cold.

His smile faded. "What is it?"

Amber shook her head, at a loss to complain. She should have expected this. After all, Nana and Nathaniel had kept separate rooms. In every way, her parents were the exception to the rules that governed society.

Christopher seemed to consider something of great importance. A look of realization settled on his face. "You don't want to live in your own rooms."

Her cheeks felt afire in embarrassment.

"Do you?" He sounded less sure.

She shook her head slowly.

His smile returned. "What a temptation. I warn you that I will find it difficult to restrain myself with you in the bed with me every night."

"You say that as if it's a bad thing." Amber winced, biting at her lower lip. *Goddess, what am I saying?*

Christopher laughed long and hard, much as he had the first time they talked in the ballroom of Lord Elmstead's manor. He laughed so hard that the bed shook in his mirth. Amber found herself smiling along with him.

She sobered at a new thought, one she hadn't allowed herself to consider before. "What will the agreement say?"

He stopped laughing and stared down at her. "Nearly anything you want it to."

His answer was so earnest and heartfelt, tears stung her eyes.

A knock at the door drew his head around. "Yes?" Christopher called out.

A man's voice replied. "Do we spend the night here or leave in time for a late dinner at Elmstead's estate?"

Amber's stomach growled at the mention of dinner. She'd not eaten at all, save the tea she'd shared with Marquita and Kambry and several cups of water...and she'd expended considerable energy with Christopher.

Christopher looked to her, arching a brow in silent question.

"I'd walk in looking the pauper," she admitted.

"Where is the skirt you wore to the ball?" he asked, unperturbed by being seen with a lowborn...one that looked the part.

"In...in the lowest drawer of Nana's bureau." But why would he ask it?

"Darren!"

"Yes?" the man in the corridor replied.

"In the lowest drawer of the bureau in Lady Reanne's room, there is a brown suede skirt." His voice lowered. "Is there anything you require from your room?"

"No. There are only a few dresses for work."

"No possessions you wish to take with you?" he pressed, his eyes narrowing.

She shook her head...then stopped. "My books. There are shelves of books in my room. My father left them to me."

Christopher nodded. "Bring the skirt, Darren...and have the guards put the books from my bride's room in the vehicle."

"As you wish." His footsteps faded away.

Christopher stroked the line of her jaw with his fingertips. "Where is the bath?" he asked.

"This is the guest master. The bath is through the door there." She motioned to the wall to the left, as one entered the room.

He rose from the bed, naked and semi-erect. Just when she thought he'd walk away, when she'd prepared herself to watch his luscious backside disappearing into the bath, Christopher put his hand down for her. Amber stared at it, at a loss for what he meant.

"A quick bath," he explained. "I promise to restrain myself until we've had dinner."

"Together?" She sounded the naïve child, and she wished she'd paid more attention to Nana's prattling about the things men and women did together.

"I'll wash your back," he offered, with a look of innocence she knew was feigned.

"I dare say you'll wash more than that." She grimaced. "I am hopeless, I'm afraid." She'd always had difficulty leashing her tongue.

Christopher's brow furrowed. "Do you want me to wash more than your back?"

"Well..." Amber sighed, resigning herself to defeat, either way. "Of course, I do."

His smile was brilliant. "Then you are simply honest." He curled his fingers in invitation.

Amber took his hand, leaving the quilt behind. They walked to the bath, Christopher growing stiffer with each step.

* * * *

"I don't know," Amber hedged.

Edward fastened the final button, leaving an enticing vee of skin, without baring her cleavage. Still, she was unbelievably sexy in the suede skirt, his wool jacket, her low shoes...and nothing else.

"You're beautiful," he assured her.

"I'm half-naked." But it wasn't a complaint. Her breathing was quick, her color high, and her eyes glittering in excitement.

"Your nipples are hard," he guessed. "You're wet and ready. Aren't you?"

She went a pretty shade of crimson.

"And no one but the two of us will know it. Everyone will think your outfit demure. We'll sit at dinner, eating and talking, a delightful secret between us. Then we'll take our leave and sate the arousal—"

"Forget what I said in the bath. You're not the Goddess's own son. You are the wickedest—"

"You love it," he countered.

She smiled, no doubt reliving his stroking hands. They'd brought each other over in the bath. Amber had watched his cum spray on her belly and breasts, her eyes wide in discovery. Edward's attempts to wash away the leavings had turned to a much more intimate end.

"Do you?" he prompted.

"You know I do."

He sobered. Was it right to do this? Amber had been mortified by the sexual games at the Bride Ball. Was he pushing for something she was uncomfortable with?

"What is it?" she asked, her smile evaporating that quickly.

"If you wish to wear underclothes, I'll send for them," he assured her. "I only wish for you to be comfortable and happy."

Confusion creased her brow.

"If anything I ask is... If any of it makes you frightened or upset or uncomfortable, I expect you to tell me that it does. You are not my mistress, Amber. You will be my wife. Do we understand each other?"

She nodded, but her smile didn't return. "Are you likely to do so?"

"I hope not," he answered honestly. "I was afraid I had, though. Do you wish underclothes? Panties and a shift...even the bustier?"

"I believe..." She hesitated, seemingly weighing something of importance.

"Yes?" he inquired, prepared to fetch what would make her comfortable personally.

"I would like to go as I am. Perhaps, I could wear the bustier for you another night?" Amber stared at him, seemingly waiting for his response.

"I would enjoy that." He offered his arm. "Shall we?"

* * * *

Amber took a calming breath and wound her hand through it, more than aware of how his jacket billowed out from her chest, leaving a pocket of air around her breasts, accentuating her nudity. Her heart stuttered in response.

"Amber?" Christopher questioned. "If you've changed your mind, I would be glad to—"

"No. It's...odd. Not a bad sensation," she hastened to add. Judging by the reaction of her body, it wasn't bad, in the least. "New. Exciting, in some ways."

His smile brought her nipples up painfully. "Good."

He led her to the door and out into the corridor. There was nothing to take with them. Even the bustier had been handed to Hein Darren, when Christopher had collected her skirt from his cousin.

The house was still, so much so that it unnerved Amber. The main room was empty, save a few of the soldiers—*royal guards,* she reminded herself—having tea with Nana. The former vaulted to their feet at the first sighting of Christopher, shooting apologetic looks at Nana.

"Ah, there you are," Darren stated, ambling from the kitchen, a short glass of whiskey in his hand. "I sent the other ladies off with Lady Amber's books."

They are safe enough then. Amber bit back a wince at the catty thought.

Holding in the grimace of disgust at her next thought was harder. How long would she be in the Montberrys' company? For how much of their journey?

Christopher placed his free hand over hers, squeezing lightly. "Would two guards be enough?" he inquired.

She stared at him, confused. What guards? What was he offering...and why?

"To assist Lady Reanne, until I engage a housemaid and lady's maid for her," he qualified.

The concept struck her dumb for a moment. "Y-yes," she managed. "That is most kind. Thank you, Christopher."

He smiled, stroking his fingertips along her cheek. "Captain," he ordered, without taking his gaze from Amber's. "Yourself and the corporal who's been so helpful."

"Yes, Highness," they answered in unison.

Amber pried her gaze away from Christopher and met Nana's glee-crinkled eyes. "Will you be all right?" she asked.

"Right as can be," Nana replied. "Why, with two young men about the house—"

Amber laughed heartily. "Nana, you are positively scandalous." And she loved her for it.

She waved Amber away, as if shooing an insect. "Off now. I expect a dedication invitation soon."

"Perhaps we should marry first," Amber suggested.

"Oh, if you must."

That reduced Amber to laughter again.

* * * *

Edward guided Amber into the back seat of the vehicle, smiling at her continuing giggles. He vowed to arrange a holiday for Lady Reanne at the palace, once they were settled in.

Darren took the front seat next to the driver, leaving them in semi-privacy. The remaining guard closed them in, then took his place as driver.

Amber's giggles tapered off, and she met Edward's eyes, her color high. His heart slammed painfully against his ribs.

He stared at her lips, then her eyes, mesmerized by the lines of her face. Their breath mingled between them, enticing him, spawning visions of Amber panting beneath him, throwing her head back and forth while he thrust inside her.

Darren cleared his throat. "The gates are coming up, *Christopher*," he taunted.

Already? How many kilometers had they spent on the verge of kissing? Edward dipped his head, indulging at last. Amber sank to the seat back, seemingly swooning, and he followed her in. In moments, they were lost in a deep, hard promise of more.

The vehicle slowed to a stop, and their lips parted. Darren exited without a backward glance, and a moment later, the guard opened the door for them.

Brand met them halfway up the front steps, his gaze passing briefly over Amber's outfit before he bowed his head to Edward. "Your parents and the Lord and Lady Elmstead await you in the dining room," he informed Edward, matching their stroll toward the house.

"Not Marquita and Kambry?" Amber asked, seemingly shocked by it...and perhaps pleased. "Not Mora?"

Brand's mouth quirked up. "Her Majesty suggested a light meal and an early night for them. They could hardly refuse, mi'lady."

Edward chuckled. "What did *Lady* Marquita do to put herself in ill favor so quickly?" He didn't question that it was she, based on her insufferably rude attitude earlier in the day.

What Darren saw in her— Oh, there was no question what Darren saw in her. She was apparently to his cousin's tastes sexually.

"I rather imagine Lady Mora was the problem. Rumor has it that the lady was a competitor for your father's attentions, in their youth."

"Ah... Now, that does sound like Mother."

They slipped inside the open doorway, and a butler closed it behind them. Brand put out a hand to Amber. She stared at it, without comprehension.

Realization came to Edward, in a flash. "Lady Amber will be keeping my jacket. Thank you, Brand."

He bowed and took his leave. "As you wish, Your Highness."

Her cheeks darkened to crimson, and Edward pulled her further under his arm, guiding her down the corridor.

All conversation stopped, as they breached the doors to the dining room. Four pairs of curious eyes turned their way, and Amber's body went still, nearly rigid in tension.

"Breathe," Edward reminded her.

Benjamin sighed. "You found her, I see," he commented. He took a sip of his drink and panned his gaze over Amber. "You led us a merry chase, young lady."

Amber nodded, her expression pained.

Elmstead motioned for her attention. "You *must* settle a wager I have with James."

"Lord Birchstand," Edward translated for her.

"If I can," Amber replied.

"How did you attend the Bride Ball without checking in with Brand or being announced?"

A smile pulled up at her lips. "I snuck in through the gardens. The sold— The guards assumed I'd gone out and come back in."

Elmstead's jaw dropped.

His wife patted his chin, urging his gaping mouth closed. "I dare say you lost five leaf on that wager," she half-laughed.

"Why?" the lord managed.

Amber's smile dimmed. "I felt Mor—I mean, Lady Mora would cause some sort of scene, if she knew I was at the ball against her wishes."

Alana sighed. "Don't stand on ceremony here, girl. Mora has never been a lady. I have half a mind to send her on, this very night.

"And oh! Has she let herself go. She's downright pudgy. Don't you think she's pudgy these days, Oriel?"

Lady Elmstead bobbed her head in a nod of commiseration.

Amber sucked in her lower lip as if restraining her laughter. Her throat jerked in what appeared to be a swallowed giggle. "If I may suggest an alternative, Your Majesty?" she offered sweetly.

His mother's attention fixed on Amber. "Yes? You have a better idea?" There was no challenge in that. Alana was seemingly ready to pounce on a new form of torture for Mora, hoping that it wasn't something she'd already tried.

"When Mora is being...difficult, I sometimes make her single spoon of sugar in her tea rather...rounded."

Alana and Oriel stared at her, waiting for more.

Amber raised an eyebrow, continuing in a conspiratorial tone. "Two or more spoonfuls usually accomplish the job well enough."

"She doesn't notice?" Lady Elmstead inquired.

Amber smiled widely. "She notices, but around Nana, she must be somewhat restrained."

No one spoke.

"I imagine she has to be even more restrained around Your Majesty?" Amber finished.

Alana and Oriel stared at each other for a moment, plotting silently.

"Two it is," Oriel decreed.

Alana smirked. "Three it is, I think, and she doesn't dare refuse to drink it." She hesitated. "I believe I'm going to like you, Amber Oakmarch."

* * * *

Amber took a dainty bite of the pasta, already stuffed. She'd gone heavy on the soup course, mistaking it for a meal in itself. Now, all she could manage was a polite bite or two of each remove.

"So..." King Benjamin intoned in a voice that left no doubt that his next words would be of paramount importance. "I imagine you'll want to marry immediately."

It wasn't a question, and Amber's heart stuttered at the finality of his words.

Christopher cleared his throat. "When did you say you wanted the ceremony, Amber?" he asked, as if they'd discussed it at length.

She placed her fork on the plate and avoided the king's eyes. "Well, I said... I've always dreamed of a winter holiday ceremony," she admitted. She peeked up at Christopher.

He nodded. "I promised what you wished. Winter holiday, it will be."

His father scowled. "You were ordered to marry within a year, Edward. Winter holiday, if memory serves, is well over a season too late."

Amber's heart sank. Her visions of a summer or fall ceremony weren't nearly as enticing, but if that's what—

"I've chosen my bride," Christopher replied calmly. "Our agreement was that I choose a bride or you choose one for me." He offered Amber a look that promised she'd have her winter ceremony.

"There will be a written contract, then," King Benjamin insisted. "Within the week."

"Of course. If Brand would assist, we could do so tomorrow."

"Tomorrow?" his father scoffed. "A contract of this sort will take days to smooth over."

Christopher stared at her, his eyes the same dreamy version he'd had in the vehicle. "Unlikely. I believe we both know what we want."

Her stomach squirmed in a most disconcerting manner. For no apparent reason, Amber was certain they were in accord. "Yes. I believe we do."

"And...perhaps Lady Elmstead would be so kind as to send her clothier to us tomorrow," he suggested.

"Of course," Oriel replied.

Amber found herself giggling. "Perhaps someone could see fit to lend me something to wear tomorrow," she teased him.

Christopher scowled. "That is a concern, I believe."

Oriel shot a look of confusion at Queen Alana. "You didn't allow Amber to bring clothing with her? Surely, your jacket isn't the only clothing the poor girl has to wear?"

That and the skirt...and a bustier. Amber cleared her throat, well aware that she was headed for scarlet. "In all fairness, I had nothing worth bringing."

There was a moment of silence, and Alana shared another silent stare with her long-time friend.

Christopher's mother nodded, her jaw tight in fury. "Four spoons, and the woman had best leave my sight within a few days, or it will surely be five."

* * * *

"Best build the dress spacious," Alana suggested. "With two and a half seasons until the ceremony, she's sure to carry."

Edward smiled at Amber's darkening cheeks. He knew she wasn't adverse to the idea of children, but everyone's fascination with the subject embarrassed her. He knew—as did she—that there were already polls going on how long it would be until she carried and whether she'd gift Edward a son on the first catch.

"As you wish, Majesty," the clothier replied, reworking her numbers.

"Her daily wear should show more cleavage," Oriel mused.

Amber glanced down at the low-cut bodice in horror, and Edward spoke up.

"I think not."

The clothier stopped writing and turned to him. "It is the fashion, Highness."

"Perhaps Amber will start a new fashion." Whether she did or not, he'd promised to make her comfortable, and he would.

"Edward," his mother began, no doubt about to insist that, as a man, he couldn't possibly appreciate the social needs of a young lady.

"A woman should dress to please her husband or lover," he cut her off.

"Well... Yes. Of course, she should. At all times." Alana motioned up and down Amber's body, currently clothed in an oversized gown that the clothier would cut down for her in time to wear tomorrow. "Your bride has a lovely body, Edward."

"She does," he agreed. It was a body that had him salivating to explore again.

"Then you'll want to see more of it," she concluded.

"I do...in the privacy of our bed. In company, I prefer to be the only man in the room to know what lies beneath Amber's dress and to anticipate rediscovering it, when we are alone."

Amber's smile was stunning.

The clothier looked from Alana and Oriel to Edward, waiting for a decision.

"No necklines lower than what she now wears," he ordered. "And a bit higher for daily wear...like the portrait of my great-grandmother that hangs in the palace."

Alana's jaw dropped in shock. "You would really torture the poor girl with the flounces and underskirts and—"

"No." He waved away her concern. "I like the illusion of inaccessibility, not the reality of it."

The clothier seemed to consider it. "Yes. I believe I know just the thing."

CHAPTER NINE

Edward took the brush from Amber's hand, grooming her hair with slow strokes. She fiddled with the combs that would hold it back.

"You're not worried, are you?" he asked.

Her smile was strained, and she didn't meet his eyes in the mirror. "Of course not. Marquita was on a drug that made her fertile, and Kambry..."

He brought the brush down again, though it was obvious her hair had long-ago been tamed smooth; she was stalling...in more ways than one. "Kambry?" he prodded gently.

"Always as regular as the spring thaw," she offered. "A woman like that is an easy catch, I've always heard."

"Are you late for your courses?" he asked. If so, was she afraid she was pregnant or afraid that she wasn't?

Amber stared at the combs, and Edward took a moment to examine her reflection. She was light on color, not pale precisely but peaked.

"Are you?" he asked again, forcing himself to continue brushing.

"No. I was always of a range. Anytime in the next week is within reason for me."

"But you ordered the servants to restock supplies almost a week ago," he noted, wondering at her nervousness.

"A woman never wants to be caught without. If I was early in the range... Better safe, I suppose."

"If you're certain." He hinted for an answer to that. If she wasn't certain... No, he couldn't rush a doctor in. If he did and she wasn't pregnant, it would make her feel worse.

She didn't reply to it directly. "Besides that, I have the full sensation that often comes just before the courses. No doubt, it will be later today or tomorrow."

Edward ran his fingers through her hair, reveling in the weight of it, the fall of unbound hair inviting him.

"When the Goddess wishes, it will happen," he assured her. He could wait for it.

She placed the combs in her hair, meeting his eyes at last. "When She wishes it. We should go to breakfast now. The servants will be waiting."

He knew it did no good to remind Amber that everything was at her whim now. He tossed the brush to the dressing table and helped her up.

Amber smoothed her dress, then pressed a hand to her abdomen.

"Hungry?" he inquired.

"Not really. I never am just before."

Edward nodded and wrapped an arm around her, guiding Amber to the door, at a loss to reassure her. With both Marquita and Kambry expecting already, she felt the pressure was on her to produce a child for Edward. Worse, everyone from his parents to servants hinted that it wouldn't be long until she did.

He noted her color again. "Are you sure you're well?" Her last courses hadn't left her looking so worn. Perhaps the doctor was a good idea, after all.

Amber laid her head to his chest, closing her eyes and letting him lead her toward the stairs. "Just tired."

Had she slept poorly? "Perhaps a nap after breakfast would be best." If she was still feeling poorly then, he'd call the doctor up from his rooms.

A smile curved up her lips, and her eyes opened again. "As if sleep is all you have in mind?"

"I could be...enticed," he teased.

Her laughter preceded them down the stairs. Edward basked in it. Her silence and nerves worried him; this was the Amber he knew best.

The dining room opened before them, a rich tapestry of scents pouring out: coffee and syrup, fruit and meats, breads and cream-covered eggs.

Amber stopped abruptly, and Edward turned to look at her in concern. Her color drained away, and she swallowed hard.

"Amber, is something wrong?" There was no question there was. He just needed her to state it, and he'd make it right.

"I...uh..." She turned from under his arm, stumbling a few steps toward the corridor, her hand out as if to use the door jamb for balance. "I don't f-f..."

She dropped in a faint. Edward caught her, easing her to the runner carpet. All around them, people exploded into motion and shouting. He ignored them, trying to rouse Amber.

A maid pressed a folded quilt at him, and Edward took it, wrapping Amber in it, then lifting her into his arms. Servants scattered before him, some speaking— probably to him, though he had no clue what they were saying and didn't care to know it.

In moments, he had her back in their bed, buried beneath two quilts. Her skin warmed slowly, and Amber stirred, her eyes fluttering open.

Edward breathed a sigh of relief. "What happened?" he asked.

"I..." She winced, as if she was in pain. "The smells were overpowering. I felt ill and...off balance, dizzy."

He stared at her, excitement warring with concern. "When were your courses due, Amber? Precisely now." She hadn't said she was certain, when he'd asked it.

She seemed to consider that. "Now...I think."

"You think?" Excitement was fast coming out the victor.

"I wasn't... I wasn't...paying attention, I suppose. I don't remember precisely when the last was," she admitted sheepishly.

"Spring holiday," he supplied. "Don't you remember your upset that our celebration was curtailed?"

Amber's eyes widened.

"You are late," he guessed, reining in his emotions. Edward wanted to shout out in joy, but it was a little too early for that.

She nodded. "A week... Good Goddess, almost two... Oh, Edward. I have never been so la—"

He knelt to the mattress next to her, enticing Amber to a deep, slow kiss.

A knock at the door broke them apart. "Highness, the doctor has come up from his rooms," one of the maids called.

Edward smiled. "Send him in."

CHAPTER TEN

"Are you certain you won't join us?" Alana asked.

Amber pressed back into the pillows, feeling her exhaustion much more acutely than she had, even days before. Who knew carrying a child was so taxing?

"Amber? Should I send for the doctor?" the queen offered.

It was a refrain Amber heard often. Any minor complaint, even a rough bout of the typical mother's sickness, sent someone scrambling for the doctor.

She didn't open her eyes. "No. I am just fatigued."

"May I join you for breakfast then?"

Her stomach protested. "I fear the scent of coffee would be too much." And Alana always had coffee in the morning.

There was a moment of silence. "If I had tea?" Her voice was uncertain, tentative.

Amber forced her eyes open, taking in the sight of the queen. Alana sat in a plush chair, her long fingers clasped in her lap, her eyes pleading. It was a side of her that Amber had never seen.

"I'd like that. Thank you."

Alana's vibrant smile returned. Did Amber's company really mean so much to her?

Amber hesitated. "Perhaps...Edward..." It was difficult to remember to call him that with his parents. "He might want to eat with his father...to discuss matters of state. I've been taking him from his duties quite a bit lately."

She seemed surprised by the offer. "He might."

The man in question opened the door and guided a rolling cart through. "There was a delay, of course," he imparted. "One of the cooks scorched the first pot of boiled oats." His gaze slid from Amber to his mother. "My thanks for offering Amber company."

"It was no imposition," Alana dismissed his comment.

Amber took a testing breath, relaxing when she found no scent unbearable. "Actually... I thought you might take breakfast with your father this morning," she suggested.

Christopher stopped, one knee on the mattress, the tray of food intended for Amber a hand's width from her thigh. "Pardon?"

"Alana and I would like to take breakfast together. We've rarely had time to talk, and... I've never had a mother to tell me what to expect of myself...now, I mean...carrying a child."

Edward settled the tray on her thighs. "Reanne never did?"

"There was no need to."

"She could visit," he suggested.

Alana's expression crumpled. She righted it, almost before Amber could notice the change.

"I'm sure I'd like that, but... I really would like a young woman's advice, Christopher."

He nodded. "I will send a tray up for—"

Alana cut him off. "Whatever you've chosen for yourself will do."

"It's boiled oats, Mother. You hate—"

"Actually, I loved them as a child...with honey, as you eat them. It's been many years since I've eaten them."

He seemed to consider that. "Very well. I'll leave you to it, then."

Edward delivered the tray he'd brought for himself to the little table beside his mother, placed a gentle kiss on Amber's lips, and left them.

Alana lifted the lid from her oats and inhaled deeply, a smile pulling up at her lips.

"If you favor them, why did you stop eating them?" Amber asked. She felt her cheeks heat. "I'm sorry. I'm much too direct, I know."

To her surprise, Alana chuckled. "Not at all. It's refreshing. And to answer you, Benjamin's mother was a noble, and I was subject to her scrutiny."

"And...she felt boiled oats beneath a princess?" How odd.

"Good only for children and servants," she agreed. "I wasn't as strong as you are. Benjamin wasn't strong for me, as Edward is, when you're uncertain." She paused, setting the lid aside and lifting a slice of lemon for her tea. "I didn't raise Edward with their snobbery. He likes boiled oats, and I never discouraged it."

"I thank you for that, but... Why did you not eat them, once she passed?"

Alana stirred her tea, seemingly considering it...or reliving the decisions she'd made. "I felt Benjamin had expectations of me. I was probably worrying for nothing, but it was my fear."

"And fear is not a rational thing," Amber noted.

The queen was abruptly far away in thought, a touch sad.

"You love him dearly, don't you?" Amber asked.

For a moment, Alana didn't answer. "Yes. I do." She stared into her oats, mixing the honey in slowly.

"Do you know..." Her smile was strained. "I don't know that he loves me."

"He has no mistresses," Amber offered.

"Oh, he's amused enough, I'm certain. I have always excelled at keeping Benjamin sexually satisfied and surprised."

"But Chris... Edward told me—"

"You can call him Christopher with me. I've always preferred it. In fact, I chose it, but the name wasn't royal. It wasn't a worthy name for an heir to the throne. Luckily, Benjamin allowed me to— But that isn't important, I suppose."

Amber nodded. She didn't ask if Benjamin's mother was the one that decreed the name unsuitable; it was certainly she.

"What did he tell you?" Alana seemed keenly interested.

"He said that a man who loves his wife has no need of mistresses."

Alana considered that, her spoon still stirring idly at her cooling breakfast. "Rather over-simplified, I'm sure. But...we should eat, before the food gets cold."

Amber picked up her spoon and sampled the oats, taking note that Alana was slow to do the same.

* * * *

"What?" Edward stared at Amber, his head spinning.

"I asked if your father loves your mother," she replied calmly.

"I heard you. I just...it's... Why would you ask it?"

Patches of dark pink colored her pale face. "He doesn't?" She seemed pained by the idea.

"My father and mother are not us," he soothed her, at a loss to comprehend her concern.

"Oh, I know that." But tears pooled in her dark eyes, just the same.

"I don't understand," he admitted. Was this the effects of being pregnant? He'd heard women were emotionally unsettled while carrying.

"You *said* a man who loves his wife has no need of mistresses. Your father hasn't taken mistresses. Not ever. He hasn't had consorts, since Alana, either. Not even when she was in her confinement after giving birth."

"I know." But he still didn't understand.

A tear wound down her cheek. "How can he not love her?" she demanded.

Edward stood there, feeling like a stag in torchlight. "Well, I imagine he *does* love her. If he didn't, he would have dissolved their union rather than putting up with her behaviors all these years."

"She only acts that way, because she's afraid your father *will* turn her out. Don't you see?"

He didn't see what she meant, at all. "You mean she's restraining herself?" he joked.

Amber glared at him.

Edward grimaced, motioning her for peace. Perhaps levity had been the wrong choice. "Obviously, I am upsetting you. I have no wish to. Explain it to me, slowly and calmly." *Goddess help my mother, if this is a game.*

"Your grandmother...Benjamin's mother shaped Alana into the image she presents. Your father seems to like her this way."

"Like it? He's like to tear his hair out some days is closer to the truth."

"Has he told *her* that?" Amber asked pointedly.

"Well..." Edward shook his head, finally working his way to understanding.

"She does love him, Christopher. Alana loves him so much that she's afraid to be something different, now that she has the choice to. If he was displeased, he might turn her out or take mistresses."

He ambled to the bed and sat next to her. "What a mess," he sighed.

"Yes, it is." Her hand settled on his thigh. "We have to do something about it."

* * * *

"Are you mad?" Benjamin asked, staring at Edward as if he believed that very thing true.

"It's a simple question, Father," Edward reasoned. "Do you love her?" *How did I let Amber talk me into this?* But he knew that a pout was all it took. Tears would have shredded him alive, and she'd been close to that.

"I've been with Alana for twenty-six years."

As if that answers the question. "And taken no mistresses. Do you love her?"

He shifted uncomfortably. "At times, I believe I do...in the privacy of her rooms or mine."

"If I suggest something that may make you both happier, would you consider it?"

Benjamin stared out the window, a plotting expression on his rugged features.

"Forget your pride for a moment and consider my words," Edward cautioned.

"Very well. I will consider it."

"Go to her rooms. Bring her a handful of the yellow roses she loves. Don't play sex games. Kiss her. Touch her softly—"

"She is your mother," Benjamin protested, turning crimson. "This is not an appropriate discussion—"

"And that is Grandmother Lia talking. I recognize the tone and the rhetoric, young as I was when she passed."

He didn't deny it. Benjamin seemed to have trouble meeting Edward's gaze.

Amber was correct. Lia had been the problem, all along. "You love her. Do what I suggest, and... If you feel that love when you're with her, *tell her* that you do. Tell her that you love her when she is...the way she is when you feel that love, whatever that may be."

His father gaped at him.

"Have you ever told her that you love her?" If Amber was correct, he never had. "Have you ever told her what you love about her? The person you wish she was more often?"

"I don't recall," he replied gruffly.

"Then perhaps it's time you make a decent memory. Past time, in my opinion." Edward walked away, before his father could protest again.

SECTION II:

SHOULD-HAVE-BEENS

CHAPTER ELEVEN

Benjamin stood outside Alana's door, feeling every millimeter the fool. He looked at the roses in his hand, wincing that he'd stooped to this. After all the times Alana had held him at arm's length, did Edward really believe flowers and chocolates were going to sway the woman? Did Benjamin?

He'd like to. He'd like to throw common sense and years of experience out with the bath water and believe that Alana held some kind feelings for him, the feelings he'd thought he'd experienced with her at the Bride Ball so many years ago.

She'd changed so quickly, nearly on the discovery that she'd conceived that night. At first, he'd assumed that Alana was reacting to their whirlwind marriage...or perhaps to the stresses of assuming the place of princess and her pregnancy. Even to the lingering effects of the Gorus tainting her system. But there had been no change in all these years, patient as he'd been, glimmers of something more he hoped he was interpreting correctly notwithstanding.

I'm a fool. I've always been a fool for her. He raised his hand to knock. *And I will be again, no doubt.*

Alana called out an invitation to enter, and he did so.

She was at her dressing table, her hair unbound as he liked it, a demure robe knotted around her body. Her face was free of cosmetics. She was beautiful.

The brush paused in mid-stroke, and she met his eyes in the mirror, hers widening in shock. She recovered quickly, that false smile curving up her lips. "Oh, Benjamin. I didn't expect you. Did you need something?" There was an invitation couched in that, one that, however insincere, raised his cock.

He ambled to her, placing the roses on the dressing table. Alana stared at them, seemingly confused by the move. Benjamin buried his hands in her hair, enjoying the weight of it, the texture when it wasn't coated in layers of spray and gel.

"Benjamin?" she questioned.

It was time to put Edward's suggestions into practice. "I love your hair this way. You should wear it down more often." He raised it to his face, drawing the scent in. "It's so...enticing."

Her breathing went ragged. "I...I never knew."

"Well, now you do. Will you?" He waited for her protest that it wasn't the style, her laughter at his uneducated male palate for such things.

She swallowed hard. "If it pleases you, of course." But she seemed off balance.

It wasn't something he saw often, and he marveled at it.

"And the roses?" she asked, her gaze straying to them, something that appeared to be longing lurking behind her imperfectly-masked expression.

"You like them, don't you?" Again, he steeled himself for a flip response, a dismissal of his effort at pleasing her.

Her hand stretched out toward them, trembling lightly, then stilling. She stroked the petals, smiling an honest smile the likes of which he hadn't seen in decades. "You know I do."

"Then why shouldn't I give them to you?" He asked it seriously, more of himself than her. *Goddess, but I have been a fool.* When was the last time he'd done something so simple and pure for her? How often had he simply showered her with praise? Was that why she'd turned from him?

A king does not openly display such sentiments. But that was his mother speaking.

Damn it, it is normal for a man to show such kindnesses to a woman he loves. Edward does it. No one thinks less of him for it.

To be honest, Benjamin had tried to talk him out of it, but his son had ignored him. *Thank the Goddess!* Edward was right, but was it too late to bridge the gulf between himself and Alana?

As if in answer, Alana masked her expression and stood, her hair sliding from Benjamin's hands. "I should get a servant to bring a vase," she decided. "They will wilt quickly enough in water, but—"

He reached out and took her shoulders, stopping her move to round him. Alana looked up, frightened as he hadn't seen her since her first days at the palace.

"Don't," he requested. "I'll bring you more, gardens of them, if you'd like. Don't...walk away from me."

For a heart-stopping moment, she stared at him. Then she nodded, and his chest muscles loosened the death grip they'd had on his heart.

* * * *

Alana waited for whatever Benjamin had to say. This entire scene was so unlike him that she hardly knew what to think. She was fairly certain he wasn't dismissing her. If he was, he wouldn't request a change in her hairstyle, would he?

But why now? Why this sudden change? Her stomach squirmed in apprehension she tried not to let show.

A princess or queen is always cool, detached, rising above the challenges life offers, laughing in the face of tribulations. How many times had Queen Lia lectured her on that very thing? How many times had Benjamin agreed with her?

The old workhorse wasn't cool and detached. She was cold and indifferent. Just because Lia's husband fucked some mistress into a second son, Matthew, while Lia lay in confinement from the first, from Benjamin... Well, the man had needs that she wasn't capable of meeting or willing to meet, whatever the case might have been. What did she expect?

But Benjamin hadn't taken mistresses or concubines, even when Alana was in confinement. Maybe Amber and Edward were right about that.

Or maybe I am wishing, as I have always wished, that Benjamin would throw off his own cloak of cool disregard and tell me there's something more than a contract and an heir.

He moved his mouth as if to speak, but no sound issued forth. Instead, he lowered his face, nuzzling at her lips with his.

Alana's heart shattered again. This was all there was. This was all there had ever been for him and likely all there would ever be. If there was more, she would never see it, so it might as well not exist, for all that it mattered.

She kissed him, throwing all of her passion at a man that couldn't care less what feelings fueled her response. No matter his feelings, she was the same fool for him she'd been at eighteen. If he wanted this, and if it meant being close to him, she'd accept it, as she had all these years. *I am a fool!*

Benjamin pulled back, shaking his head. She stared at him, at a loss. What did he want of her?

As if in answer, he kissed her again, a brush of lips that made her heart pound and infused heat into her limbs. Alana followed his lead, closing her eyes, gasping as he parted her lips and tasted inside. There was no rush to it, no urgency.

His hands slid down her back, cupping her buttocks and bringing her up against his erection. Still, he didn't move to take what he wanted. The anticipation was delicious.

Their lips parted, and they stood there, wrapped in each other's arms. Alana's entire body trembled. She opened her eyes, needing to see his expression, needing to believe that this was something more than a fuck with his convenient walking sex toy.

Benjamin appeared as engaged in the moment as she was. His eyes were heavy and darkened, hot in emotion as she hadn't seen them for some time.

"I have missed you," he whispered.

"Missed me?" But he saw her daily. He'd had her only the night before. What did he mean?

Her heart pounded in realization...or what she hoped was realization. She'd missed him, missed the man Benjamin was away from the palace, in their first week together. Could it be that he'd missed that, as well? If he had, why had he never attempted to recapture it?

"More than you can ever know."

How wrong was he about that! Alana's mind spun. After more than a quarter century with Benjamin, she suddenly didn't know what to say to him, what to do. If he admitted he liked her hair better down, what else didn't she know about him?

"Shhh," he soothed her. Benjamin guided her toward the bed, stilling her hands when she reached for the tie on her robe. "No."

That was all he said, leaving her to wonder at his strange pronouncement, while he removed his boots. He lost his balance on the second, and Alana reached out to steady him.

She hissed as one of her prized fingernails broke off in a jagged line. Benjamin went still, looking from the snagged nail to her face, seemingly waiting for something she couldn't name.

"It's just a broken fingernail," she assured him.

He stared at her for a moment, nodded, then pulled the boot free and dropped it next to its mate.

Have I been that vain? Alana suspected she had. It was no wonder he was so cold to her. Did Benjamin believe she had any feelings, beyond self-love?

She had no time to consider it in earnest. In the next instant, he was urging her onto the bed, following her down, tunneling his hands in her hair. Alana gasped at the feel of his cock pressing into her thigh, heating for him. Benjamin took advantage of her slightly-parted lips to play the tip of his tongue inside, pulling away when she tried to kiss him in return, coming at her again when she gave herself over to his lead.

It was like nothing she could remember of him. Nearly since their marriage, their loving had been driven, one sex game and adventure after another. This was... Realization left her fighting for breath.

The morning we woke together after the Bride Ball, the day we created Edward together. At least, it might have been that day; the night before was possible, as well...and the days following.

Benjamin pulled his head back, his brow furrowed. "Is it too much?" he asked, voicing concern for her.

She shook her head. It wasn't too much. It was wonderful.

"Is my weight—"

"No." How could he ask it?

"Would you rather not—"

"No. I mean... I mean, yes... I want this." She did, more than she would have thought possible, even days earlier.

He searched her face for something she couldn't name. Alana reached for his shirt, but he shook his head.

"There is no rush, Alana."

She nodded. She didn't want him to rush. Whatever brought this on, Alana wanted it to last. Memories of his promise of a slow loving their first morning together played in her mind.

As if he agreed, his lips parted hers in a slow, deep kiss. She wound her arms around his shoulders, holding to him, parting her legs to allow his cock to nestle closer to her aching center.

Benjamin's hand cupped the back of her knee, trailing upward beneath her robe and coming to a rest at the join of thigh and buttock. Alana would have arched to him, if she could have moved beneath his bulk.

He rolled to his side, taking her with him, squeezing at the meat of her backside, trailing his fingers toward the lower cleft. Alana clawed up at the back of his shirt, dimly noting another fingernail cracking.

His mouth retreated. "Just the shirt," he decided. "Nothing more."

He rolled to his back, and Alana went with him, straddling his hips. Benjamin drew her hands down to the buttons, then left them to work.

Knowing he was watching made her a slick-fingered bundle of nerves. A teasing show was impossible in her state of unbalance. Still, she managed the disrobing. Alana ran her hands under the fabric, caressing his skin, fingering the nubs of his male nipples.

Benjamin arched beneath her with a groan of pleasure. He sank to the mattress, then thrust his hips up, teasing her with his length. She undid the first button on his trousers, and his hands covered hers, stopping her.

"I said, 'nothing but the shirt,'" he admonished her gently.

She nodded, darkening.

"Goddess, I love seeing you blush. I love seeing you without cosmetics and powders. You look divine, and your taste..."

Alana looked away to his chest, working the shirt off of his arms, one at a time, reeling. Did he mean the things he was saying? She wanted so much to believe he did.

Benjamin waited until the shirt was removed, then cupped his hand around her cheek, raising her face to his. Once their eyes were locked, he thrust his hips up, as if he was testing her responses, watching for something in particular.

If he wanted to see her eyes slide shut and head rock back, he got his wish. If his groan was any indication, it was precisely what he'd hoped for.

He drew her down over him and met her mouth in kisses that made her feel as drugged as she'd been their first night together. Every millimeter of her body sensitized to his wandering hands.

A knock startled her, and Alana opened her eyes in misery. This was how it would end. Someone would call Benjamin away to something urgent, and this moment would pass, never to return.

"Leave us," he ordered without asking their business.

"B-But Majesty," Jason huffed. "General Mossglen has arrived, and her Majesty's driver asked confirmation of a mid-day departure."

The expectations pressed down on them always. It was tiring. *We are king and queen!* Perhaps... She spoke before Benjamin could.

"Cancel my driver. Send my regrets to all of my engagements for today." *The week. The month. The year, if Benjamin will make the moment last so long.*

His shock melted into a wicked smile. "And mine," he added. "Tell the kitchens we will take our meals here today."

Alana's pulse raced, and her head spun.

"Yes, Majesty." Jason left the door, his heels clicking smartly on the polished marble floors.

Benjamin trailed a fingertip from her lower lip to her chin. "How I've wished to do this."

"This?" She tipped her chin up, shivering as his finger traced her throat, then dipped into her cleavage.

"All of it. Throwing off the schedule." He moved his hand to her breast—cupping her, circling her nipple, his gaze rapt—licking his lips. "All of this. Give me the whole day."

Her breathing became a detriment to speaking. "I'll give you as long as you want."

CHAPTER TWELVE

"Dinner, Majesty," a maid called out.

Benjamin paused at the entrance to Alana's body, meeting her pleading eyes. "Leave it," he instructed. He'd ordered the same of lunch. Given the chance, he'd be doing the same tomorrow.

She didn't question him or warn that it would go cold if left too long. A moment later, she was gone.

Alana tipped her hips back and forth, coating the crown of his cock in her musk and encouraging more of his own to flow.

He understood the ache and agreed, but nothing would be rushed today. It had taken them more than an hour to dispense with her robe, and lunch had arrived while he'd been dining on her.

Feeding each other lunch had led to roaming hands and mouths. The half-empty trays banished to the corridor, Benjamin had allowed Alana to remove his trousers. She'd intended to tease him up and take him in, but Benjamin wanted the need clawing at her as it was at himself. He'd climaxed against her, then used the slick to massage her to a second...or perhaps third climax of the day.

Benjamin had delayed this moment for half the day, but he could wait no longer. It wasn't a thrust into her but rather a slide. He reveled in each muscle clenching tight at him.

Alana whimpered, her ragged nails scoring his back. Little gasps of pleasure wracked her body, and she rose against him. Approaching the pinnacle, she wiggled him in the final bit.

"Oh Goddess, Benjamin."

He nodded and eased back, coming at her as slow as the first time. She trembled, every muscle taut. The achingly slow approach lasted only as far as her first scream. His eyes slid shut, and he took her fast and deep.

Alana came apart around him, going wild in the release of an entire day of foreplay. It wasn't the 'sex game wild' he'd come to nearly loathe; she was mindless in pleasure, venting honest sounds and half-sounds of joy without reason.

He followed her over, filling her with a load unlike any he'd gifted her in years, a draining release that made his vision fuzz. His arms tightened around her at another thought.

She wouldn't have been wearing her barrier, and Alana hasn't been out of my sight to insert it. She hasn't demanded it, hasn't even hinted at its absence. Aftershocks wracked him at that.

Slow, deep kisses followed, and Benjamin stayed inside her until his waning cock could hold her body no longer. Alana let out a little cry when he slid free.

For a moment, they stared at each other. Forcing speech after such a joining was difficult. When Benjamin managed it, his voice was rough.

"I'll be canceling my appointments for tomorrow," he imparted.

Alana nodded. "Cancel mine, as well." A note of uncertainty crept into her voice. "If you wish—"

"Do *you* wish it?"

She hesitated, then nodded, watching him as if unsure of his responses and aims. He vowed to make himself clear.

"You wish to know my mind," he stated, taking the first step toward it.

"It would put my mind at ease," she offered carefully.

"Do you prefer today to the life we've always lived at the palace?"

Alana paused only a moment. "Yes." The longing in her voice warmed his heart.

Benjamin smiled widely. "Then tomorrow we start making a new life for ourselves...one we enjoy."

* * * *

Alana stopped in the bathroom doorway, her brow furrowing in confusion, crossing her arms over her silk robe. "Benjamin? What are you doing?"

In the strictest sense, she knew what he was doing. Her husband was standing at her open closet, moving along the row of clothing. Some pieces, he left on the bar; others were being deposited over a chair. In some manner, he was sorting her clothing...dressed only in a robe that matched hers.

He turned to look at her, depositing another outfit on the chair. "Do you agree that we should both be happy with the changes we make?"

Her heart pounded at such a bold suggestion. "I do."

Biting back the automatic response that it should only be so if Benjamin wished it was hard but not impossible. Terror at the possibility that he wouldn't approve of her choices made her heart skitter. If he disagreed, she'd defer, she promised herself.

He offered his hand and she rushed to take it. Benjamin turned her to the closet and guided her hand to the outfit at the furthest left. His breath warmed her ear.

"I have been removing the outfits I do not care to see you in. I want you to do the same, Alana."

"The same?"

"Keep only those you care most for, the ones you find comfortable...and the ones that make you feel as you did yesterday and this morning."

Her mouth went dry. Being nude or dressed in a silk sheath made her feel as she had since this change in Benjamin. "I have need of holiday attire," she countered softly, tensing for his frustration at being corrected.

Benjamin edged around her, drawing Alana's chin up. "You do, but they needn't be what you own now. We'll be filling your closet again with clothing more to your tastes. Do you wish dresses like Amber's?"

"Is that what you prefer?" The question was out before she could censor herself. She was deferring to him again.

"That was not the question," he replied patiently.

"But..." How to phrase it? "We must both be happy with the choices," she reminded him.

"True enough. We have to find middle ground. Do you care for Amber's style of dress?"

"Not particularly," she admitted. "It's well enough for Amber, but for me..."

"Then it isn't an option." With that, he turned back to his work, removing two of the next three outfits and setting them aside.

Alana turned her attention back to the closet, considering the first piece. It was an evening dress, cut low between the breasts. It was a perfectly serviceable piece.

Benjamin appeared at her side. "What do you think?" he asked.

"I suppose I'll keep it." She waited for his reaction to it.

"Do you love it? Or do you accept it?"

Her head spun. "Accept it...I guess."

His arm circled her waist, bringing her closer to his body. "What would you change?"

She considered it, then pulled another dress down to show him. "The skirt is fine, but I prefer this bodice."

Benjamin rewarded her with a teasing kiss that left her breathless. "Save them to show the clothier, then discard them. Only save what you love, Alana."

They went back to their work. At the first dress she rejected outright, Alana slid a glance at him. Benjamin smiled and waved her on.

In the end, only a fifth of her original wardrobe still hung, and almost a third of them remained to be templates for new pieces or to be altered. Alana stared at the pile of discarded clothing in shock.

"What is it?" Benjamin asked.

"Proof of how much we both hated what we'd crafted," she postulated.

He chuckled. "Indeed. But now we can make something we don't loathe. Starting with..."

Benjamin reached into the pocket of his robe, drawing out her barrier. He held it between them. "I notice you haven't been wearing it."

Alana swallowed hard, panning her gaze from the barrier to his face, desperate to know his mind. Was he angry that she'd chanced another pregnancy?

His expression gave no clue. "I know what I would choose to do, but it isn't my choice alone."

Words stuck in her throat. "W-what would you choose, Benjamin?"

"What would you?"

Alana took the barrier, trying to still her shaking hands. She hesitated and then tossed it on the pile of clothes to be removed.

Benjamin pulled her to his body, his cock lengthening against her. "Goddess, yes," he breathed. "When you didn't insist on it, I'd hoped..."

His mouth covered hers, and he parted her lips. Alana encouraged him, his acceptance a heady drug. Benjamin didn't rush her to bed. He held her, tracing her curves through the silk.

"After lunch," he breathed into her lips.

She nodded, though she already ached to finish.

"After lunch, we'll do the same for your bureaus."

Then his hands were at her waist, undoing the tie on her robe.

CHAPTER THIRTEEN

Benjamin played with a lock of Alana's unbound hair, working at her look of contemplation. "What are you thinking of changing?" he asked.

Whatever it was, he'd agree. The boxes of clothing, beauty products, and shoes they'd sent off had lightened Alana's mood considerably. With every item she chose to shed, she'd become more the woman he'd fallen in love with. She was relaxed, lounging nude with him as he'd once dreamed she would.

They hadn't stirred from this room for three days. They'd even had the clothier fit Alana in her sitting room, and they'd ordered an outfit from Benjamin's rooms to accomplish it.

No servants had been allowed in, save those delivering or removing what they'd been summoned for. Edward had sent word that he'd taken on his father's work, for the duration.

Alana's voice dragged him back to the lazy present. "This room. I've always disliked it, I suppose."

He kissed his way up her chest and throat, stretching out over her. "Then why did you accept the designs?"

She darkened but didn't reply.

"Mother?" he guessed. Perhaps there was more to Edward's dig about his grandmother than at first it had seemed.

She nodded.

"What would you do?"

Alana looked around. "I rather like the colors of your room," she admitted. "I was never fond of pastels, though many women are."

My mother preferred them. Lia wasn't fond of couples sharing a living space, though. "Why don't we move you into my rooms then?"

Her look of shock sent a painful twisting sensation through his gut. They'd never shared a room for longer than a night or two at a time. The last three days were the single longest period they'd spent together. Sharing a living space was admittedly one of the things Benjamin envied his son and Amber.

"If you don't wish to, Alana—"

"I do." Still, there was something guarded in her expression.

"But?" he prompted her.

"Your rooms are..."

"In need of a woman's touch, perhaps? I welcome it." He did. Little signs of Alana around would be a comfort to him.

"Too small," she blurted out. Her cheeks darkened, and it seemed she had to force herself to meet his eyes.

Benjamin sat up, passing an assessing eye over her room.

"Benjamin?" she asked, clasping her hands tight in a nervous show.

"It could be done," he mused.

"What could?"

He offered his hand and drew Alana to sitting, fitting her back to his chest. Visions of lifting her onto his cock had him semi-erect.

Benjamin forced his mind back to the discussion at hand. He motioned to the wall that separated their rooms. "Edward and Amber are planning to break through to create an adjoining nursery. We could do something similar...redecorate, change the spaces..."

She drew his hand around her waist. "It would be quite a bit of work."

"The workmen will be here, either way." He motioned to the corner of her room that held her closet and the bureaus. "A larger sitting room than either of us possesses now," he suggested. "My sitting room could become your closet space."

"And the rest of this room?"

Benjamin slid a hand between her thighs, stroking idly at her clit, shivering at her ragged breathing. "The same thing Edward intends? A nursery and a nurse's room?"

Alana moaned, moving against his fingers. "Where will we stay while the work is done?"

Something in her tone told him that Alana had an idea for it. "Where would you like to stay?"

"Birchstand," she gasped out.

That brought Benjamin fully erect. Edward had been conceived at Birchstand; their first days together had passed in bliss in the guest master in that very manor. "For a few days on each side," he decided. "I'll have James set up the guest master for us." *Our room.*

"Why only a few?" A mewing cry escaped her lips, and she rolled her head against his shoulder.

"Courtesy demands we spend some amount of time with our hosts."

She nodded, arching against him with a moan that begged more. Benjamin thrust two fingers inside her, smiling as she reached back and grasped a handful of his hair.

"I want you to myself, Alana."

She climaxed around his hand, a choked cry lighting the air around them.

"I will have you to myself," he vowed.

* * * *

Alana fussed at her gown, shooting a glance at Benjamin. He smiled, raised her hand and kissed the back of her knuckles softly.

"Why so nervous?" he asked.

Putting that into words was difficult. "A first step," she managed.

"It's one worth taking, I believe."

She did smile at that. "Yes. I think so."

He started to offer his arm, then stopped and wrapped it around her waist instead. Alana took a moment to snuggle into his chest, then started toward the dining room. She slowed from her usual swift pace, matching Benjamin's ambling gait, reminding herself yet again to savor the moment instead of rushing through it.

Servants rushed here and there, some stealing a second look though none dared to stop and stare. Alana smoothed her hair, considering that she'd broken with a sense of style she herself had forged. This "new Alana" was sure to cause a flurry of social chatter.

The dining room stood waiting, Edward and Amber already at their places. Her son dropped out of their animated discussion mid-sentence and gaped.

He recovered quickly, launching to his feet and striding to her. He took both of her hands in his own, an informal greeting he'd never used for her before. Perhaps he'd never felt free to do so. A soft kiss to her cheek took her back to his toddler years and raised a lump in her throat.

"You look wonderful, Mother. Truly beautiful."

Alana laughed, her heart light. "I'm not as young as Amber," she noted. For the first time, the little lines of maturity didn't bother her. She felt younger than she had in a decade or more.

"But every bit as beautiful," Benjamin assured her.

"To you," she replied, blushing at the compliment. "But forgive me, please. I must speak to Amber."

The two men parted to let her pass, then fell into discussion of kingdom matters.

Amber started to rise, but Alana waved her down, taking the seat to the younger woman's right.

"They are correct," Amber offered. "This style becomes you."

Alana took her hand. "Because of you, I'm sure."

"It troubled Christopher, as well."

Alana glanced at her son. "But he intervened for you."

A light blush stained her still-pale cheeks. "Yes. I suppose he did."

"Thank you. Thank you for asking it."

Amber nodded.

"Now... How are you?"

"Better. I still can't handle strong smells."

Alana patted her hand. "Which leads me to a plan Benjamin and I decided on."

Amber glanced to the men and back, seemingly perplexed. "Which is?"

"There's no reason for the pomp and circumstance of a full buffet of choices for each family meal."

"I agree."

"Then you and I will be planning a few simple choices for each day. Of course, as the pregnancy speaks to you, the cooks can make whatever you wish."

Amber considered that. "Very sensible. Organized...and definitely less wasteful."

"I thought so." Alana waited for her response. "Will you help me plan the menus then?"

"Of course... If you'll help me design the nursery."

Alana's heart stuttered. "I thought you'd never ask." She'd had no say in Edward's nursery. Now she could plan for two of them. *Goddess, but I hope we can fill the second.*

"Ask what?" Benjamin inquired, settling in the chair to Alana's right, as Edward returned to the one at Amber's left. "Oh, what does it matter? If it makes you smile that way, I'm glad Amber asked whatever it is."

Amber laughed the laugh that seemed to warm the coldest room and squeezed Alana's hand. "I rather think she smiles because of you, Benjamin."

He turned Alana's face back to his. "If so, I am a lucky man."

* * * *

Her heart skittered, and she stared at him. After a moment, Alana realized she was gaping. "Say it again," she pleaded.

Benjamin shifted in seeming discomfort. "I love you, Alana. I've always loved you."

Tears pooled in her eyes, and she pressed both hands to her mouth, trying desperately to control her giddy joy.

He stuffed his fists in his pockets. "Did I say something wrong?" The pain in his eyes made him appear half his age, about the age he was when they'd met.

Alana launched herself at his chest, wrapping her arms around his neck, laughing and sobbing at the same time. "No. Goddess, no. I live to hear it."

His arms circled her. "Do you?"

Realization struck her momentarily mute. "I love you," she breathed.

The lack of response had her heart pounding.

"Promise me something, Alana. No... Make a bargain with me."

She eased away from him, meeting Benjamin's gaze, noting his starkly-serious expression. "Yes?"

"Swear to me that we will never go another day without hearing those words."

That *did* render her speechless. Alana nodded her agreement.

His kiss was a solemn seal of that promise.

Benjamin broke away, burying his face in her hair. "I love you."

"I love you, Benjamin."

He swung her in a circle, his rich laughter mixing with hers. Benjamin was still holding her when the architects arrived to discuss the changes to their rooms.

SECTION III:

STEPSISTER

CHAPTER FOURTEEN

Darren sat, sprawled out in the chair the clothier had pulled into the showroom, surveying the latest of the outfits Marquita had modeled for him.

It was a severe cut of short gown that would bare her breasts in an instant and her slit every time she leaned forward or sat, if she wore it—as she did now—without panties. It was a tease piece, the sort of outfit exhibitionist mistresses and wives wore to sexual events.

What happened next was to the tastes of the lord in question. Usually, it was a subtle taunt to other men, a sort of social one-upmanship in the form of their contracted female companions. Occasionally, it became something more, one of the mainstays of voyeur's row.

"Acceptable," he decided. "Vincent will see you home with the purchases, Marquita."

She offered a pout that some men probably found endearing or amusing. Darren found it an incredible waste of time.

"You've chosen three dozen, at least," he reasoned, before she could voice her complaint. "It will do...for now. Go, while you can, in comfort. With your purchases and Kambry's together, there wouldn't be room for all of us in the vehicle."

Her smile returned. "Which would you like to see this evening?" she offered.

"I believe this is Kambry's day." Darren was certain she remembered it, though she pretended not to. It wouldn't be the first time she'd tried to seduce or confuse him into her bed on a day that belonged to her younger sister.

"Of course. It only feels so long ago. Tomorrow, then?" She wound a curl around her finger and struck a suggestive pose.

"The fifth," he answered. It was given that she'd spend most of the evening struggling to remember which one that was, which might keep her out of other mischief. In truth, Darren didn't care which she wore. The trappings were more for Marquita than for Darren.

She offered a forced smile, nodded, and left the room to change into day wear.

"Should we begin with the other, Hein?" the clothier asked. "Or would you care for a rest?"

As if I am exerting myself? "Send Kambry in, when she's ready."

"She is, I believe." She ducked behind the drape to check for herself.

A moment later, Kambry stepped through, dressed in a black leather teddy, complete with metal fasteners to be hooked to any number of sexual apparatus. Her blush was deep and her expression tense.

He scowled. "Unacceptable," Darren decided. "Completely unacceptable, clothier."

Kambry winced, a sure sign that she didn't understand his concern. She'd no doubt taken it as a comment about her person and not the clothing chosen for her.

"Have you no feel at all for Kambry's personality?" he continued.

"My apologies," the clothier offered. "I thought the style would be to your tastes." She seemed honestly perplexed.

"On Marquita, it would be. For Kambry... Silks, lace...soft and feminine, flowing. She is not the exhibitionist. She is..." *Solace. Private moments. Whispered words by candlelight.*

The clothier's voice broke him from his thoughts. "Angel to the exhibitionist?" she suggested.

Darren considered that. "Yes. Very much."

A shy smile lit Kambry's eyes.

"I have just the thing," the clothier assured him. She waved a stunned Kambry out before her.

It seemed forever before they returned.

Kambry was dressed in a long, dark-green silk gown that made the red in her hair stand out all the more. It was modest, clinging to the curves of her breasts and hips, drawing his eyes to her assets. He hardened forcefully at the sight.

"Hein Darren?" the clothier asked.

"Excuse us for a moment, if you please," he managed.

"Of course." She started to withdraw, most likely anticipating a lengthy break in the proceedings while he sated himself.

"Clothier!"

His bark of command stopped her halfway through the drape. "Yes?"

"Take a careful inventory. I wish to see every piece of its type."

She smiled. "It pleases you then?"

As if she cannot tell. "It most certainly does."

She departed, and Darren waved Kambry closer. When she reached the space between his knees, he drew her onto his lap.

He traced one breast through the silk, watching her eyes go unfocused in pleasure, the nipple making a beautiful show of it through the fabric.

Darren drew her mouth to his, parting her lips and enticing her into a deep, exploring kiss. He pushed the strap off one shoulder, cupping the breast and using the silk to arouse her further.

Breaking the kiss, he found himself trembling in anticipation. "You will wear this tonight."

She nodded.

"Go. Dress in something that will make the hunger keener."

Kambry stood, straightened the strap, and made for the drape with a backward glance at his lap.

Outfit after outfit accomplished just that. He'd approved nearly five dozen when his control was shattered.

The outfit was a sheer white, layers overlapping to make a maddening pattern of indistinct lines and exposed flesh. And...

"Are those panties crotchless?"

The clothier smiled. "They are."

"Leave us. Start packaging the purchases. How many have I not seen?"

"A dozen."

He met Kambry's eyes. "How many of them do you favor?"

Her blush darkened slightly. "Four."

"You know which four?" he asked the clothier.

"I believe so."

"Wrap them, as well. Kambry can surprise me."

If the unconventional request shook her, she gave no sign of it. The clothier disappeared through the drape with a murmured assent.

Darren didn't waste a moment. He unfastened his trousers and pushed them to his knees, settling back in the chair.

Kambry was nearly to him. He wrapped his hands around her waist, stopping her descent. Obviously, she thought he wanted her mouth, but he didn't.

Their gazes locked, Darren pulled his legs back and thrust them between hers, forcing her thighs wide. He pulled her astride him in a smooth motion, and she gasped, her hands pressing to his chest and her back arching.

"Take me in," he ordered.

Kambry pressed up on her toes, using his shoulders for balance. He guided his cock up for her, moaning softly at the material of the split panties taunting him.

Then he was inside her, gripped in her heat. The panties nestled to his sac, the added sensation nearly sending him over.

Darren managed to focus on her face. Kambry was in ecstasy, enjoying his length buried inside her as much as he did...or more. The first tremors of her climax said she was even further along than he was.

He didn't question that she loved the feel of his cock. He'd been with women that faked a response; he knew Marquita had...at least once. Women faking didn't make the sweet noises and expressions Kambry always had.

He rocked his hips, and she gasped out something unintelligible. In just a few minutes of this, they were both going to climax.

"You're wearing this home under your dress," he informed her.

"Yes." Kambry joined in the gentle rocking.

"I'll be removing that dress." He considered it. "In my bed, while the servants unload the car." Neither sister had come to his bed yet; he'd always gone to them.

"Yes." It was louder that time, a sign of her rising excitement.

Darren grumbled a curse. He wanted her deeper, harder. "Off. On the carpet. On your hands and knees."

Kambry complied, moaning as he dropped down behind her and wrapped his hands around her hips. He brushed the mouth of her womb with the first thrust...and the second and third.

There wasn't much Darren was conscious of after that, beyond the rippling silk of Kambry's body around his length, their rising sounds, and the certainty that he was going to feast sexually with her until the sun rose...at least. He wasn't certain he was going to make it home with her without claiming her body again on the way.

On that thought, his thinking mind scattered, drowned in sensation as Kambry climaxed. He joined her, his shout mixing with hers.

She collapsed beneath him, panting hard, smelling sweetly of female musk and sweat and sex gone right. Darren had never smelled anything half so enticing. They lay together, Darren buried to the hilt in her.

There was no hurry to dress. The clothier would have heard their sounds and didn't dare disturb them. It wasn't the first time the showroom had been used to test the wares, and it wouldn't be the last. The clothiers considered it good luck to have a patron so pleased with the wares as to demand an immediate test.

On some level, it stunned Darren that he'd proclaimed Kambry was not the exhibitionist of the two only to take her this way. One glance at her sprawled beneath him wiped his misgivings away. Already, he was aching for more.

CHAPTER FIFTEEN

Darren drove up into her, closing his mind to imagine Kambry in her place.

"Oh, Darren," she breathed.

He captured her mouth, stilling her endless string of empty words, pressing her back into the wall over the bureau to minimize the chance she'd free herself before he was done. Marquita came at him hard, believing him impassioned for her.

I should gag her, play at restraint games with her to quiet her.

He winced at that uncharitable thought. *How did I get myself into this mess?* Darren knew his father would have "I told you so" on the tip of his tongue, if he knew Darren was considering gagging one of his two mistresses to climax for her. His father had been against this contract from the start.

None of this is helping me finish. And he had to finish. If not, Marquita would make Darren's life misery, insisting that equal time of him wasn't equal time, if she didn't have his fill.

Worse, Kambry would take the brunt of her sister's displeasure. Darren had come upon them unaware several times, catching snips of Marquita's cruel humor and taunts that she would beat Kambry to the marriage bed. Had Kambry's eyes not shown her misery, Darren might have believed it a game between them, but it wasn't.

The only way to keep the worst of Marquita shut was to give her a topping off on her days for it; that left

Darren still trying to finish. The last thing he wanted was to start again. After one successful finish, he could legitimately beg off on a second.

Kambry. Remember Kambry. Her slumberous brown eyes danced behind his closed eyelids. Her sounds echoed in his ears.

His hips slowed automatically. Kambry deserved to be taken slower. She liked that...and so did he.

Memories of her climaxing in various positions sent him over. Darren kept his eyes shut a moment longer, holding to the wisps of memory that would fade at—

"That was sublime."

That simply, he was going flaccid. It was so bad, he was considering using an illegal aphrodisiac to get hard for her. The only things holding him back were the chance that he'd need to bed her more than once before it cleared his system...and the chance that he'd think he liked bedding Marquita in the drug's grip.

* * * *

"I have a surprise for you," Marquita called out.

Darren didn't turn to her, fisting his pen until his fingers ached. He bit back a sigh, his heart sinking in the knowledge that it was Marquita's night. She was surely dressed in some sex-show piece, a costume that would be lost on him.

I should dismiss her. He'd begged off two nights entirely before he decided that suffering Marquita to return to Kambry every other night was preferable to days upon days without the younger sister's touch.

Worse, the sight of Marquita, beautiful as he'd admit she was, barely stirred him. At least three times, he'd only managed to perform with Marquita by fantasizing Kambry in her place. Once, he'd resorted to gagging her.

He didn't have to look at her to know Marquita was pouting. The memory of that expression turned his stomach.

It is definitely time to dissolve our contract. My father will be displeased, but it would be worth it.

"Darren?"

"Sorry. Lost in work. You were saying?" He turned to her, pasting on the same smile he used for state holidays.

To his surprise, she was dressed for town and not for the bedroom. The reality was something of a relief.

Be honest. It is the best news you've had all day. It was, which only reinforced that it was time to dismiss her.

"Don't you want to know?" She seemed irritated for some reason he couldn't place a name to.

"Know?" He searched his memories of the last few minutes. "Oh, you mentioned a surprise. Please do." *Goddess, please don't let it be sexual. Not now.*

Her smile returned. "I'm pregnant."

A block of ice lodged in his stomach, and his mouth went dry in some emotion akin to panic.

Pregnant. He couldn't dismiss her. Goddess help him, if the child was male, he was stuck with marrying her. His head ached at the thought of enduring her moods and shrill voice for the next seventy years of his life.

Unless the Goddess is kind and kills me in the next few decades. To escape Marquita, he might decide to kill himself.

Why now? he raged silently. Why did she have to catch, when he'd worked himself up to correcting this misstep?

Marquita planted her hands on her hips, her eyes flashing in fury. "Well, aren't you happy?" she snapped.

"Of course," he managed in a voice that fell far short of sincere. "It's just...as you said, a surprise."

There was no question that Marquita was unconvinced. "Well, then," she stated. "I am fatigued."

Darren nodded dumbly. "You will likely be fatigued quite a bit."

Her smile returned but wanly. "Possibly. It isn't uncommon."

Visions of Marquita playing at fatigue gave way to the realization that this could work to his advantage. She was pregnant. She would likely want to play up her frailty, which would mean she wouldn't want Darren in her bed.

His smile was wide and heartfelt. "By all means, rest. I'll send an extra maid to you. You'll need the help, I imagine."

Marquita sighed deeply. "My thanks, Darren. It is a help." With that, she sauntered away.

He stared at the work on his desk, calculating that there was nothing pressing. Semi-erect already, Darren took to his feet. There was nothing to stand between himself and Kambry.

Except the possibility that Marquita carries a son. That thought sent a shudder of revulsion down his spine. His father was right. He never should have accepted this arrangement.

* * * *

Kambry looked up from the embroidery in her lap as the door eased open, praying it wasn't Marquita again. She'd had more than enough of her sister's gloating. This time, it would probably be a report of how overjoyed Darren was with the news that she carried.

To her surprise, Darren ambled in. He pushed the door shut, then leaned against it, staring at her.

Her heart pounded, and she had to force herself to breathe. Was he upset that she didn't carry yet when Marquita had caught so quickly? Men could be incredibly obtuse about such things, disregarding cycles and fertile windows as completely irrelevant.

Beside that, Marquita had been taking the drug to conceive. She'd had an unfair advantage in the race, though Darren didn't know it.

I knew it, and still I agreed to this! Why?

But Kambry knew why she had. Something had passed between them at the Bride Ball, something she hungered for. Even life as his mistress was enough, if Darren was a part of it.

The only nearly-intolerable part of the deal was Marquita. Could she accept being Darren's mistress when Marquita was his wife?

Only if she produces the heir first. She may carry a daughter instead of a son. No drug can promise a son.

If there was such a drug, their mother would have given Marquita that. For that matter, it would have to be outlawed, because every wife and mistress would be taking it, in hopes of cementing their positions, unbalancing the population in the process.

Then again... A shortage of women might force an improvement in their lot in life.

The question remained. Could she accept being Darren's mistress and Marquita his wife? It wasn't that being a wife gave Marquita any more hold over Kambry than both of them being mistresses. Marquita could hardly treat her worse than she did now. But if Kambry was his wife, she could request Darren rein in an unruly or unpleasant mistress. A mistress couldn't request the same of an unpleasant wife.

"Kambry? Are you well?" His voice was laced in concern that warmed her heart.

"I am," she lied, her smile wavering somewhat. She wasn't. There was an even chance Marquita carried a son. *Can I accept being a mistress and Marquita wife? Should I leave for another position, if it comes to that?*

Darren appeared before her, taking the frame and needle from her hands. She met his eyes, drinking in the stark need in them.

Yes, I will accept it, if it comes to that.

The embroidery hit the dressing table surface, and Darren drew her to her feet, guiding her away from the furniture. She followed him, already aroused and wanting.

The days he was bound to spend with Marquita were a torture. Kambry couldn't touch him, could hardly bear to think of him touching her sister, couldn't even imagine herself in Marquita's place without the reality torturing her.

She couldn't spend time with him on Marquita's days without her sister intruding and Kambry paying the price for it later. Spending time with him would have been enough for her. She felt she wilted on days she had no conversation with Darren.

Today is Marquita's day. How was it that Darren was here? Had Marquita refused him? She was pregnant, after all. She might have. If she'd turned him away, where Darren chose to take solace was none of Marquita's concern.

He circled her, coming to a halt at Kambry's back. The sound of his shirt skating off and hitting the carpet made her heart pound.

Darren's chest pressed to her back through the silk gown she wore. His hand trailed from her cleavage to her woman's curls, prompting a moan from her. Kambry reached back and fisted a hand in his hair, turning to offer her mouth.

He didn't take it. Darren's breath raced over her cheek, teasing her. His fingers made circles, gathering her gown into his hand a turn at a time. When she was uncovered to mid-mound, his index finger eased down.

She spread her legs for him, encouraging him in words her mouth and throat wouldn't fully form. The first touch on her clit sent shards of color through her field of vision, and she choked out a cry of delight, her hand tightening on his hair.

"You want to carry my heir," he whispered.

Kambry managed an affirmative response. She did want it, more than anything. If Marquita carried a daughter, and Kambry conceived his son, it would be a blessing. It was almost enough to make her forget what

Marquita would do to her innocent child, if Darren dismissed her or she chose to end the contract.

"Oh, yes...you will." He nipped at her ear.

The sound of his trousers opening made her breathing go ragged and her already heated core weep more fluids to ease his way. Darren urged her to the closer side of the mattress.

"On the edge," he grumbled.

She complied, kneeling on the edge, bringing herself to a height that positioned her for his ease. Darren thrust up into her, crying out harshly. His finger continued its massage, driving her to the edges of reason.

She didn't want reason. Kambry didn't want the reminder that even a son of her wouldn't make her wife, if Marquita also carried one. She wanted this...the length of Darren bringing her bliss.

His movements were smooth and sure, and she forced her hips up and down, meeting him fully. Darren's free hand was everywhere, touching her, enflaming her.

Her climax was blinding in its intensity, and she screamed his name. He came in a hot, hard explosion, caressing, battering, working her taut muscles looser.

In a dizzying move, she was on her back on the mattress, her boneless fingers ripped from Darren's hair. His body covered hers...then his mouth, a demanding kiss that stole her sanity and her breath. His cock breached her body again, launching her into another release and him into aftershocks with her.

His hand cupped her face, and the kiss gentled. He was abruptly the Darren she knew best...and loved, if she dared admit it. They could sit for hours, touching and kissing. It was a joy to have even that much of him. As if he agreed, his cock bucked within her.

Kambry moaned against his tongue, wrapping her legs around his waist. Darren didn't hurry away from her. He lay inside her, growing flaccid enough to slide free, then hard again against her swollen nether lips.

The next time was all slow touching and peeling clothing, deep kisses and gasps of pleasure. In the aftermath, they slept soundly in each other's arms.

* * * *

Darren smiled at the curls tickling his cheek. That prompted another decision, and he set about waking her.

Kambry sighed at the first suckling motions against her nipple, coming awake slowly. She writhed against him, venting sweet sounds of arousal.

He released her, levering himself up to take her mouth. "You'll be sleeping in my bed tonight," he informed her.

Kambry laid another kiss on his cheek, rising against him.

"I said—"

"Yes," she breathed. "Your bed."

"Do you mind it?"

The shake of her head was punctuated by another teasing kiss to the edge of his mouth.

"And if I asked you to stay longer than the night?" he persisted.

She went still, her eyes sliding open.

"Kambry?" he prompted her.

"Marquita would never stand for it."

Anger spiked at that, and Kambry's eyes widened in surprise.

"I meant no—"

"Marquita is my mistress, Kambry. If I choose to move you into my bedroom, it is no concern of hers nor a matter of law."

Horror dawned on her face. "*I* am your mistress, Darren. It may not be illegal for you to...to show a preference between mistresses, but..." She seemed to search for the proper words.

He calmed himself. Women were notoriously uncharitable when they felt one had broken with their social hierarchy. "Then I will join you here," he offered.

Her brow creased. "Permanently? It's unseemly for a lord to—"

"When I wish. And when I wish you to grace my bed... Will you refuse me, Kambry?"

"Never." It came out more a gust of air than a proper reply.

Mollified, he stroked a hand over her abdomen.

"It is only a woman's timing," she offered sadly.

He stared at her. "What is?"

"The fact that I haven't caught. I had passed my fertile cycle just before we reached your home."

Your home, as well. But mistresses weren't considered "of the estate." They were contracted employees of the lord who kept them. Darren traced swirls on her body, smiling at her beading nipples and gasp.

"And Marquita was fertile soon after," he guessed.

Leave it to women to know themselves so intimately. Would that he would have known it, Darren might have had the advantage in stacking the cards in favor of Kambry as his wife. In his examination of his thoughts and feelings, he was certain he knew which sister he'd wanted as wife and which as mistress, even when he'd faced them at their home the day he'd offered the contract.

She didn't answer. Her face went crimson, and she avoided his eyes.

Darren abandoned his play at her womb and turned her face back to his. "What is it?"

She cleared her throat. "The...the fertility drug would have extended her fertile windows."

His blood ran cold. "What fertility drug?" No one had mentioned such interventions to him. Was Marquita infertile then? It could be a reason to invalidate the contract...if she didn't already carry his heir.

"She wanted to conceive the night of the Bride Ball. Obviously, it wasn't that...effective. My...my mother wanted her to conceive, then...to Prince Edward, thinking that you were the prince, but... She gave Marquita the drug."

"Is she infertile?" Goddess but he hoped she was.

Kambry shook her head. "Simply..." She bit back whatever epitaph she was about to use. "Simply driven to conceive quickly."

"And you? Are you also taking the drug?"

He was torn. Part of him hoped she wasn't, for several reasons. Darren didn't trust the uncertain effects of such a drug on a healthy body and the babe it would create. And taking the drug would indicate a mercenary streak he never would have tacked Kambry with.

Still, the drug would make her more fertile, increasing the chances that she'd catch close to her sister. If Kambry went early or Marquita late, Kambry could beat the shrew to the confinement bed. If the Goddess was kind, she'd confine with a son.

She hesitated, shaking her head in seeming misery.

"Do you not wish to conceive? Are you trying to prevent it?" If she was, had she any feelings for him? If securing her place as his wife was of no importance to her—

"I do. By the Goddess, I do. I am not taking anything to prevent it. I swear it, Darren." There was a note of panic in her tone that made him regret the accusation.

He laid a soft kiss against her mouth, and her muscles relaxed. "If Marquita was taking the drug, why were you not?" He needed to know her mind.

A wince marred her beauty for a moment. "Lady Reanne refused to advance my mother's stipend to prepare for the Bride Ball."

"Why?" he interrupted her, interested in the politics of such a choice.

"Mother refused to act as Amber's escort. If Mother wouldn't do that one little thing for Lady Reanne, the lady would make Mother's job of preparing us that much harder."

His mind spun at the simple elegance of the exchange. Women were crafty when set to a task. "And if she would have had the money to supply you both?"

Kambry didn't answer him.

"If she—"

"Had I known you... Goddess, I would have taken it in an instant." She glanced at him, then away. "It sounds horrid, I'm certain."

"No. No, it doesn't."

CHAPTER SIXTEEN

"Why do you still share his bed?"

Marquita sneered, making an ugly mask of her lovely features. No matter how many times Mother had warned her that such exploits would cause wrinkles, Marquita ignored her. The one time her older sister had dared suggest she would find a man willing to pay her surgical upkeeps, she'd gone two days under ice packs to reduce the swelling to her cheek from Mother's hand. Mother, predictably, had told the neighbors that Marquita suffered a summer cold.

"His babe alone isn't enough to stuff you full?" she continued.

Kambry affected disinterest, though her heart pounded. She avoided her sister's eyes in the mirror, brushing her hair without pause. "I enjoy Darren's company."

"You can't get *more* pregnant, Kambry."

It was a taunt. Some days, Kambry wondered if Marquita tortured her so, simply because she no longer had Amber to make miserable. Or perhaps, she was taking out her frustration that Amber was to be queen and had cemented her place as such by catching pregnant to Prince Edward. Rumor had it that medical tests on Amber had confirmed a son in her womb, while the blood tests had proven inconclusive on both Marquita and Kambry.

Kambry ignored her sister, trying to block out the possibility that Marquita also carried a son and that she would deliver that son before Kambry labored.

Goddess help her, Kambry would accept life as Darren's mistress, putting up with Marquita or not. But how she would refrain from throttling the bitch was beyond her imagination.

"Do you hope he'll fall in love with you?" Marquita was on a tear, and nothing would satisfy her past the sight of a wound inflicted.

Yes. By the Goddess, I wish it. Kambry held her tongue. That knowledge would give Marquita the power to inflict much deeper cuts.

Marquita leaned closer. "Do you hope he'll choose to marry you, because you gave him pity fucks?"

"It's not pity." Kambry knew she should remain silent, but Marquita was crude and unkind, and Kambry had had enough of it.

"Oh... I see. You love him."

Kambry sighed, put the brush on her dressing table, and drew her hair back to braid it for the night. Yes, she loved him. Goddess, but she'd always loved him, and his attentions since she'd caught pregnant had done nothing but make her crave more.

"And what will you do, if I produce the heir?" she taunted.

"I suppose that's Darren's choice." She dared not say more. Any hint that Darren might prefer her company to Marquita's would insure that she'd try to demand he dismiss Kambry once she was wife. It was just the spiteful sort of thing Marquita excelled at.

"What is?" Darren asked, appearing in the doorway.

"What to name the babes," Kambry offered brightly, hoping he hadn't heard too much of their conversation. Would he laugh that she loved him, if he knew it?

Would he take her silence when Marquita asked it to mean she didn't love him?

"Ahhh. I see. My mother is rather fond of Erika for a girl." He moved to Kambry's back, patiently undoing the braid she'd been about to secure.

Kambry met his eyes in the mirror, feeling her face heat at the hunger in his expression. "It's a lovely name," she replied.

Marquita groaned, reminding them both that she was there.

Darren combed his fingers through Kambry's curls. "Are you well, Marquita? Should I send for a doctor?" he inquired in a tone that carried underpinnings of both concern and cool regard.

"The babe is pressing on my back. Maybe you could rub at it?"

He nodded, leaving Kambry to tend to Marquita. Her sister purred, lying against him, draping herself on his shoulder. She turned her face up to his, hinting at a kiss.

Kambry stood and went to the bed to avoid the sight of it. Marquita didn't want Darren; she just wanted to prove she could take him from Kambry. She'd likely succeed at it, too.

"My bed is so lonely." Marquita used her pouting voice, the one that had made Kambry ill in apprehension or disgust...or both, since they were children. "Won't you share it?"

Kambry knew Marquita was stroking at Darren intimately, making blatant offers of sex.

I don't want to see it. I can't stomach it.

She sent up silent prayers that Darren would refuse her, but she braced herself for his agreement. If

Darren chose to, there was no way to stop him, and making a fool of herself would only encourage Marquita to do this again. And again...and again.

"I would enjoy a repeat of the night we met," he suggested.

Her stomach rebelled, and Kambry sank to the bed. She couldn't do it. She couldn't watch Marquita with Darren. She couldn't work her sister up in a sex show and offer her to the man she loved herself. She couldn't even bear the thought of Darren loving her while her sister watched him do it. Marquita had no place in what was between them.

But she did, and they all knew it.

I can't do it!

Kambry had never refused Darren sexually. She'd never even considered doing it, but the idea of sharing a bed with both of them made her ill enough to do it.

"I couldn't possibly," Marquita protested. "That is much too acrobatic for my delicate condition."

Kambry breathed a sigh of relief. Secretly, she believed Marquita suspected the truth that Kambry would shove the dildo deep enough to draw blood, given the chance to use it on her sister.

"Nothing, then," he decreed. "Perhaps another time, when you feel up to a romp."

Silence fell between them, a tense cloud that seemed to press down on Kambry.

Marquita recovered at last. "I am a bit tired," she offered coolly. "Perhaps after a night's sleep—"

"Just the thing," he spoke over her.

"Good evening, Darren." Marquita strode across the room and out the open door.

"Good evening," he called after her.

173

Was that false cheer? Kambry waited to see what would happen when the door latched.

For a moment, stillness reigned.

"Are you well, Kambry? Do you require a tea...or a doctor?" There was nothing cold in the inquiry.

She realized tears beaded at her lashes and blotted them away with the kerchief she kept tucked in her sleeve. "It's silly, really," she attested. "The babe makes my moods so brittle."

"Do you wish me to leave you?"

Never. "Not at all."

A soft sound that might have been a sigh escaped him. "May I join you then?"

Always. "Yes. I'd like that."

He circled Kambry and settled on the bed, facing her, his expression unreadable. The kerchief slid from between her fingers, and Darren stroked it along one cheekbone and then the other.

His hand slid away, and he leaned toward her. Kambry closed her eyes, her breathing hitching as his lips pressed to the spots he'd caressed with the linen.

"Better?" he asked.

"Yes. Much."

His lips brushed hers, and Kambry leaned into him, prepared to give him the energetic romp he wanted. Anything, as long as he touched her...and as long as Marquita wasn't a part of it.

"Slowly," he breathed.

"I thought you wanted—"

"Slowly." With that, his lips closed on hers, parting them patiently. He was thorough, his mouth playing at hers while he smoothed the sheer fabric over her rounded womb.

Memories of the first time she wore this outfit for him filled her mind in startling detail, the clothier sent away, Darren pounding into her, their sounds leaving no question that he was well pleased with the wares.

Darren drew her to the bed beneath him with a groan, pulling up at the gown. His mouth left hers. "Untie my lounging pants," he requested.

Kambry focused on that task, pushing the blue silk off his hips. Darren guided her hands to his chest and planted his hands on the mattress to either side of her waist, easing inside her. She fought for an unhindered breath, biting her lower lip as his length glided within her.

He paused at the pinnacle, taunting her until her gasps became moans and Kambry wrapped herself around him. She begged for more, but he held his ground.

"You never answered her," he breathed.

Kambry met his gaze, pleading for understanding. What had she not answered? How much of Marquita's foul humor had he overheard? Did he believe her guilty of it, too, as he'd believed her guilty of taking the fertility drug?

* * * *

Darren couldn't tell if she was lost in misery or confusion. Kambry's expression shifted endlessly.

"Do you love me?" He'd wanted to demand it, but it was a plea, at best. He was begging for a mistress's love.

No. I'm begging for Kambry's love. I'll beg for this. I'll go to my knees and... There seemed no end to what he'd do to hear her profess love for him.

The damned tears were back in her eyes. It was definitely misery, but why did she feel it? He understood the first well enough; she hadn't wanted him to take Marquita up on her offer. But what was this?

"Do you? Please... The truth, Kambry. No games."

She nodded, swallowing what was probably a knot of tears, but she offered no verbal response. Was she agreeing to answer him truthfully or giving him an answer? He had to know for certain.

"Kambry? Do you love me?"

"Yes," she breathed. "I love you." She sobbed, looking for all of paradise as if he was breaking her heart.

"Don't," he soothed her. "There's no need."

"Is there not?" she hitched out.

Darren stroked her hair, reasoning that he should leave her body to discuss this, certain she'd misinterpret the move, if he did. "Have you never questioned my tenderness for you?"

Kambry seemed confused by that.

"I have realized... No. Goddess, but why is this so difficult to say to you?"

"D-Darren?" Her chest moved in sharp little intakes of breath. If she expelled breath—and he assumed she did—he couldn't mark the passage.

"I love you. Damn it all, I think I've felt the stirrings of it from the beginning, but I was stupid enough to get into this mess, and now... Convincing you how I feel is nearly impossible."

Far from calming her, his announcement sent her into tears. Sobs wracked her body, and she buried her face in his chest.

Darren's cock made the decision for him, shrinking until it released her. He rolled to the side, taking Kambry with him, letting her spend her emotions in a heated spate. When she laid trembling and hitching in his arms, he tried again.

"Do you hate me?" His heart ached that she might.

"How could I?" There was something weary in that statement.

He sighed in relief. "Then we'll work this out."

"How? You gave your word. We *all* gave our word."

"We could—"

"What if Marquita carries your heir?"

I was right. I am breaking her heart. "I don't know," he admitted. He loathed himself for saying it. Kambry deserved better from him.

"You do know. You gave your word."

Darren pulled her tight to his body, at a loss to reassure her that married to Marquita in name was all her sister could hope for. He couldn't even get hard for the shrew anymore and hardly could in the days before she'd turned up pregnant. Marquita might get his name and position, but his heart would always be Kambry's.

"You must keep your word," she decided.

But only the letter of the word. Many men didn't sleep with their wives. If it came to that, Darren would be one of them.

CHAPTER SEVENTEEN

"Are you certain, mi'lady?" the doctor asked.

Though the door was closed between them, her voice carried easily through. "I don't want him here," Marquita screeched.

Darren's jaw tightened in anger. He was certain Kambry would want him at the birth of their child.

It is my child! Damn the woman, she has no right to refuse me the first moments of my babe's life.

Unfortunately, the doctor believed otherwise. He believed the laboring woman had the right to choose.

The hack. "I should find another doctor for Kambry," he grumbled. Did he really want someone this stupid tending to Kambry and their child together?

"He is the best Haven has to offer," his father stated, appearing at his side. "He's no Philip or Douglas Wheatstand, but he's a competent and caring physician."

Darren grunted his agreement, torn between the best care for Kambry and his anger at the medical professional.

"Come have a drink with me," Matthew suggested.

"She's close." He couldn't leave now. He had to know.

"The servants will come for you when it's finished. It's not imperative that you—"

"It is!" *Goddess knows it is. Please let it be a girl.*

Marquita screamed, a sound more of frustration than of pain.

"A few more pushes," the doctor instructed.

"A few more," she mocked him, though breathlessly. "A few more. I will pen those words and shove the parch— Oh! That hurts!"

"Just push. The head is emerging now."

"Good," she snapped.

Darren winced at the thought of being married to Marquita, even if it was in name only, even if his sweet Kambry shared his bed every night and presented him with dozens of babes.

"That drink," his father drawled, "is waiting. It sounds as if you may need it."

"I'll consider it." *If she presents me with a son, drowning my losses may be preferable to admitting my failure to Kambry tonight.*

He considered following in his father's wake, taking the drink for fortification. The squall of an infant brought him up short. His heart pounded erratically, and the internal litany of pleas for a girl made his head spin.

"You have a daughter," the doctor announced.

Darren placed his hand on the wall, letting out a breath he hadn't realized he'd been holding. His lungs ached in response. His entire body went weak in relief.

No matter what happened now, he wouldn't have to marry Marquita. Getting rid of her was going to cost him a fortune, but it wasn't impossible.

"Do not bring it to me," Marquita ordered. "There are nurses and nannies for that."

A maid answered, her voice mirroring Darren's confusion. "The babe needs a feeding, mi'lady."

"And ruin my breasts? There are bottles for that. Beside that point, I can be ready to bear again in a year, if I'm not wasting away my resources by nursing."

You will never have the chance to bear for me again. The thought energized him, and Darren straightened.

The door opened, and a maid stepped out, a bundle of babe in her arms. She met Darren's eyes, paling.

He was aware that he was a frightening sight. His muscles were clenched tight and his teeth grinding.

Darren put his hands out, motioning for the maid to place his daughter in his arms. She hesitated, then settled the blanket-wrapped mass in his care. Expectation hung heavy between them.

The babe was light, probably the result of Marquita's obsession with her weight while she carried. She squirmed, seeking him out with big, blue eyes, golden wisps of hair dusting her forehead.

"Hein Darren?" the maid asked, nearly squirming herself.

His daughter yawned, and he managed a weak smile. Whether he meant to dismiss Marquita or not, this was his daughter. No one would begrudge him a child of a mistress he'd openly claimed. *I hope.*

"Have the cradle moved to my rooms...and send the first bottle and nappy to Lady Kambry's immediately. I will be there."

He turned without giving her time to question him, his long stride eating up the distance from one sister to the other in a few short moments.

Kambry looked up at his entrance, paling at the sight of the babe in his arms. She stared, her breathing ragged, apparently faint in apprehension.

"I'm naming her Erika," he breathed.

She collapsed to the pillows, covering her face with her hands. Something that might have been a laugh or a sob fled her shaking form.

"Will you look at her, Kambry?" Darren prayed Kambry would agree to be the mother Marquita would not. If she refused, it would be much more difficult to claim the child as his own. A wife could make such a thing socially and practically problematic. And Kambry would be his wife.

Her hands retreated, and she straightened. "What happened?"

"She wants no part of mothering my daughter. Not nursing. Not...not even holding Erika. She called my babe 'it,' as if..."

"I don't doubt it," Kambry bit out. "To Marquita, Erika is a failure and nothing more. She doesn't see the innocent child...*her* child."

Darren tried to dissect what she was saying. He prayed the stress that Erika was Marquita's child didn't mean she was refusing.

As if the conversation disturbed her, Erika started to fuss. Kambry waved him over, taking Erika from Darren's hands as soon as he'd reached the bedside. He breathed a sigh of relief at her performing a search for something that would cause the babe's unease; Kambry hadn't agreed, but she hadn't dismissed Erika, either.

She tickled the babe's cheek, grimacing as Erika rooted and latched onto a finger. "She needs to eat, Darren. We should—"

"The bottle and nappy will be here soon," he assured her. Where was the maid? The bottle and nappy should have been her first stop. Did it take so long to warm the milk?

She nodded, rocking Erika, murmuring assurances that the babe couldn't possibly understand.

"I'd like to keep her," he admitted. "I need your agreement to make that possible. Will you give it?"

Kambry didn't hesitate. "We must."

We. Not "you must." We.

It took a moment for the hard edge to that statement to sink in. It had been more an order than an acceptance. There was anger in her tone that unbalanced him. It wasn't like Kambry to be angry. Hurt? Yes, but not angry.

"Kambry?"

She closed her eyes, stroking Erika's back. "Do you know what Marquita and my mother will do with her, if you turn Marquita out?"

He sank to the bed beside her, his stomach rebelling, abruptly glad he hadn't imbibed. "She'd be a servant like Amber was, I suppose." The idea of his daughter serving that harpy and the harpy's mother—

Kambry opened her eyes and met his gaze, tears threatening. "If she was lucky, and that's unlikely. Amber was sheltered by Lady Reanne."

"*That* was sheltered?" Amber had had nothing of her own, save the books her father had left her...and likely only those, because Mora and Marquita didn't read, because they felt it quaint that Amber read. She'd worked from sunup to sundown and beyond, serving her family to avoid being turned out...tormented, taunted...

His head spun.

Kambry's nod broke him from his recitation of Amber's standing.

"I don't understand." He hoped he didn't. "What worse thing would happen to Erika, if we didn't insist on keeping her?"

"My mother's term for it is..." Her jaw quivered, and she seemed unable to continue.

He braced himself for something distasteful. "Go on."

A tear slid down her cheek. "Dis... Disposing of a bastard," she choked out. "You can't let them, Darren. You can't." A note of panic crept into her voice at that.

Words stuck in his throat, and several equally-horrible possibilities warred in his mind. He was afraid to ask whether an orphans' home or an "accidental death" was closer to the truth. Even exposure to the point of death wasn't outside the realm of possibility, he supposed. Perhaps Kambry didn't know which her mother meant. Either way, the question would upset her further.

Darren nodded. "Erika is never to leave my sight with Marquita or her mother. I don't care what it costs me; she is *our* child, Kambry. If-if you would agree to—"

"I will." Again, it was definitive, unswerving.

He stroked his fingertips along her cheek. "Will you feed her, while I speak to my father?"

Kambry nodded her agreement.

Darren rose, planting a soft kiss on Kambry's forehead. He strode away, his mind mired in plans and laws.

Matthew was in the study, an after-dinner whiskey in his hand. "A girl, I hear," he noted with a raised eyebrow that reaffirmed his qualms about the original deal, as posed. "You may have better luck with Kambry, though. The sooner this is settled with a wife in place, the better."

Darren steeled himself for an argument. "Whether Kambry carries my heir or not, I'm making her my wife."

"We've discussed this."

"I'm dismissing Marquita. There is no chance she'll ever give me an heir."

"Because she labors badly?" his father asked in disbelief.

"Because she only wants my name and position. She is cold and uncaring to myself and Erika. She—"

"Erika?"

"My daughter," he explained patiently.

"Women often lack the motherly emotions for several days or weeks after a birth," Matthew dismissed his concerns. "True, your mother loved you so much it made her cry in joy on her confinement bed, but not every woman feels so much."

"This is not parting depression," Darren informed him.

Matthew waved him off. "You will see. Even the hardest woman, when faced with a child—"

"She came into the agreement planning to dispose of my daughter, if she failed to make the place of my wife. That is not a fleeting thing. That is...is premeditated and heartless."

His father went still, his hand fisted on his glass so hard that his knuckles stood out white against his tanned skin. "You believe this?" he asked.

"I know it."

Matthew drained his whiskey, wiping the back of his hand over his lips. He was silent, nearly brooding.

"I won't give Erika up," Darren stated. "If it costs me double—"

"It will," his father added. "Double or more. I knew it would go badly when this scheme involved Mora."

"Marquita's mother?" Darren had heard enough about Lady Mora to guess that few held her in high regard. In fact, he hadn't heard a single favorable comment about the lady yet.

Matthew nodded.

"I don't think I understand." No. That was inaccurate. Darren definitely didn't understand.

"When Benjamin was searching for a wife, Mora wanted the position."

"She was chief competitor to Alana." Darren had heard that from Edward while they'd stayed at Elmstead's manor, after he'd convinced Amber to contract with him.

"It was a bitter rivalry that had every woman in the kingdom taking sides and every man taking bets. Most of the ladies took Alana's side, though she was lowborn. Even then, few people liked Mora." There was no amusement in his tone.

Darren took a seat. "Go on."

"It was meant as... Prank is too tame a word for it. It was underhanded and riding the rail between legal and not. Of course, it's highly illegal now...thanks to Mora."

"What is?" Why did nothing his father said make sense?

Matthew took a deep breath and started in again. "Our father threw a series of Bride Balls, hoping to find matches for both Benjamin and myself. There is nothing quite as thrilling to a young man as a sexual event."

"Yes, I know." Darren hoped never to attend one again, but he remembered well how caught up one could become. His own difficulties were at least partly to blame on his actions in the heat of the ball.

"Mora slipped an aphrodisiac into Benjamin's cup, expecting to seduce him at her most fertile. Aphrodisiacs weren't illegal then, as long as both parties were willing, and Mora reasoned... What Benjamin didn't know he'd befallen wouldn't harm her. He'd been drinking heavily and might have believed it was the alcohol alone."

"Uncle Benjamin was affected by an illegal aphrodisiac and bedded Mora?" Darren asked, horrified by the concept.

And I considered using one to sleep with the viper's daughter? Oh, the Goddess has a vicious sense of humor, some days.

His father laughed harshly. "Not precisely, no. You see, Alana intercepted the cup and drank it down. It was a very potent mixture, and... Let's just say that Benjamin was very appreciative...publicly and privately."

"That seems to have ended well." Rumor had it that Alana was pregnant again, and Benjamin was strutting around like a prize buck.

"The rest of that night is rather confused, even to me, and I was sadly...present for it. As near as the guards were able to piece it together, a group of the *ladies* decided to repay the prank."

Darren groaned at the thought of it. "Who did they pair her with?"

Matthew didn't answer. He refilled his glass and emptied it again.

"You?" *Good Goddess.*

"In my defense, they drugged us both...heavily. If the testing is to be believed, at least twice the dosage we should have been given. More likely three times or more, but after hours...

"I vaguely remember more than one undressing me and teasing me up, but it was Mora who got the fill of it." He paused, swallowing hard. "More than once, I've been told.

"Somewhere along the way, your mother shamed them into admitting that they'd gone too far. The others were charged with caring for Mora, and..."

"You and Mother?" he guessed.

"I'd had quite a lot of the aphrodisiac," Matthew admitted. "In the morning... Goddess, but I still wanted her. We were married within two months and expecting you soon after."

"It ends there?" Darren had expected more.

His father sighed. "I wish it had."

There was a tense moment of silence between them.

"Mora arrived at the door two months into your mother's pregnancy, showing herself."

Darren's mind rioted, and he forced himself to reason that Marquita was younger than he was by a full two years; she wasn't his sister, thank the Goddess. His calmer mind assured him that his father never would have let him take a close relative as a lover.

Matthew waited for his mind to process that before he continued. "She had the results of the paternity tests in hand. How she managed that without my knowledge is still a mystery to me."

"It was your child, from the night you were drugged." Darren didn't question it.

"It was a boy. She..." He reached for the decanter again.

"I believe I could use one." Did he have an older brother somewhere, heir but for a twist of fate?

Matthew poured two, handed one to Darren, and took a seat next to his son.

His younger son.

On that thought, they both drank deeply. The whiskey burned a fire trail down Darren's throat and then his gut.

His father started speaking again, as if to unburden himself. "Mora seemed certain I would turn your mother out for her. After all..." His voice went bitter. "She carried my heir...if I chose to claim him."

"You didn't, obviously."

"I love your mother. Whether she carried a son or a daughter, I wouldn't have hurt her for anything, even the certainty of an heir."

"As I love Kambry."

Matthew managed a weak smile. "I hope she carries a son. This will be much easier and less expensive, if she carries your heir."

"How expensive was it for you?" Darren asked bluntly.

The rest of the whiskey disappeared down his father's throat. Darren followed in his wake, certain he was about to need a drink. Better to beat it to the need.

"Without my agreement, the babe was useless to Mora. Had it been Benjamin's child, he'd be Hein, and neither of us would be. But it was *my* son.

"Mora wanted to be my wife, at least in name. A position as my mistress was beneath her aims."

"You offered that?" Darren asked in disbelief. "You offered her a place as your mistress to claim your son by her?"

"When I learned what she intended...yes. I offered it. I would have given her a cottage, somewhere your mother would never have had to see her. Mora refused outright."

"She terminated?" he guessed.

Matthew laughed harshly. "I offered... Servants, money, a place in the country... Mora told me that she wouldn't spoil her body for a bastard she'd have to pawn off on someone anyway. She left the proof behind with me to consider.

"She waited a week for me to change my mind. Then she had the notice of termination sent to me. I still have it. I should have burned it long ago, but I couldn't."

Darren wanted to offer comfort for his loss, but how did a man do that, when the loss was so deep and the reminders so present?

"Maybe her inability to produce an heir for Montberry was divine justice. I've prayed for the last two and a half decades for her to pay for what she did to us...your mother and me."

Darren took a calming breath. "I will never release Erika to them. I'll ask Uncle Benjamin for a judgment first. I'll have him petition the Counselors on my behalf." Though the final judgment would be handed down by the Counselors, they took the wishes of the king close to heart.

"You may have to." He sighed, laying a hand on Darren's shoulder. "The Goddess was kind in giving you this chance. Don't let the young bitch play you as her mother played me."

CHAPTER EIGHTEEN

Darren sat in bed, half-asleep, Erika cradled on his arm, a bottle in her mouth. She sucked in bursts that announced her descent into dreams. He hadn't slept well in three days, but he refused to have his daughter raised by nurses and nannies, as Marquita had suggested.

Kambry had been no end of aid, even taking on babe duty while Darren napped, but she was late in her term. He drew the line at compromising his second child to make caring for the first easier. Though he wanted Kambry in his bed, she would only get unbroken sleep in her own.

The door clicked open, and Darren looked up, prepared to send Kambry back to bed.

It wasn't Kambry in the doorway. Marquita stood, wreathed in light. Darren controlled the urge to shout her out, his jaw clenching in fury that she'd dared come here.

"You wanted something?" he asked.

"You didn't come to see me." She feigned hurt at it.

"I've been busy with Erika." *And you made it clear you didn't want me near.*

Marquita's nose scrunched up in dislike, and he took perverse pleasure in the fact that she hated the name he'd chosen. Kambry liked it, and Kambry would be Erika's mother.

She sighed. "There are nurses and nannies to care for her. You needn't lose sleep over her."

"Erika is my daughter. She won't be raised by servants." That was one thing Darren had no complaints about; his parents had always been there for him.

An unpleasant smile settled on Marquita's face. "You've decided to make me your wife? How wonderful."

"I've decided nothing of the sort," he assured her.

Her smile disappeared. "I don't understand."

Darren held his tongue, wanting solid legal advice and backing before he made his move. Moreover, Kambry still carried, and he wouldn't chance this selfish bitch harming her when he dismissed her.

"Darren?" she prompted him.

"We will discuss the future at the end of your confinement. You should rest." With that, he waved her away.

* * * *

Kambry looked up at the sound of a light knocking, swallowing a lump of fear.

It can't be Marquita, she reasoned. After her sister's visit to Darren's rooms, he'd set guards with orders to keep Marquita and Mora away from both Kambry and Erika. At the moment, both were settled on her bed, which meant at least four of his guards were in the corridor. There was no way her sister could make it to the door.

It's probably a servant.

They usually announce themselves.

The knock sounded again.

A guard knocking for a laden servant?

"Yes?" The apprehension persisted; Kambry couldn't admit the person blind.

"Lady Sirana to see you, Lady Kambry."

Shock stole her ability to speak. Darren's mother had studiously avoided spending time with her...and with Marquita, to be fair. "Come in," she invited.

Rising from the bed was no easy task, and she'd only half accomplished it when Lady Sirana strode in.

The lady stopped and stared, her brow furrowing. "What *are* you doing?"

Kambry settled on the edge of the mattress, sighing. "Making a poor attempt at rising to meet you, I'm afraid. My body does not currently support my manners."

"Which is why pregnant women who show do not rise for anyone but the king and queen, and confined or nursing mothers rise for no one."

She winced at the rebuke, no matter how softly delivered it was. "The former sadly missing from my mother's instruction," she offered by way of explanation and apology.

"But easily corrected." Sirana dismissed the lack as inconsequential. There was no snub in the comment, though Kambry knew the lady and Mother had some history of animosity.

Sirana crossed to the far side of the bed and looked down at Erika, a wistful smile curving her lips. "May I?" she asked.

Kambry paused in the process of settling back into the pillows. "Erika is your granddaughter." Why would Sirana ask permission to hold her?

"And you are her mother, I'm told." She deferred to Kambry as such. It was enough to make the head spin.

Answering such a statement was problematic. "Darren says it, but..."

Sirana settled on the mattress, her gaze locked on the babe. She offered Erika a finger, cooing out a compliment as a pudgy hand circled it. "Do you wish to be her mother?"

"Of course, which means Marquita will stop at nothing to deny me that wish...and Darren that wish, once she scents his aim. Marquita doesn't often lose."

"Neither does your mother. That doesn't mean they can't be beaten."

"If you don't mind—"

"I do." It was delivered kindly but with a finality to it.

"May I ask one thing?"

"I don't promise to answer, but I won't be offended by the asking."

Kambry took a calming breath. "Fair enough. I imagine Darren doesn't want me to hear the tale?"

Sirana raised her head, smiling sadly. "I imagine you're correct about that. Darren worries. We all do."

"My mother was in rare form," she muttered.

That prompted a heartfelt smile. "And the question is?"

"Which of you won?"

Her smile disappeared, and she swallowed down what might have been a lump or a sob. Kambry had given up hope of an answer when Sirana offered one.

"It couldn't properly be called a win for anyone. On some level, I think we all lost and we all suffered." She looked as if she might say more but didn't.

Kambry stared at Erika, her heart aching. "That's what I'm afraid of. If Marquita looks to lose what she wants, everyone will."

Sirana's hand closed over hers. "You fear you'll lose Darren?"

"I hope not," she admitted. "But the loss would change him, and I shudder to think of what it would mean for Erika."

"Which is something you shouldn't be worrying about, in your condition. Let Darren handle the details. Let me handle them."

Kambry nodded solemnly. It did no good to argue it; Darren's entire family treated her as if she was made of glass.

"In the meantime, we have a wedding to plan."

That pronouncement left Kambry gasping for air and missing at every word she sought to use.

"You will let me help plan it, won't you?" There was something of a plea in that.

"I highly doubt my mother would care to," she blurted out. Her face burned in embarrassment.

Sirana laughed heartily. "Then you'll need a replacement."

Kambry joined her, her heart light. "I suppose I will."

CHAPTER NINETEEN

"Sira stopped by." Alana mentioned it in a voice that was falsely nonchalant.

Benjamin raised his head, abandoning the report in his hand, his attention piqued. "There's something wrong?"

She settled on the arm of his chair, as she'd often done before they married. "Darren wishes to remove the parental rights of one of his mistresses. He needs to know his legal rights, before he proceeds."

His jaw dropped; forcing it shut took more than a moment. "That's a serious situation," he managed when he recovered enough to form words.

"He has reason to believe she means to harm the child."

"Does he have evidence of it? As much as I hate to admit this, without proof, there is not much I can do to aid Darren with the Counselors." Benjamin anticipated her crestfallen look; he ached that he couldn't favor her with a simple solution to the problem.

"He has two witnesses to the conversation," she offered hopefully.

"I take it one is the other mistress?" he ventured. He'd seen that more than once.

She nodded, fussing at her skirt in an attack of nerves.

Benjamin sighed. "It's a conflict of interest, Alana. She stands to gain, if the judgment goes to Darren." There was little question of that, though he loathed the fact that he had to suspect it, that he had to err on the side of solid proof without chance of taint.

"The other doesn't have a conflict." She wound her fingers through each other, yet another nervous show.

"Alana?" He wound an arm around her waist and drew her onto his lap.

"In fact, she dislikes both mistresses," she added. "The witness less so than the accused, but neither are allies."

"Sirana is the other witness," he guessed. He folded Alana into his chest. "She has a conflict of interest, as well." He knew it would upset Alana to think of a child in danger, considering her condition. Still, he needed proof that wasn't suspect.

Alana shook her head. "Sira isn't the witness."

"Matthew? Darren?" There had to be some reason she was stalling off on revealing the witness to him.

"Amber."

For the second time in a hand of minutes, she rendered him momentarily speechless.

"I know it's a bad time to question her; the wedding is only two days away. Darren hopes to stall off on the proceedings until the end of his mistress's confinement, but the battle will come...in days...in weeks, at most."

"While Amber still carries," he mused. It was decidedly a bad situation. "I'll have to make her testimony as painless as possible, if it comes to that."

"It will. You know who the mistress's mother is, and I'm told this one is cut from the same cloth."

She didn't say Mora's name, as if she found forming the syllables distasteful. That probably wasn't far from the truth. The last time Mora had interfered in the royal family's lives, she'd nearly destroyed all six of them, by Benjamin's estimation.

Alana nestled her cheek to his chest, seeking comfort silently. "Should we warn Edward that this is a possibility?"

"No. They have enough to worry about with the wedding closing fast."

She nodded her agreement.

Benjamin forced his mind back to the subject at hand, needing all the information he could gather about the situation. "I take it he means to dismiss the mistress."

"Of course."

"And keep the other?" That would give her a pressing reason to lie.

"Marry the other, as I understand it."

He considered that. "Problematic, considering his contract...unless we know she carries his heir?"

Alana shook her head. "The blood test showed nothing conclusive...nor did the sonogram, and Darren won't permit an amniot draw for a definitive answer."

"I can't fault him that one. The risk is too high for the return. I wouldn't allow an amniot draw on you, either."

The blood test was less precise than the amniot draw. If it indicated a male child, it was foolproof; if it didn't, it was inconclusive as to the sex of the child.

If the blood test wasn't definitive—and the sonogram wasn't—there was no way to be certain without an amniot draw. Unless amniot was called for to establish some other genetic marker, most couples would rather be surprised than risk losing the babe to an elective procedure.

Edward had been confirmed by blood test and sonogram. They'd decided to allow the Goddess to surprise them this time.

Alana fidgeted again, a sure sign that she was about to suggest something he wouldn't care for. Benjamin cleared his throat and motioned for her to speak her mind.

"There is one thing we can do to help, I think."

Here it comes. The subject she doesn't want to broach.

* * * *

"A few more moments, Highness," Trent called out.

Edward smiled at Amber's nervous fidgeting. "We'll be right there."

The runner turned and strolled out, leaving them alone in the library.

Edward gathered Amber into his arms. "Why the nerves? We've been living as a couple for so long." Was it that she would be officially named as Princess Amber? She'd switched to Lady Amber, easily enough.

"I look ridiculous," she moaned.

He laughed, adding an extra squeeze. It had been difficult refitting the traditional gown for a woman as heavy with child—*children*—as Amber was. In truth, the result was rather uncomfortable-looking.

"It's only for the ceremony," he assured her. "You can change for the feast."

Amber pulled at the bodice, sighing when the tight, sleeveless satin continued pressing in and up on her full breasts. The high waistline was pushed higher still by her rounded womb.

Edward rubbed at her lower back, and she groaned, nestling her cheek to his chest.

"Are you very uncomfortable?" he asked. Though it would be a breach of protocol, Edward would delay the ceremony and let Amber change her dress now, if she was too uncomfortable.

"No. I suppose not."

Edward stroked the hard swell of her womb, enjoying the peace of the moment.

Darren's voice came from the doorway. "I hear congratulations are in order."

Amber sighed. "We're not married yet."

His cousin's laughter was deep and rich. "Not that. I meant the babes. I hear that the doctors suspect two boys, that they've confirmed one, at least."

Amber groaned, folding herself into Edward's chest, as if she meant to go to sleep. And she might; carrying twins was exhausting.

"Is she well?" Darren asked, concern stealing his levity.

Edward sat on the edge of the sofa and pulled Amber into his lap. "Just tired. Perhaps we should arrange a nap between the ceremony and the feast."

"Good." The relief in his voice was unmistakable.

"Are you saying you want to distance yourself from the throne?" Edward teased.

Darren hesitated. "It has crossed my mind, of late," he confided. "But that's a subject for another time."

There was something serious going on here, but Edward let Darren have his space to unravel it at his leisure. Pushing him would likely be a bad choice.

"Did you bring Kambry?" he asked instead, keeping his voice low so as not to disturb Amber.

It was a given that he hadn't brought Marquita to the celebration. She was still in her confinement, recovering from the birth of a daughter almost three weeks earlier.

"No. She gave birth last night. I may not stay long. I should get back to her."

"Really?" Edward raised his head, trying to analyze Darren's expression. It was troubled...or pensive. "Will there be a wedding?"

"I... It was another daughter. My father is livid. Marquita is smug, as always. Kambry... She's too tired to decide what she feels, right now."

Edward could see something momentous building behind Darren's lips, sealed inside. "What do you think about the situation, Darren?" he asked bluntly.

"I think... No, I know that I'm marrying Kambry anyway." He darkened, looking as if he'd just been caught in some misdeed.

"You're taken with her."

"I am. We sit for hours, just as you are now."

"Will you dismiss Marquita? Or will you chance her producing the heir first?" No wonder Darren was so subdued. Considering his contract, these questions were costly ones, both emotionally and monetarily.

"I can afford to pay her a handsome sum to be rid of her, and I will. I... It's always been Kambry, I think."

"Then why didn't you offer for Kambry alone?"

Darren sank to a chair across from him, looking as if the weight of the world rested solely on him. "Lunacy, I suppose. I was taken with the idea of what they'd offered. They are both beautiful women, in their own ways."

"But beauty isn't everything," Edward finished for him.

Amber sighed. "I hope not."

"You are beautiful," Edward chided her.

She didn't argue with him, thank the Goddess.

Darren ran a hand through his hair, looking ten years older than he had the night of the Bride Ball. "Marquita hasn't aroused me in months," he admitted. "But Kambry... Her confinement is going to be torture."

Edward nodded. "What about your older daughter?" From what Amber said, he knew Marquita would abandon the babe to whatever fate had in store for her...or something worse that even Amber couldn't put a name to.

"I love Erika, and so does Kambry. We intend to raise her as Aliya's sister. Marquita will make a fuss for more money, but she doesn't want the babe. She never really has."

He nodded. "All for the best, then."

Trent appeared in the doorway again. "It is time, Highness."

Edward started to lift Amber to her feet, but she was heavily asleep. He settled down, caressing her back.

"Highness?"

"There will be an hour delay," Edward informed him.

"But Highness," he started to protest. "The guests are—"

"My bride is exhausted. She needs to rest, for my heirs' sake...and she will. An hour." *Or more.*

"Yes, Highness. I will inform the guests."

Darren chuckled.

"You find this funny?" Edward asked.

"No. It was the right choice."

"Then why are you laughing?"

"Because, now I know it's the right choice. If you'll excuse me..." He stood, unbuttoning his jacket. "I don't belong here, Edward. I'm going home to Kambry. Appearances be damned."

"And that, cousin, is the right choice."

* * * *

Amber yawned, stretching to the hands rubbing her sore back.

"Feel better?" Christopher asked.

"Much. Yes," she mumbled, half awake. She opened her eyes, wondering at how much darker the room was. "Has the sun gone into hiding?"

"No. It's still shining brightly."

She worked her way off Christopher's lap, with his assistance. "How long did I sleep?"

"Nearly two hours."

Amber's heart skipped a beat or two. "Oh, no," she moaned. "I'm late to my own wedding."

His hands wrapped around her shoulders from behind. "No, you aren't. The wedding was delayed for your comfort and health."

"What of your mother's comfort?" she countered. "What of her health?" Was anyone thinking of Alana, as Christopher was thinking of her?

"Only you would worry about that."

"That's not true. I'm sure your father worries about it."

"True. She's early in, not even showing yet," Christopher assured her. "Now, will you stop arguing or delay the ceremony further by continuing to argue the rights and wrongs of this?"

Her horror melted in light of the fact that he was teasing, and she knew that well enough. "This isn't over, Your Highness."

He smiled against her cheek. "I hope that is true."

Benjamin strode into the room, visibly distressed. "Edward... Amber..." he greeted them with slight bows of his head. "I'm afraid I have to ask a bit of your time today."

Amber nodded. "If it's important, of course." She'd already wasted the time of others. It was the least she could do.

He crossed the room to her, taking her hands in his. "I need you to give testimony to the Counselors, just after the ceremony."

Her heart stuttered. "Testimony? Me?"

Benjamin nodded, his expression starkly serious.

"About what subject?"

"There was a conversation. I've been told you were a witness to it, and as the only disinterested party, we need your testimony as to what was said."

Her head spun. "What conversation?" What could be so important?

"There was a discussion of some sort between Mora and her daughters, before the Bride Ball." He left off, seemingly waiting for her reaction to that much.

Her breathing hitched, and her stomach dropped out. She pressed a hand to her mouth, then drew it away. "Good Goddess," she managed. "What has Marquita done?" She grasped at Christopher's hand for support, tears stinging at her eyes. "She found out that Darren intends to dismiss her and did something to her babe? Please, tell me she hasn't."

Benjamin reached out to steady her. "No, thank the Goddess, but Darren believes she will. You feel that strongly that she will harm her own child?"

The two men together guided her back to the sofa, and Amber sank into it, her stomach churning so badly it ached.

"I have no doubt of it."

Benjamin nodded. "Then the Counselors will have to hear your testimony."

Christopher closed a hand on her shoulder. "I suggest we get Ivyvine to run a few tests, as well."

Amber smiled weakly. "I'm certain this is simply due to shock," she assured him.

"Yes, but there are other things we can do to help the cause."

CHAPTER TWENTY

Darren looked up in surprise at the maid rushing toward him.

"Is something wrong?" he asked. The manor suddenly seemed too still. What had happened?

"There was a...disturbance, Hein."

"Disturbance?" Without asking for more information, he started up the stairs toward Kambry's rooms.

The maid hurried along. "Lady Marquita and her mother, Lady Mora, tried to burst in on Lady Kambry and your mother. There was something of a scene when the guards refused them entry."

His heart stuttered, and Darren broke into a trot. "Is Kambry all right? What about Aliya and Erika?"

"All well," she reported. "Lady Mora and Lady Marquita were ordered under room arrest by your mother. She is caring for Lady Kambry and the babes."

He nodded, breaking into a run and outdistancing the maid. The guards cleared the way for him with a slight tip of their heads, and Darren bolted into Kambry's room.

She was asleep beneath a pile of quilts, showing no signs of abuse, thank the Goddess. He took a calming breath, looking for his mother.

Sira sat in the padded rocker, feeding Erika a bottle. "She's fine, Darren," she assured him. "They're all fine."

He nodded, striding first to Aliya's cradle, then to the bed, checking on them, all the same. Kambry sighed at his touch, but she didn't wake.

Darren sank to her side on the mattress. "Tell me what happened." Depending on what he heard, he might have to ask Benjamin to leave the wedding festivities to seek a judgment.

"Marquita demanded her child, and the guards informed her that, by your orders, she was forbidden to see Erika without you."

He winced at what probably followed. "She had...words for the guards, I am sure."

"The guards, you...Kambry most of all."

"What words?" What foul thing had Marquita accused this time?

"She threatened Kambry's life, Darren. This has to end."

His blood ran cold at that. "I agree. Send Vincent for Father and Uncle Benjamin. Wedding or no wedding, a judgment has to be made on this."

* * * *

Kambry woke to find herself cocooned in quilts in the middle of Darren's bed. Her head spun, and she fought for a coherent memory stream that would lead her here.

"I moved you while you slept," Darren assured her.

He was sitting in a comfortable chair, his feet propped up on an ottoman. One of the babes was curled to his chest, but wrapped in the blanket as she was, Kambry couldn't tell if it was Aliya or Erika.

"I had the babes brought here, as well. They won't be leaving, and you'll all be much safer on this level than the one your sister and mother currently inhabit."

"What will we do now, Darren? Marquita is trying to take Erika away. She's reasoned her way to your plan now." Just the thought of it made her ill. She'd come to love Erika, come to dream fondly of the idea of raising her two girls together.

"I've asked for a judgment. My uncle should arrive within the hour with the Counselors' decision. I don't care what it costs me, Kambry. If you're willing, you will be my wife, Marquita will be dismissed, and Erika will be ours...for a reasonable amount, if the Counselors side with us, or everything I have, if they don't."

"I wish it," she answered.

He nodded. "Then let's get you into a robe and move this chair into the sitting room. The proceedings will take place here, in your confinement, if we've been driven to it."

* * * *

Darren tucked the quilts around Kambry and looked to the two nurses and four guards standing in the doorway. "The doors are to remain locked. The six of you are to remain in the bedroom, no matter what you hear on this side of the doors. Am I understood?"

"Yes, Hein," the Captain responded.

The head nurse nodded her agreement.

"If Aliya wakes for a feeding..." He glanced at Kambry, waiting for her nod of approval. When she gave it, he turned back to them. "A bottle this one time won't harm her. I don't want my daughters in this room."

"Yes, Hein." That time, they said it in unison.

His orders given, Darren waved them into the bedroom, listening until the lock clicked shut.

"They'll be safe," he assured her for the third time.

"I know." A weak smile pulled up at her lips. "You're such a good father, Darren. I always knew you'd be."

He crouched to her level and laid a gentle kiss on her lips. "And you are an excellent mother to twin daughters."

His father bustled in, looking tense. "They took advantage of your absence," he grumbled. "Just what I'd expect Mora to do."

"No swaying the proceedings, Matthew," Benjamin teased, striding in. He took Darren's hand for a handshake, cocking his head to one side. "I believe you're right," he mused.

"What?" Darren asked, perplexed by the comment.

"Your father told me how much you've matured in the last year. I do believe he's right."

Darren's cheeks heated. "I hope so. I truly do. And...I'm sorry for pulling you away from the festivities. If this could wait— I had planned to wait until the end of Kambry's confinement, the end of Marquita's, at least."

"Don't be an idiot," Edward chastised him from the doorway. "We were on our way out to the Lake Serenity house anyway. We'll simply spend the night here and move on tomorrow, if that's acceptable to you."

"Acceptable? It's wonderful. Mother was going to invite Alana for a visit anyway."

"Speaking of the lady." Matthew met his wife at the door, taking her in his arms. "Are you well?"

She smiled. "As well as one can be with Mora underfoot and intent on mischief. Can we get started? The sooner the judgment is rendered and the deal struck, the sooner I can exile that beast from my home."

"Please," Darren requested. The sooner this was over with, the better.

Edward raised an eyebrow. "One suggestion, cousin."

"Yes?"

"Don't question anything. Keep your mouth shut and play along."

"I concur," Matthew added.

Darren's heart raced at that, but a search of the faces around him gave no clue as to the meaning of it. "If you say so."

"I insist," Benjamin closed the subject.

"If you insist," he managed shakily. With a squeeze to Kambry's hand, he steeled himself for the coming tensions.

It was the strangest scene Darren had ever thought to see. No. Even his imagination wasn't this rich and varied.

Darren stood at Kambry's side, ready to act as her personal guard, if the need arose. His mother sat on a desk chair pulled to Kambry's other side, and Matthew stood at her shoulder, looking similarly prepared to protect his wife from harm.

Benjamin had forbidden Alana from attending, even when she'd begged for the chance to watch Mora get her comeuppance.

Amber had expressed no wish to see the judgment delivered, which meant Edward hadn't had to order her away. Darren didn't question that his cousin would have done so, if forced to it.

"Is Amber feeling better?" Benjamin asked.

"Much," he confirmed. "But I've sent her to rest, nonetheless. Mother is sitting with her."

"Impatiently waiting news, I'm sure."

"Problem?" Darren asked. He hoped the trip to Willowmarsh hadn't been a hardship for her.

His father shook his head. "Simply the stresses of the day."

Darren relaxed. "We should get this done. Kambry doesn't need the stresses, any more than Amber does."

"I agree," Benjamin intoned. "We've already sent the guards for them."

Out of courtesy, the small sofa had been left empty for Marquita. No matter what else she was, she was a woman in confinement.

She made a show of her fatigue, crossing to the sofa and settling into it with a sigh. Her eyes flicked to the more comfortable chair her sister had been afforded, but she kept silent, proving her intelligence and sense of self-preservation.

Mora settled beside her, patting her daughter's hand. She took inventory of the assembled royals and the guards at the doorway. "If we could settle this insanity," she hinted.

"Insanity?" Sira countered. "Your daughter threatened the life of another within my home. She threatened violence."

"My daughter is a confined woman being denied her child."

"A child she's made no attempt to see in three weeks?" Darren snapped. "A child she ordered taken from her sight at birth and has since relegated to whatever chance might offer her for care?"

"I knew you'd care for her, Darren." Marquita affected a wounded person at that accusation.

Mora wrapped an arm around her. "Marquita is suffering parting depression. Any fool could see that."

"A simple blood test could confirm that...or refute it," Matthew suggested.

Sira raised an eyebrow. "And death threats are to be taken even more seriously, with proof that the subject is unbalanced."

"She's my sister," Marquita protested. "Threats of harm or death are common occurrences between siblings."

Darren offered Kambry a sideward glance, wincing at her squirm and blush.

She cleared her throat. "I won't deny I've been threatened   before,   but   never   with   quite this...vehemence."

"You see?" Mora replied. "Sibling squabbles aren't that unusual, now are they?"

"But threats to an innocent child are," Benjamin offered gravely.

There was a moment of tense silence.

"I would never," Marquita decreed. She shot a look of hurt at Kambry that might have passed for sincere with anyone who didn't know her well.

Benjamin crossed the room and offered the decree, signed by the Counselors of the Four Quarters. "According to Princess Amber's statement, you did. You and your mother both. The Counselors take such threats very seriously."

Marquita took it, seemingly stunned. She didn't read it.

"Your parental rights have been stripped and guardianship of your child awarded to Darren."

Her face darkened and then screwed up in anger.

"This is outrageous," Mora fumed.

Sira rolled her eyes. "Voiced by the one most closely acquainted with the condition," she muttered.

Mora shot a mutinous look back, and Matthew moved between them.

"Based on the testimony Princess Amber has already given, the Counselors were unanimous in their decision," he informed her. He stressed Amber's title, as if sending warnings or poking reminders that their former servant by circumstance was now their better.

"How could they?" Marquita wailed. "I've been forbidden to state my side?"

"You've been forbidden nothing," Benjamin countered. "Well, short of Erika, that is."

"It's unseemly," Mora complained. "There's been abuse of power here."

Edward stepped in calmly. "No such thing. A child was in danger, and decisive action was taken. It would have taken hours longer, had the Counselors not been gathered for the wedding. Your actions fortuitously coincided with the event."

Fortuitously? Darren bit back a snort of disgust. They'd planned their attack for a time when both he and his father were out of the household.

"I've got no recourse?" Marquita cut in. There was a cold edge to her eyes and voice.

Benjamin sighed. "By law, you have the right to appeal the Counselors' decision, to plead your case to them personally. A slim chance exists that you might overturn the decision, but an equitable dissolution of the contract with award would serve everyone nicely."

Marquita seemed to mull over the suggestion. "It would have to be a formidable award for the sacrifice of my child," she murmured. "For surrendering my rights to her permanently. At least...four times what is typically awarded for Darren's station in life."

Darren started to protest it as unconscionable. No award was more than triple the typical, and that was in cases of criminal acts.

Edward cut him off cleanly, when barely a syllable had passed his lips. "You'd accept that? You'd release Erika to Darren and forfeit all rights of parenthood and of contract for the settlement of four times the typical award for his position?"

She hesitated, perhaps weighing the chance that she could get more against the chance that she was harming her odds at appeal by agreeing to a price on her child. In the end, Marquita offered her hand in agreement. "Done," she informed Darren, her eyes narrowed.

He started to shake his head in refusal, stilling in confusion at the nods from Benjamin and Edward. A glance at his father revealed that Matthew concurred, though the request was scandalous. He unfisted his hand without looking away from his parents and crossed the room to the shrew. His arm resisted raising, but he forced it up and grasped Marquita's hand, meeting her eyes at last. "Done."

Her smile turned his stomach.

I promised anything. It's worth it for Kambry and my daughters.

Benjamin offered Marquita his arm and guided her toward the door. "Forty thousand will be delivered to you within the week," he assured her.

Darren snapped his head around, noting his father's sly smile in shock. Marquita's protest sent his focus back to her.

"Forty? It should be two hundred, by my reckoning."

Mine as well. But Darren dared not admit it. Whatever his family had come prepared to do to aid him, he would accept with thanks.

Edward furrowed his brow as if in confusion. "Two hundred? If Darren was Hein Darren, that would be a correct assumption."

Darren's head spun, but he held his tongue, waiting to see how it would play out.

"He *is* Hein Darren," she replied, as perplexed as Darren was himself.

Benjamin feigned shock, then realization. "You didn't attend the celebration."

Marquita yanked her arm from his. "Of course not. I *am* in my confinement."

"And so obviously debilitated," Sira offered dryly.

Mora shot her another warning look. "And what difference would that make, King Benjamin?" she inquired with a cool reserve about her.

"Why...the announcement, of course."

He should have been an actor. Goddess, but he's playing her well.

She spoke through ground teeth. "And what announcement would that be?" she played along.

"Alana carries a son," he imparted happily. "The blood test was conclusive."

"What if she doesn't produce a viable child?" Marquita snapped. "The queen is rather old to be carrying."

Kambry sucked in a breath at the rude and unfeeling comment. It was considered bad luck and bad form to insinuate a coveted child would be delivered less than perfectly.

Sira was less restrained, glaring down the young woman as if she meant to lay a blow across her mouth. Darren had no doubts the women Sira influenced would hear of this insult and have some punishment of their own for Marquita.

Benjamin's jaw tightened, but he didn't reply to the snub.

Edward did. "How joyous that her doctor disagrees."

Marquita didn't respond, leaving Darren to wonder if she was oblivious to the fact that she'd angered him or uncaring of it.

Edward continued in a matter-of-fact tone that put Darren on edge. "After Amber's...reaction to the stresses of the day, the doctor insisted on a few tests between the ceremony and the celebration. The sonogram was conclusive; both of my children are male. Moreover, Amber was found to be in impeccable health, as were my sons," he added before Marquita could insinuate that it wasn't the case.

Benjamin cut in. "It would be highly unlikely that we'd lose two of the three young heirs...and that Amber would prove unable to carry again. With two heirs in Edward's generation...or Goddess forbid, two in the next, if there was some unforeseen circumstance, Matthew is not Hein. He has been officially recognized as Duke Matthew Willowmarsh."

Matthew tipped his head to Mora. "Since there is no possible way for me to accede to the throne, I publicly announced my new status, in advance of the births that will push me away, and the Counselors acknowledged it." He paused only a second. "With my new status, Darren was reduced to the Honorable Lord Darren Willowmarsh."

Darren bit at the inside of his mouth, holding in laughter at the shock on Marquita's face.

"So, you see," Benjamin offered with a sad smile and a sigh. "You are mistress to a lord, one day to accede to Duke, we hope. Your settlement, as agreed before all these witnesses, will be based on Darren's current status, that of a lord."

Mora's face went so tight in anger, it appeared it would crack beneath the creams and powders. "I assume Kambry will be offered the same settlement and be free to move on to a position suitable to a lady of standing?"

Darren opened his mouth to protest that a lord of a line to be Duke in his time was hardly beneath the daughter of a Duke...or perhaps to the presumption that Kambry meant to leave him, simply because her mother and sister were upset.

Kambry didn't give Darren a chance to spout out whichever won the race to his lips. "I'm accepting whatever contract Darren offers, Mother." She knew what that contract was, but she played innocent of it well enough.

"You are the daughter of a Duke," her mother thundered. "You could make a coveted position."

"I have the only position I covet." There was something soft and loving beneath the steel of her words.

Darren smiled and took her hand laying a kiss on her knuckles. "The position is yours...only yours."

"I won't spend another night in this house," Marquita grumbled.

Sira's face erupted in a vicious smile of victory that announced she'd just been gifted what she'd been waiting for. "Vincent will see you back to Oakmarch...or wherever you intend to go. You can take what you can carry this night. The rest will be sent along for you."

Marquita gaped at her. "I am a confined woman," she protested.

"And you wish to leave. You are an adult and no longer under contract with my son. If you wish to leave, leave in comfort. If you wish to stay until the end of the confinement, you may do so in the quarters assigned you and under guard."

Mora placed an arm around her shoulders, guiding Marquita toward the door. "Come. Giselle will prepare you a soothing tea and help you to bed."

Edward snorted. "Giselle and Coraline are the servants I engaged for Lady Reanne. Unless Reanne orders them to pamper you, I would highly suggest you use a portion of your settlement to engage a servant of your own."

The two women turned to him, their mouths moving as if they had words they couldn't lay tongue to.

Edward's expression left no doubt that he was serious. "In fact, I believe I'll send Reanne's favorite corporal along. They so enjoy visiting together."

Darren gave up and howled in laughter. *And the guard will make sure Reanne is safe from any plotting and threats the duo might dare to send her way.*

SECTION IV:

POISON, LIES, AND NO-WIN

CHOICES

DEDICATED TO...

Grimm, the first love of my fantasy life, as it is for so many fantasy authors.

Tamer, the love that was meant to be.

CHAPTER TWENTY-ONE

Benjamin's cock came up at the feeling of Alana on his lap, her laughing body vibrating against his.

It had to be soon, appearances be damned. The game of decision was amusing enough and a social nicety, but he'd long ago decided that only Alana would do.

Her face dipped close to his, and he captured her lips in a kiss that released his frustration and need...at least a modicum of them. It left them both ragged, and sweat coated his bare chest, most likely from clenching his muscles in restraint.

Mora's chattering broke the moment, and Alana levered herself onto the arm of his chair, giving the other contender room to sit on the opposite arm. Her smile faltered at the sight of the noblewoman, with her fine clothes and augmented body. Alana recovered quickly, smoothing the simple blouse and skirt most of the lowborn in attendance wore.

Another reason it has to be soon. Alana was becoming disheartened by his failure to choose formally, unsure of her appeal.

Mora offered the cup in her hand. "It's warm in here, don't you think? I thought you might like a drink."

Before he could take it, Alana did so. "My thanks," she breathed. "I'm frightfully parched."

"But that—"

It was too late. Alana had tipped her head back, baring her graceful neck, draining the contents of the cup in a few hearty swallows. That accomplished, she handed the cup back to a horrified Mora. It was a bold move, riding the edges of uncouth, but contending to a prince was thinly-veiled civility, at its finest.

Benjamin bit back a laugh at the tactical prowess that had won Alana this round of the chase for his attentions. How could he choose another, when such a witty and inventive woman had captured his heart? The words to dismiss Mora were on the tip of his tongue when one of the other ladies saved him the trouble by drawing her away.

"Mora? I need a word."

He worked at the mystery of Mora's upset and distraction without success. Surely it wasn't Alana besting her that caused the reaction; that had happened many times before. The hair rose on the back of his neck in warning, but his alcohol-muddled mind couldn't work its way to an explanation for his unease.

Mora engaged in a whispered discussion with her fellow, and Benjamin turned back to Alana, noting the pain in her eyes. It had to be tonight, propriety or no. When Mora returned, he'd make a public show of choosing Alana. If the Goddess was kind, he'd be taking the latter to his bed after that.

* * * *

The drink went straight to Alana's head, and she wondered at what vintage it might be. Wine, even strong wines, didn't usually affect her this quickly.

She'd only been drunk once before, but she didn't remember it feeling this good. Her entire body sang in a pleasant awareness.

Benjamin's hand settled on her thigh, then trailed upward. It clasped lightly at her hip, and he pulled her back into his lap. "Where were we?" he growled playfully. His mouth closed on hers, and Alana shifted closer to him.

She shivered at the touch of his ready cock through the silk trousers that comprised the whole of his outfit. Every night of the event, she'd prayed she'd feel that length, but Benjamin had decreed only the one he'd ultimately choose would.

And Mora is still a contender for his love. Mora, with her cunning and cold resolve. Alana wished there was a way to open his eyes to Mora's true nature.

That an unlikely proposition, she had to make her own sincerity clear to Benjamin. She threw herself into the kiss, moaning at him surrounding her in textures and scents.

He was so potent, he made her head swim. The need for more rode at her, and Alana tangled her fingers in the crisp hairs that bisected his chest.

Benjamin came at her mouth more avidly, urging her on. Emboldened, Alana touched him, moaning as muscles tensed beneath her palms and fingertips.

Her body burned and ached for an end to the game. His kiss wasn't enough. His hands exploring over clothing wasn't enough. Alana cupped his rigid length between their bodies.

Benjamin broke off the kiss with a half-swallowed cry. She forced her eyes open, meeting his questioning gaze. He wasn't stopping her, so she stroked him through the silk.

Her heart pounded in apprehension. Would he rebuff her? Dismiss her and choose Mora? This was presumptuous, but her need was maddening in its intensity.

The kiss resumed, a harder, hotter kiss that announced his interest. Benjamin guided her around to face him, and Alana placed a knee on either side of his body, stretching her skirt to its limits. One of his hands fisted in her hair, and the other grasped at her hip, drawing Alana to his body.

The temperature in the room jumped abruptly. The heat between them followed in kind.

Alana pulled at the fasteners on his trousers, and Benjamin wrenched his mouth from hers. He shot a startled look between their bodies, then met her eyes, swallowing hard.

"Here?" he whispered.

"Anywhere." *Anything.* "As long as it's now." She shifted her hips against him, making the offer.

He pushed up at her skirt, and Alana opened his trousers. His cock strained against her hand and she grasped it, moaning at the feel of him.

Benjamin positioned her over the crown, then guided her down. Alana's breathing hitched at the first touch. She forced her hips down, gasping his name as he arched off the seat and filled her.

She held to his shoulders, her fingernails biting skin, her eyes sliding shut. His cock filled her, stretched her, eased the ache.

"Goddess, Benjamin, yes," she urged him.

* * * *

Benjamin froze in disbelief. It couldn't be... But he knew it was true. Alana was a virgin. *Well, she was, until I—*

"Goddess, Benjamin, yes," she pleaded.

At least I didn't hurt her. Thank the Goddess for that.

There'd been an even chance she was untouched...perhaps less than even, all things considered. When she'd agreed to exhibitionism, he'd assumed she was experienced.

Alana rose and fell over him, scattering his senses. Who knew a virgin could move this way? If this was what she did to him untrained, her sexual education might well kill him.

A hoot of appreciation opened Benjamin's consciousness to other sounds from the assembled crowd. That brought a measure of sanity to his fevered mind.

Benjamin shook his head, cupping Alana's face. "No, Alana. Let me—"

"Let me," she purred.

Any thoughts he'd had about a virgin being too skittish for exhibitionism fled. He couldn't decide if she was too involved to notice their audience or uncaring that it existed. If Alana wasn't bothered by it, Benjamin wasn't going to force a stop.

It was a wild ride, and the end was kinetic. Alana threw her head back and screamed at the first jet of his seed into her. Her contractions gripped him hard, and he roared in possession. She was his, and the Goddess help anyone who stood in his way.

Her eyes slid open, and the look of longing made his heart stutter. She was innocent of what her expressions did to him, how they turned him into clay in her delicious, little hands.

She's innocent. That fact finally made it through the haze in his mind. Benjamin glanced around at the attendees of the Bride Ball, some watching them avidly...some less overtly...none oblivious to the spectacle.

It's unacceptable. Benjamin eased her skirt over her buttocks, shielding all but the sight of the root of his cock extending up between those silken thighs.

Alana whimpered at his touch, her eyes pleading for more, her body still gripping and releasing in the throes of waning climax.

"In my rooms," he offered. "Will you accompany me—"

"Yes."

"Highness," one of Alana's supporters addressed him. "Highness, I must—"

"When Mora returns, tell her to move on to other pursuits," he announced. "I've chosen Alana, if she'll have me."

Aftershocks ripped through her, and tears misted her eyes.

Alana laughed in delight. "Oh, yes."

"But Highness, I must tell—"

"Enough."

She fell silent, though she shifted nervously.

Benjamin set Alana on her feet, carefully covering her. He fastened his trousers, glad he'd chosen purple. Gold would have shown the smears of red more clearly. At any respectable distance, the stains on the purple would be mistaken for clear female fluids, and the masses wouldn't have leave to gossip about watching Benjamin deflower his wife.

He took to his feet, wrapping an arm around Alana. The woman he'd dismissed twice dared to approach him again.

Benjamin motioned her to silence before she could speak, glaring her down. "One more time, and you will find yourself in a cell."

She dipped a quick curtsy and scurried away.

CHAPTER TWENTY-TWO

Matthew looked around at the hoot of a voyeur coming from the direction opposite voyeurs' row. His jaw dropped at the sight of Benjamin and Alana.

He knew his brother had been at the edges of madness for the girl, and it seemed the game had ended with an explosion of repressed passion given wings. The two hadn't even made it as far as voyeurs' row.

That should calm the old man. At least, Matthew hoped it would.

It wasn't that Matthew was adverse to the idea of a wife or mistress. He simply hadn't found a woman he'd consider for more than a night or two with a male barrier.

He sank back into a sofa, closed his eyes, and sipped at the glass of punch, grinding his teeth at the sounds from voyeurs' row. *This was definitely not the place to find one.*

Benjamin had caught lucky with Alana. She wasn't the usual Bride Ball fare, and she doted on him. But how many like her could there be?

As if in answer, a feminine shape settled next to him on the sofa.

And it starts. Benjamin has chosen Alana. Most of the ladies willing to settle for a noble match paired off in the first four days of the event. As the second highest-ranking man in attendance, the focus of the remaining royalty-chasers has fallen to me.

He smiled. Then again, he wouldn't balk at a bed partner for the night. On that note, he opened his eyes to survey the first of his choices.

There were actually two of them, both dark-haired, both pretty enough to spark his interest.

"Care for some company, Hein Matthew?" one asked, running a finger down her cleavage.

"Company is all I'm seeking, I'm afraid." It was stated bluntly...a bed partner with no chance of a contract in the making. They'd either accept his terms or withdraw. He'd lay odds that one of each would occur.

The closer's hand settled on his thigh. "We'd be interested in no ties."

He flicked a glance at the other. "Which do you suggest?" His tastes were better known than this. Sex shows were amusing enough, but he preferred hands-on single action between the sheets.

"Hmm..." her cohort purred. "Perhaps a taste to allow an unbiased choice?"

"Now that is enticing," he admitted.

The first rose and circled his body. Matthew shifted to the center, allowing them to bracket him.

There was no fanfare. In a heartbeat, there was a warm woman pressed to his chest, their mouths meshing. Matthew wrapped his arms around her, testing the feel of them moving together.

He eased away. "Nice fit," he murmured.

She offered a vixen's smile and slid into her vacated seat. Matthew raised his glass to cleanse the palate.

The second took it, laughing. She offered another glass that held a gorgeous burgundy. "Try this. James gave it to me himself. It's a *much* better vintage."

He took it and inhaled, chuckling. "Birchstand's best." It was just the thing to celebrate his brother's contract—fine wine and fine women. Half of the slim glass disappeared down his throat.

The next kiss was even more avid, as if they were trying to outdo each other. They probably were, since he'd made it clear he was only choosing one for the night.

He raised the glass, stopping to stare at the level. It was full. His lips quirked up in a smile. "Trying to take advantage of me?" he teased.

The first cupped her hand under the stem of the glass and guided it to his mouth. "Most definitely."

Matthew considered that and took a sip of the wine instead of a mouthful.

The next quarter hour passed in deep, carnal contemplation.

With each trade, the play became more intense and involved.

Matthew threw himself into the game. He wanted this. He needed it. He didn't care which one he took to his rooms. He'd take them both, if they were willing...as long as he sated himself soon.

The one currently nestled to him stroked his cock, and he reasoned he wouldn't make it that far. "Voyeurs' row," he rasped out.

She laughed, walking her fingertips up his abdomen. "We prefer privacy in the sheets." She left his lap and shot him a look of invitation.

"My rooms, then."

The other hefted the wine bottle. "One for the trip?" she suggested.

Matthew pushed the bottle aside and dipped toward her lips. "Just what I was thinking." *I could finish here. Benjamin had it right.*

She placed a hand on his chest, signaling a stop. "I think we've had enough...here. The sooner we reach your rooms, the sooner the real fun begins."

He released her with a growl, taking to his feet...too quickly. His head spun. Matthew replayed his consumption in confusion; two glasses or so of good wine and one of spiked punch wasn't enough to do this.

They sandwiched him, hands roaming. The need slammed into him so hard it nearly floored him. Sweat beaded on his skin, and the air scorched in his lungs.

"Hein Matthew?" one asked.

"It's hot," he breathed. "So hot."

"Lodi?"

The other took his arm and guided him toward the corridors. "We'll open a window, Hein. In the meantime..." She passed him the wine bottle.

"Lodi!"

"Just something to wet the mouth," she explained.

Matthew nodded, raising the bottle and swallowing down two mouthfuls. He was thirsty. He was hot, and—by the Goddess Herself—he needed to get laid...hard, fast, and probably more than once.

The trip to his rooms was punctuated by touching and tasting...both of mouths and wine. The cool stone of the corridors soothed his bare feet.

At times, he swore there were more than two women with him...more than two pairs of hands touching him, but that didn't make sense.

The door closed behind them, and Matthew turned to the one at his right, seeking her mouth.

The other—Lodi—took the bottle from his hand and set it on the table near the door. Her hands worked at his suede trousers. "Time to get undressed, Hein. Time to cool the fire."

He was on fire. There was no denying it. The one in his arms led him toward the bed, and Matthew stumbled along with her. His balance deserted him, and they sprawled to the mattress together.

Hands worked at his trousers, yanking them down and off. Other hands stroked his bare cock, his buttocks, spread his thighs to play at his engorged sac...

Matthew pushed his partner beneath him, pulling at clothes, desperate to bury himself in her.

She ripped her mouth from his. "Lodi, hurry." She let out a sharp cry that overlapped with the sound of tearing fabric.

"Get him to his back," someone ordered.

Hands pushed and pulled, forcing him off his partner. Matthew reached for her, falling back at the mouth sucking him in. It wasn't perfect, but it took the edge off.

"Take off your shirt."

"What?" another woman gasped.

"Give Hein Matthew something to amuse himself with until his partner is ready for him."

"P-partner?" he managed. *Ready?* She likely had to insert her barrier.

The mouth was ruthless, and Matthew reached for the woman's hair. His hands were diverted by a grip at the wrists, guided forcibly to a full pair of breasts...augmented but acceptable.

He worked at his position numbly...one woman gripping his wrists, one suckling him, the soft globes of one kneeling beside him...and still hands stroking at him? Climax loomed, and he closed his eyes to the patchwork reality of his rooms.

"You want a soft pussy, Hein?"

He nodded, moving his hips restlessly. "Whose?" she pressed.

"Yours. Hers. Any. I don't care," he growled. "Just stop teasing me."

She chuckled. "He's ready."

The mouth retreated, and Matthew thrust up in response, needing to follow...needing to find a replacement.

One of them straddled him, and a hand positioned his cock at a ready body. Matthew didn't have time to buck into her; her downward thrust stole his breath. She rode him hard, venting screams and pleas for more. Matthew grasped at her hips, guiding her.

The end came quickly, making his head swim in the rush of orgasm. Every effort to open his eyes and look around resulted in a sickening swirl of half-formed images.

"Do you want more?" a voice teased.

I must be dreaming. This is paradise. "Yes."

Another voice overlapped his; he didn't try to identify it.

Acknowledging that it was familiar was enough.

Someone brought a cup to his lips, offering a fortifying drink, and Matthew gulped it down.

"Would you take any cock offered, Mora?"

Mora? Matthew scowled and shook his head in disgust. What was Mora doing sullying this fine fantasy? *Maybe it's a nightmare.* He barked in laughter at the thought.

"Any," her voice rasped.

"Hein Matthew?" That taunt came from the one they called Lodi. "Any pussy?"

"I hate her," he grumbled, but the need clawed at him, and he started thrusting into the body gripping him, beyond questioning who it was, beyond caring. What did it matter? This was certainly a dream...a fevered phantom.

"I'd rather take a...a driver," Mora cursed.

Matthew had heard her say something similar before. It was a gardener last time...or a horse trainer. Mora loathed him nearly as much as he loathed her; it was impossible for her to surpass him in that regard.

A ruthless mouth played at his, and Matthew buried his hands in a wealth of hair. His cock demanded more of the heat surrounding it, and he pistoned harder.

A voice brushed at his ear, a voice he didn't recognize. "What delicious irony, Hein Matthew," she suggested. "What would you give to see that bitch Mora kneeling between your legs, sucking you, begging for your cock? Taking you in every orifice and moaning for you?"

It was a perverse sort of dark pleasure in the making. He pulled away from the foraging mouth and groaned. *That would be no nightmare.*

236

"She'll do it," the voice promised. "She'll love every second of it, and she won't be nearly as haughty, knowing you've mastered her."

He arched up with a roar, giving his fill.

A further voice teased at his raw senses. "Suck him, Mora. Suck him, while we prepare you for more."

Matthew opened his eyes, faces going in and out of focus. How many were there? Ten women? Fifteen? The one straddling him was the slowest coming. It looked like Mora, but it couldn't be; he'd never fuck her.

"What are you doing?" a shrill voice demanded.

A hand touched his throat, a cool hand on his heated flesh. A sickening trail of gold danced across his vision, and Matthew closed his eyes on a groan.

I must be ill...fevering. His stomach lurched. *I'm hallucinating, perhaps dehydrated.*

The body around him started shifting again. "Stop," the shrill one ordered.

Matthew found himself halting mid-thrust, seeking out her eyes...blue eyes...big...luminous...wreathed in a mist of pink and gold.

Her hand cupped his cheek, soothing some of the inferno. "Goddess, no. You had no right to do this to him."

There was a hint of something sad in her voice. Matthew opened his mouth, intent on asking why she was sad. He'd even offer to fix whatever it was, just to see her smile for him.

Her voice came first...angry...furious. He furrowed his brow, trying and failing to follow the chain of events that would cause such a change in her.

"You had no right to do this to him!"

A swing of gold sent his eyes sliding shut.

"Don't! Don't even *attempt* to justify this. Just get out."

"What should we do about—"

"I don't care. You created this situation; you correct it." There was a heartbeat of silence. "But you use that poison on no one else tonight. I don't care if you take turns fingering her, if you find no one willing to bed her. That's your problem and not mine."

"And if we refuse?" The hinted violence in Lodi's question had his muscles tensing to fight.

"I'll go to the guards myself." There was steel in that, a deadly calm that relaxed him.

"Very well. I believe Mora has been taught lesson enough."

"Or nearly so," another offered in a tone that promised unpleasant happenings to come.

The woman straddling him retreated in an awkward movement. Matthew gasped, groaning out a protest, reaching blindly for one of them...any of them he could reach, but there was no one close enough.

"Are you certain?" someone taunted. "If we leave, he's your problem, you know."

"Just go. I'll seek a doctor for him if I cannot handle this alone."

There was confusion of movement and sound. The door clicked shut, and silence stole into the room. Matthew was sure he was alone, until the hand touched his face again. He knew before he opened his eyes that it would be the golden-haired goddess.

She whispered to him, a balm on his ragged senses. "I'll care for you. You have my vow." A beat of silence fell. "By the Goddess, it was wrong."

Sailors told stories of sea angels with blue eyes you could drown in. Matthew was certain that was the turn this strange delusion had taken. She was his sea angel. The stories said they cared for half-dead sailors...and loved them well.

"I'll return in a moment," she promised, gliding from his side.

The ache in his gut nearly doubled him, and Matthew panted it back. *Goddess, I hope she comes back nude and ready.*

* * * *

Sira returned with a bowl of hot water and a cloth, intent on cleaning Hein Matthew and caring for him, fuming at what Lodi and the others had done to him.

She went still at the sight of him, laid out on his bed, shifting uncomfortably. His cock was stiff, twitching in need still, though he'd given Mora his fill at least once.

Someone must care for him, she reminded herself. That's all this was, a moment of solace...with a nearly-perfect male specimen.

Pushing that thought away, Sira sat beside him and placed the bowl on the stool. She wrung out the cloth and, taking a deep breath, stroked it along one strong thigh, watching the muscles tense. Hein Matthew moaned, rising to her touch.

Sira blushed, well aware that she was teasing him. She would have to make the job quick and efficient. She wet the cloth again and went to work, trying to be detached, while he writhed beneath her, moved to her, seeking her touch...and finally climaxed to her hand as she cleaned his sac and length.

"Goddess," she breathed. Her hands shaking, she wet the cloth again, stroking it along his chest and stomach, cleaning the evidence of his latest climax, thankfully not much. It was probably a sign that he'd already poured out quite a bit.

His dark blue eyes opened, and he stared at her, his cock bucking against her hand. His expression was intense, verging on violence.

Sira eased her hand away, self-conscious at touching him. "I only mean to help," she assured him. "Do you wish your doctor?" Not that she had any clue how one found a doctor in a royal or noble household. The idea of explaining all of this to a guard was enough to send ice to her stomach.

The Hein stared at her, his muscles bunching and releasing, his eyes boring into her, challenging Sira to explain herself.

"Do you understand me?" she asked him. How far had the drug clouded his mind? If he couldn't give her a coherent answer, she would have to fetch the guards for him.

A slight nod was his only reply.

"Do you need something? Do you want your—"

He moved fast, faster than she would have thought possible in his state. His hands locked around her upper arms, and the cloth slipped from her fingers.

Everything seemed to happen at once. The Hein dragged her across his body and onto the bed. Her foot struck the stool and sent it tumbling, water splashing the floor and the entire mess of bowl and stool landing with a crash.

In the next instant, she was beneath him, his weight pinning her to the bed, his face a whisper from hers. Sira pushed at his chest, hoping he understood enough to recognize her plea for freedom. His head lowered toward hers, and she moved, trying to work from under his bulk.

His hands tightened, sending shards of pain down her arms. She stopped on a gasp, meeting his gaze, manic eyes that showed he had no idea what he was doing. He was in the throes of the drug, needing, and she'd been stupid enough to try to care for him herself.

Why didn't I go for his doctor immediately? Because I didn't want to leave him alone that long? It had seemed like a good idea at the time, but now...

His hands loosened slightly, and he lowered his head again, tipping it to one side so that his lips touched the soft skin under her jawline. It was so tender, so unexpected, Sira let him.

The first nip brought her back to her senses, and she tried to lever him off with her fisted hand. The growl that escaped him sent her heart pounding. He nipped again and again, alternating between that and a series of little kisses and licks at the spot.

Sira bit back a groan, her body coming to life for him. This was a guilty little pleasure of sorts, and it was one she'd gladly give him.

Hein Matthew released one of her arms, cupping her knee with the now-free hand...forcing upward, dragging her skirt along with him. "My sea angel," he breathed. "My angel."

She gasped in realization. He was too far gone. He thought she was offering...for some reason. Was it because she hadn't fought his kiss at her jawline?

"Hein, please," she whispered, pushing at his chest again, not that she could budge him. Sira just wanted to get his attention.

His head came up, and he stared at her. Words stuck in her throat. He was beautiful and frightening, an exotic mix that made her head spin.

His hand moved higher, and she stiffened, well aware that Hein Matthew was far too close to his goal, and with him naked and her naked beneath the knee-length skirt, this could escalate quickly.

"Hein, please. This isn't—"

The kiss was hot and hard, announcing his intentions...and his needs. Sira had never been kissed this way before. It was consuming. Her body burned, and she understood what he felt...or at least a little of what he felt. If his drive was stronger than hers, he was truly afflicted.

As if in answer, he shifted his weight to one side, using the break between their bodies to push her skirt to her waist and bare her to him. Her legs clamped together in mute protest, and his hand tightened against her thigh, pushing outward, twisting brutally. Sira fought the move, squealing into his mouth at the spike of pain.

She calmed herself. He didn't know what he was doing. His senses were in a riot and his thinking mind an uncertain quantity. For that matter, her thinking mind wasn't faring well.

I have to talk him down.

With that in mind, Sira tried to extricate her mouth from his. That proved harder to accomplish than she would have thought possible. Her head was already pressed hard to the mattress, and when she tried to turn her face away, his hand left her thigh and cupped her cheek to keep her from turning away, his mouth tilting to take her deeper.

The urge to bite him was strong, but she resisted following through. He wasn't thinking. He could hurt her for it. Beside that, she didn't want to hurt him, unless it became necessary.

At a loss for something that would cut through his madness, she scratched hard at his chest. His mouth left hers, and he arched his back, moaning.

His eyes opened, and Sira held her breath. He seemed to be lucid. Perhaps it had worked. She took a deep breath, preparing to reason with him.

"Hein Matthew—"

"Matthew," he invited. His eyes softened, pleading with her. "I need you."

Sira bit her lip, her heart aching. Did he need to sate the drives the drug had instilled in him with any female body, as he had with Mora? Did he need her...or someone like her, personally? Was the "sea angel" meant as a pet name, or was he lost in a fantasy where she was one of the mythical creatures? There was no answer to any of those questions, but whatever the case, he needed comfort she could offer.

Goddess, I want to offer it. I want him to need me, at least for the night.

When he knew his mind, it was unlikely he'd look twice at her again. Sira was the daughter of a minor noble, lowborn but for a small parcel of land they owned and the king's favor on them.

She unbuttoned two buttons on her shirt, offering herself silently. Hein Matthew swept it to one side, dipping his head down to latch onto a nipple, suckling hard at her body.

Sira worked at the buttons, shifting against him as she dragged the shirt off. He moved to the other breast, stroking insistently at the first. It was a brutal pleasure, twinges of sweet pain mixing with bolts of ecstasy.

The Hein pulled at the tie on her skirt, indicating that he wanted it off, as well. He released her breast, helping her out of it. Then his mouth closed on hers, his tongue sweeping inside her. Sira held to him, dizzy in arousal, meeting his kiss in a daze. His hand eased beneath her leg, and he guided her thighs apart. Sira didn't fight him. She didn't want to fight him. He needed her—not a mindless, violent need but rather a soul-deep longing that was infectious.

His fingers circled at her clit, bringing her hips off the bed with a mew of delight. Sira stroked her hands down his chest and arms, learning his body by touch. Just when she would have explored his cock, he moved.

Sira clawed at his chest and back, a sob escaping her at the slice of pain cutting her in two. The Hein hesitated only a moment, a moan escaping his clenched teeth. Then he was moving, his entire body contracting with each ramming motion.

A scream built in her throat and burst free, an exquisite pleasure-agony making her lightheaded. Hein Matthew growled, his hands closing on her hips, forcing himself further into her in a move that stole her breath.

"I need you," he whispered. "I need..."

His roar sent shivers of sensation down her limbs. His heat erupting into her wrung little cries from her. A sharp spike of some emotion she couldn't name assaulted her, and tears escaped her eyes.

In the aftermath, Sira lay trembling in his arms, gasping at the bucking of his cock in her full and aching sheath. His lips parted hers, and he came at her, ravenous. She wound her arms around him, encouraging him.

His renewed thrusts left her panting, fighting to form words. "H-Hein—"

"Matthew," he growled. His hips sped, his cock sliding in and out of her battered core, staking a claim she couldn't begin to understand.

She nodded, closing her eyes, exhausted, riding the waves of sensation with him, wondering how many times he'd need to escape the drug's hold.

CHAPTER TWENTY-THREE

Matthew swallowed a metallic slick, wincing at the aches in his joints. Was he ill? He rotated his shoulder, and individual wounds seared him, prompting a hiss of discomfort.

Wounds? What happened last night?

He replayed what he could remember.

There had been a Bride Ball. He'd been drinking, but not heavily...not as heavily as Benjamin had been, at any rate. His mind protested that with a memory of him drinking directly from a wine bottle, but it was fuzzy and indistinct.

He moved on, disconcerted at the gaps and lack of clarity.

Most of the women had been either draped on Benjamin or running interference for the two top contenders to the place as the next queen of Lenvia, Mora and Alana. There had been a few who'd showed interest in Matthew, late in the evening. They'd brought him a drink and made promises.

Fractured memories of walking between them, trading kisses with both... Matthew shook his head, trying to dislodge it. He'd been unsteady...and horny...exceedingly so.

More memories followed. There were more than two, many more. Hands and mouths had played at him, an indecent foreplay orgy. Matthew wished he could forget that he'd taken part as much as he wished his memories of how he'd found himself in the situation were clearer.

Faces bobbed in and out of his visual record, one prevalent...Mora. Goddess, but he loathed that woman. Still, in the faint recollections of her, Mora was over him, meeting his mad thrusting, laughing, moaning, cooing...

Matthew opened his eyes, needing some reality but the one his mind had concocted for him. The room went in and out of focus for a few gut-clenching moments. When it cleared, little details supported the vision. There was a bottle of wine on the table by the door, a single glass settled next to it.

I wonder what the royal doctors would find if they analyzed it? A sick twisting in his gut accompanied the certainty that he'd been drugged.

His stomach vowed to empty at the first provocation, and he postulated it wasn't his disgust that accomplished it. Most aphrodisiacs were mild poisons. His stomach lurched again. *Or powerful ones.*

A soft sigh brought his head around, and his heart pounded in anticipation of Mora feigning his agreement to bed her.

It wasn't Mora. The lady in question was one he'd spied across the room several times the night before, but he didn't know her name. She wasn't one fawning over Benjamin, though she'd milled in and out of that crowd several times.

He took a moment to consider her. Her skin was a fresh pink and her lips a few shades darker. Her hair glowed like the gold silk of his father's cape in the morning sunlight.

His jaw clenched at her lack of clothing. Wisps of memory taunted him, less than those of Mora but enough to confirm for him that he'd tumbled her as well.

"How many?" he whispered. How many had he bedded in his drugged state? How many had laughed and taken a ride, at his expense?

Matthew turned over her, fighting the urge to throttle her. She gasped, her eyes flying open. At the sight of him, a lazy smile graced her lips.

Then her gaze locked with his, and the smile disappeared.

She shrank from him in fear, pressing deep into the mattress.

She'd better fear me. She had also better tell me what I need to know.

* * * *

It took a moment for Sira to decipher the expression on Matthew's face. Her heart started to pound, and she recoiled from his anger.

He planted his hands on the mattress on either side of her, caging her in, looming over her.

"Matthew?" she managed, her voice squeaking a bit.

"That would be *Hein* Matthew," he informed her, one eyebrow rising in challenge.

"H-Hein," she repeated, nodding her understanding.

"How many of you?" he demanded.

"Wh-what?" What was he asking?

"How many of you was I tricked into bedding, after you drugged me?" His voice rose at that, and his expression promised pain to anyone who stood in his way.

Sira shook her head. There was no answer she could give him.

"Tell me," he ordered, his muscles tensing to do harm.

"I don't know. I wasn't a part of it," she pleaded.

"Then you admit you drugged me?"

"I admit *they* drugged you. I was only trying to help you."

Matthew snorted in disbelief. "I see how you decided to help."

"You—"

He tensed, and she pushed herself as far into the mattress as she could reach.

"I what?" he growled at her.

"You won't remember," she decided miserably. That alone could spell her doom, if he decided to press charges.

He wasn't mollified. "I remember much more than you might hope I would." That sounded of a warning.

"If you remembered, I wouldn't be worried. Your reaction proves you don't remember...at least not me."

Matthew visibly calmed himself. "And what are you claiming I should remember?"

"You grabbed me. You pulled me into the bed with you."

"I had no choice."

A sob welled in her throat, and Sira swallowed it down. "Perhaps not," she conceded. "The drug was apparently very powerful."

Her agreement seemed to mollify him...for a moment. "How many?" he repeated.

"I don't know. I know only...only the one I interrupted." Her face burned at the memory of Mora riding him.

"Mora," he spat. "Did you think it funny?"

She shook her head, misery eating at her. "It was wrong. I told them. I told—"

"You had no right," he whispered. His expression eased into confusion. "You had no right to do this to him."

Sira didn't reply to him. Either he remembered it, or he didn't.

Matthew pushed away from her, settling with his back against the wall, scrubbing his hands down his face. "You said that. Didn't you? It was your voice...your...face. I know it was."

She nodded. "Yes. I did."

His eyes closed, and he laid his head back against the wall. For a long moment, he said nothing more. "Go. Leave me." It was weary, the voice of a man exhausted in body and spirit.

Sira knew that feeling, since she suffered it herself. She didn't question him further. She pushed from the bed, pleasant and not so pleasant aches slowing her progress.

Her shirt was hung over the foot of the bed. She pulled it on and went searching for the rest. She had her shoes in hand when she found the skirt shoved under the bureau. She retrieved it and started to pull it up her legs, stilling at Matthew's voice.

"Come here."

She finished pulling it up and half-turned, trying to gauge his expression. It was one she couldn't fathom and didn't want to delve too deeply into...something between shock and suspicion, perhaps. She didn't go to him, tying up her skirt instead and blousing the shirt over it.

"I said to come here," he repeated, none too gently.

"I don't think that's a good idea," she replied calmly, heading for the door. She could put her shoes on elsewhere.

At the sound of him moving, she ran, bolting into the corridor and down the wing toward the doors and freedom...or at least the illusion of it. A glance back told her that he'd stopped to dress and hadn't followed her in the nude.

She'd almost reached the central staircase when someone grasped her arm and dragged her into one of the dormitory-style rooms set up for the young women in attendance. Sira stumbled in with a squawk of surprise, coming face to face with Lodi. She pushed the older woman away with a grumbled curse on her entire family.

Lodi released her, shooting a sheepish look at Sira, then at the crowd of "ladies" behind her. "I take it he's angry," she guessed.

"Don't you think he has the right to be?" Sira snapped back, raising one shoe and slipping her foot in with unsteady hands.

"Perhaps."

"Per... Perhaps?" Sira fairly screamed that at her, lowering her foot.

Lodi motioned for silence, and several of her cohorts winced, shifting nervously.

"Are you mad?" Sira asked in a calmer voice. "How could you do this?"

"Mora had to face censure, so she wouldn't try something so underhanded again," Lodi reasoned, seemingly unperturbed by the outburst.

Nuay nodded her agreement. "She had to be taught a lesson."

Sira felt her temper coming uncorked. "With a *willing* man, perhaps. But this was hurtful, criminal. It was—"

Lodi interrupted her. "Have you told him who we are?"

"Hein Matthew hasn't asked...yet." She worked on the other shoe, finally sliding it on, and lowering her leg.

"And when he does?" she challenged, straightening, as if Sira would back down from such a threat in her mood.

"I will turn you over in an instant. You had no right to do this. Neither will I go to prison as conspirator to something I had no part—"

The door behind her opened, and Sira stiffened. She didn't turn to look. She was afraid to. Whether it was Hein Matthew or his guards, the next few minutes were going to be ugly.

"And...here you are," he drawled. There was a moment of silence. "How convenient that I recognize several faces...and all in one place."

Lodi's look of confidence faded, and she paled alarmingly, backing off several steps.

Sira didn't question why. The heat at her back was answer enough. She swallowed hard, all too aware of Hein Matthew close enough to... She didn't want to contemplate what he would do when he laid hands on her again.

His whisper teased at her ear. "I gave you an order," he reminded her.

Tears pricked at her eyes. Sira nodded, envisioning a prison cell. Here she was, with the conspirators. The Hein had no reason to trust her. The cell was probably her fate.

His heat receded somewhat. "Let me get this in perspective. You ladies were angry with Mora, because...?"

No one answered. Hein Matthew ambled around Sira, turning halfway toward her and catching her eye. His expression demanded an answer.

"She was trying to use the drug to seduce Prince Benjamin," she reported.

Nuay had told her as much when she'd dragged Sira off to "witness Mora's comeuppance." If everyone would see prison time, Mora wasn't going to be left behind. The drug wouldn't have fallen into Lodi's hands, if not for Mora's plans to use it.

Hein Matthew's eyes widened, and he motioned to someone at the door. "Check Benjamin," he ordered. "Check him now."

Footsteps pounding away were all the clue she needed that guards were in the corridor. She wondered how many, then decided she didn't want to know.

The Hein recovered quickly, his eyes narrowing. He crossed his arms over his bare chest, and Sira looked away, the memory of tasting that chest too raw and close for comfort.

"You wanted Benjamin for yourself?" he asked.

The silence was nerve-wracking. Why didn't someone answer him?

A throat clearing brought her attention back to the Hein. No one was answering, because he was staring her down, addressing her personally, as far as anyone with manners would assume, given his stance.

Sira shook her head. "It was obvious that His Highness was taken only with Mora and Alana," she offered. "I was hoping for Alana, personally."

"So was I," he admitted. Hein Matthew motioned around the room, without taking his eyes off of Sira. "These are the ones who drugged me? These are the ones you were arguing with last night?"

She hesitated, realizing that no woman would trust her, if she did this. The Hein waited for her answer, his arms tensing.

"Yes." Sira's stomach twisted in the combination of hunger and apprehension. "I don't know which... I didn't see which one or ones actually did it; I wasn't there when they...drugged you. But yes. They were the ones I was arguing—"

"Honestly-given and well-stated, I believe. Gentlemen, I have heard enough."

A hand closed around her arm but loosely, and Sira closed her eyes, torn between looking at the guard and simply following him to her fate.

"If you would," he began.

"That one comes with me, Johnus."

Sira started shaking, wondering if this boded well or poorly for her. Considering his anger that she'd disobeyed him, it probably boded ill.

The hand retreated, and another circled her opposite arm. She didn't question that it was Hein Matthew's.

"Come with me," he ordered gruffly, drawing her along.

Sira stumbled. He paused for a moment, and she opened her eyes, realizing the futility of trying to follow along without watching where she was going. She reconsidered that when she caught sight of the Hein's expression of exasperation. She looked away at the guards, and he started leading her again.

He offered no conversation, and neither did she. What was there to say?

At his room, he ushered her inside and closed the door. He led her to the stool, now at the center of the room, then seemed to reconsider and turned her toward the bed.

Panic bloomed in her, and Sira planted her feet, shaking her head. Whatever he was doing, she wanted no part of it.

Hein Matthew pulled her to face him, locking his hands on her arms, just tight enough to restrain her but also tight enough to press at the existing bruises he'd left, reminding her that he was strong and angry...and powerful enough to explain away taking retribution on her. His jaw tightened in fury.

Sira expected him to point out that she hadn't minded the night before. He didn't.

"Are you sore?" he challenged.

She considered that. She was sore, but why would that matter?

"Are you?" That time, it was stated in a calmer voice, and his grip eased.

"Yes."

"Then you'll want the bed. I will take the stool." He released her, settling on it, as promised.

Sira stared at him, confused by his sudden show of concern. She backed toward the bed, sinking to the edge, her eyes locked on him.

Why? What do I think he's going to do? Vault across the room and attack me?

Hein Matthew shifted, finding a more comfortable position, and she backed away along the mattress, admitting to herself that she really did fear it. And why wouldn't she? He'd been physically attacked and made a fool of, and he thought her part of it.

A pained expression settled on his face. "You were virginal."

He didn't question it. Sira wasn't certain if he intended her to answer, so she took the safer route and nodded.

A series of curses streamed from between his clenched teeth. Hein Matthew panned his gaze up her body. "Did I hurt you?"

Sira stared at him, her brow knitted so hard the muscles complained.

"You were virginal, and I had no self-control. You say I grabbed you, that I pulled you into the bed. Did I harm you?"

* * * *

Matthew's heart pounded, and his palms went slick with sweat. The scratches on his chest burned a reminder that he'd almost certainly done something she didn't sanction.

If I've hurt her, I will push for the most severe punishments my father and the Counselors will allow.

She shook her head slowly. "No. I'm not hurt. Just the normal aches of a..." Her cheeks went crimson, and she averted her eyes again.

"Are you sure? I can call a doctor, if you—"

"No. Please. I'm certain I'm fine." Her half-choking voice called her a liar.

"Did I force you? Did I force you to a single thing? Please, do not lie to me about this." *Goddess, this could drive a person mad.* His memories were fractured; he could be certain of so little.

What would he do, if he had? How could he make amends for it?

She didn't raise her head. "No. You...you seduced me, to be sure, but I was willing."

"That isn't what I asked," he grumbled. "I asked if I forced you. Did I..." He wasn't certain how to phrase it delicately. Perhaps the doctor would be best.

"You did ask—"

Matthew snapped. "Did I hold you down? Did I—"

"Yes."

His heart stuttered. "I...what did I...?" Her expression was so heartbreakingly innocent and lost, it tore at him. *Goddess, what have I done?*

"When you pulled me into the bed, you held me down. Hein Matthew, I don't understand—"

"They will pay for this," he vowed. "They will spend the rest of their days in cells...no matter how short a time that may be."

She paled, and her shaking intensified. "I don't under—"

He stood, intent on holding her and calming her. She scrambled to the far side of the bed, her breathing harsh and uneven, her eyes wide. Matthew put up his hands in a calming gesture, and she relaxed, her small hand unfisting against the quilt, her delicate fingers splaying out on the dark fabric.

A memory of that fist pressed to his chest ripped through his mind. *Hein, please. This isn't—* He'd silenced her with a kiss, a brutal one.

Goddess, please let that be a phantom, a nightmare and not fact.

"I don't understand," she repeated, seemingly pleading with

"I think you do," he replied calmly. *At every move toward her, she runs from me. I must have frightened her to death, scarred her for the act, perhaps scarred her to men, in general.*

She shook her head, tears pooling in her eyes.

"How far did I force you?" he asked, easing toward her.

She didn't retreat from him, not that she had anywhere else to go but over the footboard and out the door again. "I don't understand." Her eyes widened. "You think... No, it wasn't like that. You didn't..." She paled a shade.

"I didn't?" Matthew prompted her, taking another step toward her.

"You didn't...rape me. You kissed, yes, but... You must know that I was convinced and not unwilling."

He nodded, settling to the edge of the bed. She gasped but didn't move away from him.

"I will not harm you," he promised. "You have my vow on that."

She nodded, taking a deep breath.

Matthew eased his hand over hers, squeezing lightly. "You don't know what to expect from me."

"No," she replied weakly. "I don't. Are you still..."

"Still?" he prompted her.

"Angry with me? I didn't... I swear to you that I had no part of it," she added miserably. "I only wanted to help."

A spike of guilt pierced deep at that. After what he did to her...however she wanted to minimize it, his treatment upon waking had been deplorable. "I know you did," he offered.

Her eyes closed, and her body relaxed. He noted the dark circles under her eyes, her pallor, her shaking. This was his fault.

No. It is their fault, and they will pay for it.

Matthew raised her hand to his mouth, pressing his lips to it, a silent promise that he would make this as right as he could.

Her eyes opened, and a tear spilled down one cheek. With that one drop, he knew he could never take away what she'd suffered.

And what she still might. Goddess, what a mess this was. "If you carry..." he began.

A second tear spilled. "I will ask nothing," she promised. "Your actions were not your own. I know that."

You will have everything I have to give.

But now was not the time to argue with her. Considering the circumstances, she might choose not to carry the babe at all, and the law would allow her termination...now or in the future. "You will contact me when you know for certain," he replied.

She nodded, seemingly miserable at the asking.

I have a right to know.

But had he forfeited that right? Only she could say, and this was the wrong time to ask it. He wanted to growl at the way his hands had been tied and his choices taken from him.

"I will have my guards see you home. I have to attend to...to the rest."

"I understand."

There was one more thing he had to know. "What is your name?"

She stared at him, a fresh tear dropping from her golden lashes to cheeks that were starting to redden in response to the salt tears. Matthew resigned himself to the fact that she might not want to answer him, that he might have to learn her name from someone else.

"Sira," she whispered. "Sirana Firloch."

CHAPTER TWENTY-FOUR

Alana woke to wisps of sensation she didn't recognize.

Something soft was trailing over the tip of one nipple. "Benjamin," she whispered, holding to the sweet dreams of moments before.

"Open your eyes," he requested. "I want to see them as I love you."

It wasn't a dream.

Alana opened her eyes to the sight of Benjamin leaning over her, stroking the petals of a red rose over her breasts. Startling memories of him teaching her all manner of sexual positions and practices made her head spin.

"How many times did we?" she managed. And what *was* the strange taste in her mouth?

Benjamin chuckled darkly, moving the rose to the sensitive bud between her legs. "Not enough."

She moaned, rising against the flower. "Do you like it?" he teased.

"I prefer yellow roses, but..." She gasped at the stroke against her nether lips.

Benjamin tossed the rose away and turned her beneath him. "But?"

"Any touch you grant me is paradise."

"Slowly," he breathed. His lips parted hers, and his tongue offered lazy promises that made her spinning head more acute.

Alana explored his body, committing him to memory, reveling in his attention to pleasing her.

When his cock eased in, she whimpered, sore and sensitized to intimate pleasures.

"Slowly," he promised.

She nodded, holding to him while he produced sparks of bodily paradise within her.

The corridor door burst in, and Alana startled. Before the first soldier cleared the sitting room and made it to the bedroom, Benjamin had a sheet pulled to their hips.

"How dare you—" he started to rant.

"Are you well, Highness?" a captain asked.

"What? Of course, I am. Now, if you don't mind—"

"I'm afraid we can't, Highness," a major intervened. "If your...companion would be so obliging as to dress and accompany us, we will—"

"Are you mad?" Benjamin thundered.

Alana sank closer to him, wondering the same thing.

"Your brother was drugged, Highness. Illegal use of a powerful aphrodisiac. The conspirators claim the attempt was made on you, as well. That being the case—"

"No," Alana breathed. "Oh no." *Goddess Mother, please tell me he wasn't drugged.*

* * * *

The horror in Alana's expression told Benjamin all he needed to know. She knew nothing about the plot. She'd had no part in it. Not that he had reason to doubt it, of course. Alana was the last person he'd suspect of such machinations.

"We'll have to question the lady," the major stated.

Her eyes went wide and wild. "I didn't," she attested. "By the Goddess, I swear I—"

"I don't believe the accusations," Benjamin assured her.

She took a calming breath and buried her face in his shoulder, trembling hard. The reaction made him want to tear the major limb from limb.

As if speeding toward his own demise, the man spoke again. "Believe it or not, I must insist on a doctor for you, Highness. If there is no sign of the drug, I can forgo on questioning the lady."

"I tell you, I haven't been drugged," he roared. Were they deaf?

"The sex show last evening was quite out of the ordinary for you," the major offered delicately.

A retort died in his chest. *It was completely out of character for Alana...completely unexpected for any virgin.*

Benjamin shifted his weight and guided her head back to meet her frightened eyes. "I believe you," he whispered.

Alana shook her head. "I didn't, Benjamin. I would never—"

"I believe you."

Tears dotted her lashes. She nodded.

"What are the symptoms Matthew reported?" he asked calmly. Benjamin held her gaze, watching her expressive eyes for a sign he hoped he wouldn't see.

The major started listing them. "Urgency for the act, confusion, a feeling of being overheated in a comfortable room—"

Alana's mouth opened, then shut, and she swallowed hard, her breathing going ragged.

"—a metallic taste in the mouth, indicating Gorus or Rallex—"

She went a sickly shade of pale, and she swallowed again, looking as if she had to faint or vomit.

"—nausea—"

"Enough," Benjamin commanded. He smoothed Alana's hair, smiling weakly.

It was Mora. He didn't question it. Visions of Alana downing the wine meant for him taunted him. He'd sensed danger then. He'd known something was wrong, but he hadn't seen the signs of it.

My poor Alana...poisoned in my place.

Memories of the insistent woman who'd tried to speak to him followed. *She meant to tell me, and I didn't let her. What did the delay do? Did it harm Alana?*

"Highness?" the major asked. "Prince Benjamin?"

"Send a doctor for Lady Alana. Send *my* doctor, my father's personal physician." She would have the best.

They didn't move.

"Now! And leave us to dress."

They retreated, closing the door between the two rooms.

Alana blinked, and a dislodged tear dotted her cheek. "It was real," she pleaded. "It was real."

Benjamin nodded, wiping away the tear. "The drug may have loosened your sensibilities, but I have no doubt it was real, Alana. You are still my wife, if you wish to be."

"I do."

He laid a kiss on her lips. "We need to dress. Once we know you're well..."

"Yes?"

"I intend to continue where we were interrupted...if you feel up to it."

* * * *

Benjamin tried to focus on Doctor Ivyvine's words, but Alana kept drawing his attention away.

She was dressed in her skirt and one of his shirts, the sleeves rolled to her elbows. He'd insisted that she meet the inquiry in his bed, a stack of pillows behind her and a light quilt drawn to her waist. The one time she'd tried to rise, she'd been struck by nausea. It was an aftereffect of the poison, he'd been told.

"Highness," the doctor demanded his attention.

He abandoned the sight of a young journeyman healer hovering over Alana, asking her questions to better gauge her condition, and forced his focus back to his father's personal physician. "There's no question that Mora drugged her, then?"

"I can't say who, but your testimony is consistent to it. It wasn't a full dose, but enough to cloud her mind and bury inhibitions," he confirmed. "Had you taken the cup instead...perhaps half a dose for your weight, I'd estimate. It would have been enough to make you more open to the suggestion...more than open to it, if you'd imbibed enough alcohol in addition to it."

"I had," he added, to be certain it made its way into the doctor's report. "Is she still...clouded now?" At what point had it been Alana coming to him so avidly and not the drug pushing her to him?

"I can't imagine she would be. Gorus berry processes out of the system in a matter of hours, unless one is overdosed on it, and Lady Alana was not, thank the Goddess."

Benjamin's heart eased in relief. She was naturally so responsive then; that was good to know.

He motioned to Alana. "But the nausea persists? Was there some damage done?" *And how will I forgive myself, if there was? If my inattention and the delay caused it?*

"It's still a mild poison. Not enough to cause permanent damage," he hastened to add at the first sign of Benjamin tensing. "It will persist for a day...two at the outside." Ivyvine sighed. "Your brother will be feeling its effects for a week, I'm sure. The younger Wheatstand says he's drowning in the poison, even now, weakened as it is by time."

And drowning in guilt, misplaced as it is.

The guards had brought word of the latest fiasco to Benjamin, since he'd been unwilling to leave Alana's side to seek information on his own. *Goddess, how much of the poison did they give Matthew to cause him to attack a woman?*

He promised himself to speak to Matthew when Alana was settled. His brother likely needed someone to verbally beat sense into him again.

Alana's protest drew his head out of contemplation of his brother's soft heart and back to the bed. He strode for her, noting crimson patches in her pale cheeks.

"How dare you," she choked out. "How dare you insinuate—"

Ivyvine's journeyman made placating motions. "I must ask in such cases, Lady Alana. Nothing more, I assure you."

Benjamin stopped over them. "Ask what?"

Alana's voice wavered in anger. "He insinuated I'd taken others. He—"

"No such thing," the young man offered patiently. "I—"

"Phrased it badly," Ivyvine cut him off. "Apologize for your tactless handling, please, Roger."

The journeyman tipped his head to her. "My apologies, Lady Alana. I only meant to ensure no one had...taken advantage."

Benjamin ground his teeth at the thought of it. "She was virginal our first time and hasn't left my sight since. There is no possibility."

Ivyvine smiled, no doubt postulating the king's pleasure at having such news delivered to him. "Well, then. We needn't trouble Lady Alana with tests to confirm it." He motioned to the sitting room. "If you would, Highness?"

Benjamin drew her hand up and kissed the palm. "I will be close. Call if you need me."

* * * *

Alana's heart leapt at the assurance. She watched him stride into the sitting room: confident, proud, beautiful...

"Lady Alana?" the damned journeyman called to her. She turned her gaze on him with a sigh. "Yes?"

Roger studied a pen and notebook and not her. Though his attention unnerved her, his avoidance was worse.

"When is your fertile window, mi'lady?"

"What?" Why would he ask such a thing?

He met her gaze, seemingly pained. "Do you know your cycle?" he rephrased the question.

"My courses, but... I'm no lady of means, Journeyman Roger."

She didn't know his family name to address him correctly; he might be an Ivyvine and might not.

For that matter, he was addressing her incorrectly. Benjamin had called her "Lady Alana," but she was lowborn and not a lady, by birth. *I suppose the future wife of a prince has to have a title of some sort.*

Alana forced her mind back to the subject at hand. "I've had no testing to determine the rest. Nor am I taking drugs that would enhance or time it to...needs."

"When did your last courses begin?"

"Mun the ninth...or perhaps the eleventh."

"You're certain?"

"If I was certain, I would produce an exact date. I know it was before mid-month. Is that precise enough?"

His expression said it wasn't. Roger motioned to one of the techs, and a syringe settled in his hand. Alana looked at it in apprehension.

"What are you doing?" He'd already tested the level of Gorus in her system. Why would he need more blood?

"Just a bit of blood, mi'lady," he offered in a soothing voice.

"I can see that. I am asking why you need it."

"It is procedure. I must confirm your cycle. In cases of illegal use of an aphrodisiac, it is considered primary evidence."

"To prove motive, but I didn't drug Benjamin to win a child."

His jaw tightened in some strong emotion, but he kept it reined otherwise. "Or to prove hardship inflicted. Please, allow me to draw the blood." The fact that he was asking proved he couldn't do so without her permission.

Carrying Benjamin's babe would be no hardship. As his wife, it would be expected that she do so, and she wanted to.

Still, it was procedure, and Benjamin was intent on seeing those responsible punished...all of the guilty, including Mora. She offered her arm. "You may."

The draw was quick, and he left her side, whispering instructions to the techs that would analyze the sample. Alana had never realized such tests could be processed out of the office or lab, but royals seemed to have whatever they wished or needed.

She let her eyes drift shut, riding the edges of sleep, whispers and the whirring of machinery lulling her away.

"Lady Alana?"

She forced her eyes open, biting back her frustration. It had been a long night of revelry and exploration, followed by a morning of medical tests and endless questions. Could no one allow her a moment of rest? "Yes?"

He didn't approach the edge of the mattress this time. In fact, Roger fidgeted, looking as if he'd rather face a firing squad than her.

"Yes?" she repeated, her voice more subdued.

"The tests show... You are at the close of your fertile window, mi'lady."

Her heart stuttered at the news. Then there was a chance she'd carry from it. Would Benjamin be happy at the news? It was so soon. He probably wasn't ready for this. Alana wasn't certain *she* was ready for it.

A horrifying thought followed. She'd been poisoned. Would the poison harm a child just forming? She stuttered out that question, barely breathing.

"No. No, the babe would be fine, if one..."

She collapsed against the pillows, sending thanks to the Goddess for it.

"I have to offer, Lady Alana. Please, understand that this is the law."

"What is?" she squeaked out, her calm ripped away that quickly. *Oh, this is sure to be unpalatable.*

"Carrying a child produced under influence of an illegal aphrodisiac is classified as an undue hardship." He hesitated, letting that much sink in.

It's not. Not if it's Benjamin's child. And it would be. There was no question of it.

He cleared his throat. "The law demands, upon proof that you may carry from this...crime—which the cycle indicates, of course—that I offer you early terminating measures."

"No," she gasped. Her hands went to her womb, covering it, protecting the child that might be.

Roger nodded. "If you carry and find it a hardship, you may choose termination at any point up to—"

"No!" How could he even suggest it, when she'd made it clear she wanted no part of it? "Get out."

"Alana?" Benjamin's voice crossed the distance between them.

"Lady Al—"

"Get out. Now." Her heart pounded, and bile rose in her throat. At the sight of his hand approaching, she batted it away. "Don't touch me." This butcher was endorsing the unthinkable to her, offering to kill what she'd always wanted, a family...with Benjamin. She didn't want him in the same room with her, let alone touching her.

Benjamin appeared between them, pushing the journeyman away from her bedside. "What did you do?" he shouted.

"It's the law, Highness," Roger protested.

"The law needs changed," she breathed. It didn't. It was good that women were offered such choices, but women who'd refused them shouldn't be subjected to further pressure and reminders.

Benjamin's inquiry was preempted by a curse from the doctor.

"I'm sorry. Roger is young...learning. Roger, leave us, please."

Alana relaxed at the sight of the journeyman's retreating back.

"You have my most abject apologies, Lady Alana," Ivyvine continued. "In service to Their Majesties... He's never had to make this offer before."

"Do you share his sentiments?" she breathed.

"I am old and experienced enough to temper the laws with compassion, mi'lady. If you have refused and mean to refuse in the future, I see no reason to trouble you with hurtful reminders."

"Apology gratefully accepted."

Benjamin turned and sank down beside her, cupping her cheek in his hand. "Do you feel up to telling me?" he asked.

"He offered—" The words stuck in her throat, and her stomach lurched at the thought of it. "Doctor

Ivyvine, if you could... I can't bear to think it, let alone say it."

Benjamin raised her hand to his cheek, warming her silently.

Ivyvine cleared his throat. "When there is a chance a woman will carry, in a case of illegal use of an aphrodisiac—"

"Terminating measures," Benjamin finished for him. He guided her hand to his lips. "If you're about through, Doctor."

"Of course, Highness. Just follow the instructions I've given you, and contact me, if there is any negative change."

He nodded.

Ivyvine executed a formal bow to them and headed for the corridor. The techs followed silently, their rolling machines in tow. The door closed, and the silence beat at her.

"Are you angry?" she managed.

That seemed to drag him out of deep thought. "Angry? At what, precisely? So many things have happened to draw emotions out."

"That I refused? It's so soon, and you might not want..." She couldn't meet his eyes.

"I'm relieved that you refused."

"Are you?"

He smiled widely, then placed a soft kiss on her knuckles. "Ecstatic that you did." There was the promise of something sinfully decadent in that voice.

She pushed toward him, laying a trail of kisses up his throat and jaw.

"Alana?" Benjamin whispered against her lips.

"Slowly," she invited.

CHAPTER TWENTY-FIVE

"Mi'lady," the guard prompted gently, offering his hand to help her to her feet.

Sira took it and stepped out of the vehicle with a wince. Her exhaustion made the cloak she was wrapped in feel as if it weighed as much as a sack of grain. She looked at the house, sighing. How would she explain this to her parents?

She startled in the realization that the guard was peering at her, seemingly memorizing every expression. Sira averted her eyes, afraid to postulate on what he was thinking about her.

He led her up the path, using his larger body to block as much of the wind as he could. The move was so solicitous, it nearly made her laugh aloud. He was protecting her to the door, but she'd likely be under house arrest for the rest of her life, once he took his leave.

The door flew open, and her father rushed out. He motioned the guard away and pulled Sira to his body. His hand stroked at her hair, and he murmured his assurances that she was home.

She shivered at the welcome, wishing it would last. But once he learned the sad truth of her stay at the Bride Ball, his attitude was certain to change.

"The message arrived?" the guard asked.

"It did. It did, indeed."

Sira leaned into her father's chest, too tired to make much sense of the conversation.

"The doctor should be here soon."

"He's inside."

She tried to roust herself from her stupor to question that.

What doctor was here? Why was he?

He brought the move to an end by lifting Sira and carrying her into the house. The guard followed, shutting the door behind them.

"Must you stay?" her father complained.

"I am ordered to take word back to His Majesty immediately. My apologies for the intrusion."

"Then stay here. My younger daughter will fetch you a drink."

Sira held to her father's shirt, her attempt to open her eyes ending in a dizzying rush that rolled her empty stomach. She buried her face in his chest, feeling weak, spent.

She sighed at the bed beneath her, trying to sink closer to sleep. It was a wish destined to go ungranted, it seemed. Voices buzzed around her, growing louder.

"Go, Vic," her mother ordered.

"She's my daughter," he protested.

"Do you think she wants you to see this?"

"See what?" Sira mumbled, opening eyes that focused unreliably, so the tableau of her worried parents faded in and out.

"It is best that you wait outside," another voice suggested calmly.

Sira turned to him, startling at the sight of a strange man staring down at her. She straightened the cloak, well aware that her costume still lay beneath.

The man's kind, blue eyes narrowed, and he ran a hand through his thinning, gray hair.

"Don't look at her," her father ordered, sounding nearly panicked.

"I must look at her." The voice was soothing. The tone was light, hinting at a joke unspoken.

"Who are you?" she managed, her tongue thick and her eyes drooping. For some reason, Sira felt as if she was the one that had been drugged, but not with an aphrodisiac. It felt as if she'd been given a sleeping potion.

"My name is Doctor Philip Wheatstand."

The doctor... "Why...?" Sira closed her eyes, trying to make her overtaxed brain function.

"Go, Vic," her mother ordered again.

Her father grumbled something unintelligible and then walked away.

"Good," Wheatstand breathed. "Now, let's get her out of these clothes."

Sira forced her eyes open, her breathing going ragged at the hands closing on her. "No." Why were they doing this? She'd told Hein Matthew she didn't require a doctor. "He didn't... I told him he didn't."

The doctor took a step back. "I see what he means," he whispered, seemingly troubled. "Young lady, you must understand. I am charged with examining you. If you would like, your mother can help you remove your clothing and wrap you in the cloak or a quilt, but I must examine all of you. Do you understand me?"

She shook her head. "I don't want this. I don't need it. He held me. That was all he did." It was hard to catch her breath.

"There are charges... You know about that?" he asked.

"The aphrodisiac. Yes, I know."

"How severe the punishment for those that used it will be based, in part at least, on what I find. This is necessary."

She nodded, glancing to her mother for signs of anger. There were none. If anything, Mother looked as weary as Sira felt.

"I'll help you change, if you wish," she offered, a strained smile pulling up at her lips.

Sira hesitated and then nodded. In her current state, it might well take her five times the normal to disrobe. She glanced toward the doctor, and he turned his back, giving her privacy...for the moment.

It was slow-going, even with help, mainly because Mother moved cautiously, as if afraid Sira would break at the slightest jarring. At last, she offered a quilt. Sira shook her head, pulling the cloak around her. It smelled of Hein Matthew, and no matter the misunderstanding that morning, Sira found his scent a comfort.

"Doctor," her mother prompted him.

He turned, panning his assessing eyes over her. "I will go slowly and explain what I am about to do," he soothed her.

Sira took a calming breath, praying it would be over quickly.

Wheatstand settled one knee on the edge of the mattress, leaning over her. "I'm going to check for injuries...just your face and neck."

"Go on," she managed in a strangled whisper.

His hands pushed at her mussed hair, and his head swiveled to take in every detail. His fingertips pressed at a tender spot beneath her jawline, and Sira winced. He stopped and tipped her chin up, peering at it.

Memories of Hein Matthew nipping at her sent a pleasant heat through her that she found disconcerting. "It was—"

"Shhh," Wheatstand soothed her. "There is no need to explain it."

Sira didn't nod her agreement. "Your arms, please."

She slipped them out, pressing the cloak to her chest. He turned them this way and that, noting several bruises on the insides of her upper arms. Wheatstand took his time, examining her hands, her fingernails, in particular. Sira found herself squirming under his inspection.

Wheatstand released her arm, standing straight. "Your chest...please, mi'lady."

Her heart pounded so hard it made her head spin faster.

"Sira?" her mother asked. "Sirana?" A hand touched her throat. "Doctor?"

In a flash, he was in motion, as was Sira, scrambling the opposite direction. She teetered on the edge of the bed, her mother wrapping her arms around her to keep Sira from falling off. Sira buried her face in her mother's shoulder, seeking escape, well aware that the cloak was gaping open, exposing her to Wheatstand's eyes.

"Allergies?" the old doctor asked in a low voice.

"No," her mother replied.

A sharp pinch at her thigh forced a cry of fear from her. Then it was gone. Sira held to her mother, pleading for her to make the doctor go as she had

Father. Her muscles relaxed in a wave of warm fluid. Hands lowered her to the bed.

"Is she sleeping?" Mother asked, as she would have when Kiri was a napping babe.

"No. It's mild. If she wishes to, Sirana can open her eyes. I fear... I believe she has no wish to."

Mother stroked at her hair, humming a lullaby.

Hands roamed her chest and abdomen, touching her breasts much less expertly than Matthew had. The sensation of being bathed followed, hot cloths stroking her intimately, much as she'd stroked him.

Fingers pressed at a sore spot on her inner thigh, and Sira turned her head away, grimacing. Incoherent sounds in her mother's voice flew at her, making the sense of unreality more acute.

Something breached her, and Sira tried to shut her legs, babbling out something incoherent, even to her. Her body wouldn't respond to her commands. It ached. It felt tight...whatever breached her too big. A twinge of pain cut through the fog, then a second, and she screamed. Hands held her shoulders to the bed.

"Stop," she begged, gulping in air. "Plea...please, stop."

Then the offending object was gone, and she collapsed to the pillows, her teeth chattering in the sudden cold.

"Cover her. Keep her warm," the doctor ordered. "Sirana, I need to take a blood test to determine—"

"No," she managed. "No more."

"As you wish."

The weight of the quilt on her was a comfort. Sira slipped closer to sleep.

"Is there damage?" her mother asked.

"It was a rough ride for a first time," Wheatstand surmised. "Physically, she will heal. I fear the hardest wrongs to right will be the mental scars."

He paused. "There are other decisions she may have to make, but not today. She's too scattered to make a rational answer to anything right now."

Sira wanted to ask what he meant, but her mouth no longer followed the commands of her muddled mind. In moments, sweet darkness took her.

* * * *

Matthew looked up at the knock, his heart sinking at the sight of the elder Wheatstand. "How bad?" he asked. The expression on Philip's face was assurance enough that he'd been right to send the old man to Sira and allow his son Douglas to handle the examination on Matthew.

Wheatstand took his time, settling in the chair across from Matthew with a weary sigh. "I thank the Goddess you were not responsible for your actions," he summarized. "I thank Her that we can prove it...and you should thank Her, too."

Matthew found forming words a physical impossibility. His breathing was harsh in his own ears. *Dear Goddess, what have I done?*

"Had you been, and had she chosen to call charges down, I would have no choice but to supply my honest assessment of it. As it is..." He faltered.

"I..." He buried his face in his hands, visions he hoped were fabrications taunting him. *Sira screaming... Matthew thrusting hard into her, while she did.* "It was rape then?"

"I cannot state it, but the evidence is consistent, in many ways. Had she come to me claiming it, I would agree it was plausible."

Matthew raised his head, posing the question with a look.

Wheatstand sighed. "There are bruises...on her arms, where you held her down; there's no question she told the truth about it. And that you guessed at the scratches correctly; there are signs of it on her. There are others..." He hesitated, shooting a weary look skyward. "If I was to guess, I would say you bit her."

His stomach rebelled, and Matthew was abruptly thankful he hadn't eaten at Douglas's suggestion that he do so. "A love bite, I hope?" But he knew it wasn't. Wheatstand wouldn't have considered that of note.

"No... A bite, but a small one, as if you caught only a few of your teeth in her. I can barely see the scrape of them in the bruise."

Matthew groaned. "Can this get worse?"

The doctor didn't answer that, lending to his greatest fears being realized.

"What else? What else did I do?" he asked bluntly.

"There is a bruise on the inside of her thigh."

"From? Can you tell?"

"Were I to guess, I would say...perhaps..."

"What?" Why couldn't the man simply say it?

"This is only a possibility, but it is consistent with a man forcing a woman's legs apart...or attempting to do so."

Matthew's mouth went dry, and the foul taste of bile rose up strong. "And...the rest? Did I? Did I cause her pain?"

Wheatstand pulled out a flask and drank deeply. He didn't meet Matthew's eyes. He didn't speak.

"Did I rape her?" he demanded.

"She says 'no,' but the swelling and bruising, the tearing..."

"Tears? She had..." His stomach warned that he would have no appetite for weeks, if he'd heard it correctly.

"Small ones, and I've treated them. Thank the Goddess I'd already— I had to sedate her to examine her, so the treatment was not as traumatic as it might have been. She tried—"

"To run from you," Matthew finished for him.

Wheatstand nodded, taking another swig of the alcohol. "She shies from touch, from meeting the eyes of men, those she knows and those she doesn't. She wouldn't even allow the blood tests to...establish her cycle."

"Rape," Matthew forced out. There was little question now that it had been. "Then that is what we have to report it as." Damn what people said about him. He'd accept their scorn, rightly or wrongly applied to him.

"I already have. There was little choice but to do it."

His jaw tightened. "I hope they rot."

* * * *

Sira straightened, her limbs aching, though she was just waking from sleep. Her bladder demanded attention, urgent attention at that. Though she'd like to stay tucked under the quilts, it was time to rise and take care of her needs.

The room felt unnaturally cool, and she pulled on a robe over her sleeping gown. Though it was light out, the house was silent and still. She considered calling out to someone, then decided to toilet first.

The walk down the corridor was a puzzle to her. Every muscle and joint in her body protested. Her arms were sore, her legs, even her stomach. Was she sick?

Sira stumbled, catching herself against the wall, shaking her head to clear it. Her vision shimmied and jumped alarmingly.

She felt drugged. She felt—

Sira grasped at the door jamb, the memories of the last day returning in a rush. She was drugged, and she was sore...with good reason.

The toilet beckoned, and she staggered toward it, shutting the door with one hand while she braced herself up against the sink with the other. She dragged her sleeping gown up and settled on the chilled seat, relieving herself in a rush.

The pain assaulted her a moment later, and she whimpered, crossing her arms over her stomach, rocking forward in an attempt to weather it. Goddess, but who knew she would hurt this much? The idea of patting herself dry brought a shiver of dread, but there was little choice.

A tentative knock sounded at the door. "Sira?" her mother called out. "Do you need me?"

It was on the tip of her tongue to refuse. This was mortifying, in the extreme.

She swallowed down her pride and admitted to herself that she needed help. "In a moment," she replied. She needed help to rise. That much was certain, but she wanted to clean herself first. Sira patted at her tender body with the tissue, half-swallowing a sob.

"Sira? May I enter?"

She dropped the tissue in the bowl, then spread her sleeping gown over her knees. "Come in."

Her mother opened the door, silently assessing. "Have you finished?" she asked.

Sira nodded. Her head spun at that movement, and she pressed a hand to it, hoping to right the world.

Getting Sira back on her feet was easier with two than with one, as she'd hoped it would be. Her mother guided her back to her room, settling Sira beneath the quilts. That accomplished, she started speaking.

"Are you hungry?"

She wanted to answer in the affirmative, but her stomach was less certain. "A little," she managed.

"Soup and bread, then."

Sira made to rise, but her mother pushed back gently. They stared at each other, Sira's heart pounding in conflicting emotions.

"Doctor Wheatstand's orders," she offered.

"He won't..." Sira managed. "He won't want to... Not again."

Mother sat on the edge of the bed with a sad smile. "No. Unless you worsen, I believe he's done his job. You have medicines to take that will help in healing."

CHAPTER TWENTY-SIX

Matthew stared at the note, conflicting emotions pulling at him. He'd read it ten times. He would probably read it another hundred, searching for clues to her feelings that weren't there.

He closed his eyes, seeing the words in her flowing script.

My courses came on schedule. As promised, I'm sending word.
Take care, and may the Goddess watch over you.
Sira

Conflicting emotions made his newly-righted stomach roil as if the poison held him tight again.

She hadn't caught from their night together.

On some level, that relieved him. Sira wouldn't be forced to choose between bearing a child conceived that way and terminating one. Many of the dirt-nobles and lowborns considered termination for any reason against the Goddess's wishes. The idea of her carrying for religious reasons was enough to make him heartsick. Knowing she didn't carry meant that one less worry.

A rebellious streak screamed that she hadn't caught. His reasons for it were impossible to unravel.

It could be that he wished something good would come of it. A new life that she might rejoice in—and he might, if she were willing to share such a wonder with him—would give a positive bent to the thing. It would mean there was a meaning, no matter how the Goddess had managed to affect such a miracle.

Further good would come in the monetary aid he could lend to such a child. Offering Sira money for her suffering was a poor attempt at righting this wrong, he knew, though the money would ease her life in general. If she carried, it would be within the realm of believability that he would claim the child and support it. He could provide Sira with servants and comforts he dared not offer under other circumstances.

Or, maybe it was his continuing madness clouding the issue. It had been a little over a week, and he still dreamed of her. He'd hoped the dreams would end when the drug left him completely, but they hadn't.

No. I didn't hope it.

Had the dreams been of his attack on her, he would have done so, but they had been dreams of himself and Sira in slow, heated embraces, engaging in kisses that warmed the sheets.

He shifted, cursing his erection aloud. It was unseemly that he was thinking about her this way. It was morally corrupt that he did...on some level, at any rate. Though he couldn't reason himself to why it was—past his guilt, which wasn't a moral issue but rather an emotional one—he was sure there was some path to the decision he wasn't seeing.

Matthew folded the note blindly, finding the creases he'd pushed to the edges of tearing without his eyes to guide him.

He simply wanted to know she was well and comfortable. If he managed that, he'd leave her to her life and try to reassemble the wreckage of his own into something honorable again.

"Hein?" the guard he'd summoned intoned.

His heart ached that he was sinking to this. "I want you to make inquiries," he ordered.

"Of what type?"

"Of Sirana Firloch."

* * * *

Matthew knocked on the door, certain that he wouldn't be welcome, but he had to see her. It opened, and her father stared at him, dark eyes narrowing in challenge. He waited to see what Matthew had to say, neither dismissing him nor inviting him in.

"Good day, Firloch," he intoned.

The man bowed his head in response.

"I came to..." *What? What excuse could he have?*

"You wish to see her." He didn't question it.

Matthew nodded. "If Sirana is of a mind to," he conceded. "If you would allow—"

"Stay here. I will ask her." The door closed between them.

His heart ached at that. Typically, people rushed to admit him. It was another sign of how ruined he was that he wasn't trusted to enter their home.

Time dragged along, every moment an agony in which he was certain the dismissal would come. He turned away, looking at the fall colors. The door opened behind him, and he turned back, his heart aching at her refusal to see him already.

And she was there...still pale though not as markedly, her expression uncertain. She was beautiful, unblemished, but haunted no doubt.

"Hein Matthew," she greeted him with a bow of her head. Her eyes met his briefly, then darted away, her color deepening.

He hooked his hands behind his back, a silent reminder not to touch her. "Sirana."

Silence fell between them for a moment.

"Are you well?" he forced out, only one of a million questions he wanted to ask her.

She nodded, her smile strained. "Well healed, I think."

But she wasn't. The reports said she didn't venture from home, that she never did. Her mother had only just started admitting a few lady visitors, none Sira's age; no men entered the house, save her father, not even the lord's business partners and allies. Her curtains were always drawn tight. It wasn't right for a young lady to be so isolated. It wasn't natural.

She met his eyes again, a faint look of longing shining out.

But longing for what? What did she want of him?

When he didn't answer, she turned...but not inside. Sira walked along the front of the house, toward the working buildings at the side. Matthew followed, at a loss to explain her actions.

She entered one, stopping at the far end, not facing him. He waited at the door.

"Sira?"

"I'm...sorry that you've been so vilified in this. I never meant for it to happen. I tried to tell them what happened that night, but no one would allow me to speak. No one..."

Her apology stunned him. "There was no need to make you endure it. The physical evidence was—"

"Misleading." She turned to him, her hands clasped, seemingly tortured. "Have you never questioned it? Hein Matthew, how *could* you accept this without even asking if you were guilty of what you claim to be?"

"I hurt you."

"You did," she conceded, "but not in the ways you believe. Not in the ways others believe of you." Again, tears dotted her lashes.

"I am about to use your refrain, I'm afraid. I don't understand what you're saying."

"You should. I was clear enough the last time I told you. You didn't... You didn't rape me. Why is this so hard to comprehend? Of the two of us, who do you believe remembers the night, as it was?"

"Neither," he answered honestly. The doctors had told him as much, had said that her memories might have been reordered to fit her attempts to hide herself from the truth of it.

She sighed. "Perhaps, but I cannot agree."

Her upset ate at him. "You wish to do this, don't you? You wish someone would let you talk about it." If she said yes, could he be the one she unburdened to? Would it help or hurt his sense of guilt?

Sira nodded.

Curiosity warred with terror. *I did this, however oblivious to it I was at the time. It is my mess to wipe clean.* "Then tell me. Tell me what really happened that night." He doubted he'd get the whole truth, but it was worth it, if it eased her upset.

She took a calming breath. "I did argue with them and send them away. I did try to help you. I know you remember a bit of both."

Newly-recovered memories of her bathing him and him climaxing to it played out in his mind. Matthew nodded grimly. "I remember it."

"I thought you were cognizant, so I offered to get your doctor. Not that I knew how to find the man without spending a night or more in a cell for it, but I offered."

He winced at her candor. With Matthew incapacitated, she was likely correct, on that point. The guards would have detained her, until some accounting could be made of the situation and her innocence proven...if that was possible.

"You said you understood me. I offered to get help for you, to get you whatever you needed." She paused, biting at her lower lip lightly.

"And that was when I forced—"

"You grabbed at my arms and pulled me down. Yes. I've told you as much."

His stomach rumbled in warning at the vision in his mind.

"You only clamped down and left bruises when I tried to escape from beneath you."

"And you say I'm not guilty of—"

"You are that far, but I've always said it."

Matthew motioned for her to continue, hoping she'd speed through the rest.

"You laid kisses at my jawline. I was so shocked by your tenderness that I allowed you to, and—"

"Tenderness?" he scoffed, well aware that he shouldn't question her version, not without a doctor to handle her reaction to it.

She took a step toward him. "You were."

"I was so tender, I left more bruises," he noted, loathing himself for doing it, loathing himself almost as much for saying it.

"The nips beneath my chin followed. Yes, they hurt, but the way... There was pleasure mixed with the pain. Had anyone bothered to ask it, I would have told them so."

His heart skittered, and he shook his head. That had to be in error.

"You're like everyone else," Sira accused, seemingly hurt by his denial of her version.

"No. Tell me. Please..." If it would give her ease, he would listen to her tale.

"I didn't protest it. I did push at you, but I didn't refuse you."

"It's no better," he muttered. *Why am I doing this? Why am I opening myself to how much a bastard I was to her?* Drugs or no drugs, he had to face that he had committed these crimes against her.

"You started raising my skirt, and I realized..."

"Go on."

"I realized there would be no barrier between us, if you did."

"Then you didn't want me. Sirana, you know what rape means, I'm sure," he reasoned.

"Will you let me tell the tale or not?" she challenged.

Matthew opened his mouth to speak, then shut it, nodding. *Perhaps this is my punishment.*

"I started to talk you out of it, and you kissed me."

"If it is the moment I remember, I ravaged your mouth. There was nothing kind in that moment. Do not make it over so, I beg you."

"If you remember it, how is it that you don't recall me responding in kind? Dear Goddess, have you no concept of what an appealing male you are, when you are intent?"

Memories he'd dismissed played at his mind. He'd dreamed of them for weeks, waking hard and wanting, cursing himself for writing off his crimes against her so completely, damning himself for being aroused all over again by the act...without the drugs to blame it on.

"You do remember," she whispered.

"I remember...something. It's hard to make sense of it," he qualified.

"Then let me make sense of it."

For the first time, his sense of dread was overpowered by his need to know. "Please," he invited her.

"You did hurt me once more, a hurt you intended, in your state."

He braced himself for the truth of it, barely breathing in his tension.

Sira continued. "You wanted to be in me so badly, you tried to force my legs apart to get there. Yes, it hurt. I won't deny it, but you didn't force them apart. You didn't force your way in."

His breath left him on a dizzying rush. Goddess, but that was good to know. "I'm sorry," he whispered. "I can never tell you how sorry I am that I hurt you."

"You had no choice in the matter. And I allowed much of it. If I had screamed, Ma...Hein. If I had screamed, someone would have—"

"Likely not...and you did scream. I remember it." His misery returned that quickly.

"You remember so little," she whispered.

He nodded, agreeing with her assessment. "Please...tell me." Oh, how the tables had turned. Now, he was begging her for information, wanting to hear how he could have done her such damage and not have her damn him for it.

"I scratched you." She faltered, her face going crimson and her eyes pleading with him. "I...I was at a loss to break through the fog over your mind. I never meant to hurt you."

"I believe that." Would that he had never meant to hurt her. "You scratched me," he repeated numbly. "And did I... Did I do something in return?"

Sira nodded. "You pulled away and looked at me with such longing... You said that you needed me. I didn't know if you needed me, because the drug was driving you mad or...or if you actually saw something in me that you needed, but either way, it was a sentiment I couldn't ignore.

"I started undressing for you, meeting your passion, inviting it. By the time you entered me... Yes, it was rough. It hurt, but there was something more...something I fear I will never be able to name."

Matthew tried to digest that. "You could have ignored it. You could have continued to deny me," he countered. "Why didn't you?"

"Because you were driving *me* mad. Because I wanted..." She looked away, her throat working on what was surely a sob.

"You wanted what?"

A sad smile turned up her lips. "I wanted that passion to be personal to me. I know it was foolish to want..."

His heart raced, though he couldn't tell which of his chaotic emotions caused it to. "No. It wasn't foolish, at all."

Tears pooled in her eyes, and she wiped them away in what appeared to be annoyance. "It was. I should have realized a man like you couldn't possibly..." She took a calming breath. "Of course, it was foolish."

"That I couldn't possibly be what?" he asked, his mind rebelling at the answer he wanted to hear.

Sira didn't answer him.

"Couldn't possibly want you?" he asked calmly.

She stared at her white-knuckled, clasped hands. "Don't lie to me about this," she stated bitterly. "It's not right, you know."

Matthew went to her, breaking his own counsel by raising a hand to her cheek. "How I wish we could start over," he mused.

"Then you don't wish to." Sira jerked in what was probably a silent sob.

"Oh, I wish to." He did. He'd wanted to, for varying reasons, since the morning he'd woken with her in his bed.

Sira raised her head, her eyes assessing, seemingly shocked into silence.

Matthew lowered his face to meet hers, stroking his lips along the line of hers. She sighed, her eyes closing.

"I want so much to start over," he breathed, closing his eyes and pressing his forehead to hers.

"Then we should."

Matthew turned his head and dipped it down, seeking her agreement. Her lips parted to his, a slow, solemn kiss that grew deeper and hotter in moments. He released her, panting in the force of his arousal. If this was what he'd felt that night, his madness might be more attributable to her potency than his state.

"Matthew," she whispered, not quite a question.

He captured her lips again, one hand settling on her shoulder and the other cupping her cheek. His cock hardened, aching to nest inside her again, a slower joining that they both could revel in.

"Release her."

The voice came without warning, drawing Matthew out of his daze. He turned to find Sira's father standing in the doorway, his hands fisted and his body tensed to fight.

"I said, 'release her'."

The choice was taken out of his hand when Sira nestled closer. Matthew wrapped an arm around her, mindful of the fact that he might have to leave her to block blows. He wouldn't allow her to stay in the middle of a fight, if it came to that.

Firloch's eyes widened, and his fists loosened. "Sira?"

"It is not what you think," she stated, though her voice shook at the admission. "For well over three weeks, I have told you all that it's not what you believe, what you want the evidence on hand to support."

He shot a look promising death at Matthew.

"If I may?" Matthew asked, hoping to diffuse the situation. Firloch didn't reply, so he continued. "Nothing excuses the pain I caused Sirana. I know that. I came here...looking for some way to accomplish that, pitiful as such an attempt was."

"And you think this is it?" he snapped.

"I wouldn't have thought we'd ever end up in such a situation, after the night of the Bride Ball. But not because I didn't want to touch her," he hastened to add. "I thought I had ruined any kind feelings Sira might have harbored for me." He met her eyes, smiling at Sira's blush. "Imagine my surprise to learn that, not only was I wrong about what transpired that night, I was wrong about your daughter's capacity and caring."

"Where were you?" he challenged. "Where were you, when she could barely put one foot before the other? When she wouldn't meet my eyes? When she couldn't face the world outside of her bedroom? If you cared so much—"

"I didn't think I had the right to see her," Matthew admitted, reliving his own days and nights of misery.

"You didn't, and you don't."

Sira wrapped a hand in Matthew's cloak. "I believe that is my decision," she offered.

For a moment, her father said nothing. He simply stared at her in disbelief. Then he recovered himself. "You cannot be serious."

"The choice to accept a position or trial position is my own," she reminded him.

Matthew kept his mouth shut. All three of them knew that her father could block such a move, if he appealed it to the king and Counselors...if the old man agreed with him. If it came to a challenge, Matthew wasn't certain which side his father would lend his might to.

Firloch stared at Matthew. "Is such an offer forthcoming?"

Matthew didn't hesitate. "If Sira would accept it."

Both men looked to her, and Matthew held to his mask of royalty as she paled. Was she going to refuse him?

"A trial, for now," she agreed. "I believe... I believe we need to get to know each other away from Bride Balls and drugs that affect us, before we commit to more."

"And what sort of contract would you be offering?" Firloch continued.

Again, Matthew knew his mind. "One that makes her my wife."

Sira seemed surprised by the proclamation.

CHAPTER TWENTY-SEVEN

Sira wrapped her arms around Matthew's waist, pulling herself flush to him, licking her lips at the press of his cock to her belly through the layers of sleeping clothes. His mouth sought out hers again, making promises he'd yet to keep.

It had been over a week, and their time together still consisted of nothing more than touching and kissing, talking and sleeping under the same sheets.

She'd climaxed; Matthew had made certain of that. She'd come to his mouth and his hands, and he'd come to her hands, but he shied at every move toward sating himself in her. He shied even at both of them being completely nude at the same time.

That had to change. If she was to be his wife, Sira was going to carry his heir, and no amount of fear on Matthew's part was going to stand in the way of that.

He reached for her sleeping gown, and she pushed his hands away, working at the tie on his lounging pants instead. Matthew groaned into her mouth, giving himself up to her. His pants loosened, Sira worked them down his hips to his thighs, urging him to his back on the mattress.

Her mouth watered at the sight of him, and her heated body ached to feel him inside her again. She was healed; she knew she was. Sira had even tested it...carefully, with her fingers in the bath, at a time when Matthew was otherwise occupied.

He reached for her dominant hand guiding it to his shaft in silent request. Sira started stroking him, smiling as his eyes slid shut and his hips rose to meet her. This could work.

She shifted her weight, straddling his thighs, just below his jutting cock, far up on her knees so she wasn't resting on him. Matthew's eyes shot open, and his breathing hitched. Sira started stroking again, making no further move to mount him, and he relaxed.

No doubt, he thought himself safe from temptation, because she was dressed for sleeping. What he didn't know, couldn't know, was that she'd removed her panties when she'd begged off for a toilet break earlier. She would taste his length, if she had to trick him to it; it was likely the only way she would.

He watched her pleasure him, his breathing going ragged in his need to come, his body moving with her. Finally, his eyes closed again.

Silently, slowly, Sira eased her sleeping gown higher. Matthew's panting and his grimace announced how close to the edge he was. It was time.

She eased his cock back slightly and encased the head and first finger-width of his shaft inside her. Matthew cried out harshly, coming up off of his back so that he was nearly face-to- face with her. The motion forced more of his cock into her, and he went still, his eyes half-closed in pleasure, his muscles bunching.

"You shouldn't," he gasped out.

Sira paused, enjoying the stretch of her muscles around his cock. In answer, she pushed down further, moaning at the delicious sensation. "Goddess, yes, I should," she breathed.

"Sira," he reasoned.

She silenced him with a single motion, the slide of her sleeping gown up her body and off over her head. He stared at her, his cock bucking against her walls.

"You want to. You hunger to do this. Don't you?" Sira tossed the sleeping gown away, noting that his eyes didn't track it.

Matthew started to shake his head in a negative response, then stopped. "You know I do, but it's too soon. You're not healed."

Sira answered by sliding further down his length. It was sweet torture.

"Does it hurt you?" he asked. "By the Goddess, tell me the truth."

"A light ache and no more. Matthew, my body must adjust to you. All women do."

He nodded, his jaw tight. "If it hurts you—"

"I promise to tell you."

"Then take me in."

Sira moved slowly, forcing his cock into her, stilling at the sharp little twinges where she had been torn the first time.

"It hurts you," he accused. "It is too soon. We will wait—"

"No," she panted out, easing back a bit and settling further.

"Oh, yes. I'm going to take all of you."

"If you can."

"I can." She didn't question that it was true; she'd done it before. Instead, she slid back and down again.

Matthew's hips jerked up, and he pulled back, a guilty look on his face. It was unacceptable.

"Again," she pleaded.

"Sira—"

"Again, Matthew."

His hips rose to meet her, and she moaned in delight.

He hesitated a moment, then thrust up again, assessing every expression, every movement. At his next rise, she pushed down onto him, smiling at the touch of his body that announced she'd very nearly taken him to the hilt.

"Deeper," she urged him.

His cock bucked at her inner walls again. He breathed her name, bowing up from the bed to comply. He stayed there a long moment, his breath fanning hot and fast over her mouth.

Sira tipped her head to one side and tasted his lips. That kiss led to another and a third, each more involved than the last. She wrapped her hands in his hair, and his hips started to move, slowly at first, then gaining force as their kisses did likewise.

"Tell me," he demanded at a break between them.

"This is what I want...what we both want."

His mouth came at her, unrestrained. His body followed close in its wake.

Climax whispered, then roared through her, her scream muted against Matthew's questing tongue. His cock erupted within her, stealing her breath.

He collapsed back to the pillows, dragging her along by virtue of her grip in his hair. His chest rose and fell in ragged breaths, and his arms circled her back, holding Sira to him in his most unguarded moments.

"Goddess, I have no control with you," he berated himself.

She laughed. "Who said I want you to have control? If this is you lacking in it, I fully support the idea."

Matthew turned over her, his eyes hard. Her heart rate jumped in alarm, then settled. This was Matthew...no drugs, no madness, the same man who'd refused his needs to give her ease and comfort...to allow her to heal.

"Like this, Sira?" There was a bite of something unforgiving in that. "Can you ever face the thought of me over you again?"

"How can you face me over you?" she countered. "The memories of—"

"The memories of what I did to you are worse...and better, which doesn't help my sanity," he admitted.

She tipped her hips up, watching his frustration and torture melt into something soft and dreamlike. "I can face you over me, because it's you, Matthew."

He buried his face in her hair. "I just want to hold you."

A plan took shape. "For now."

"And afterward?" he breathed in a voice that sounded of exhaustion.

"Do you still want me as your wife, Matthew?"

"Yes. By the Goddess, yes." His hands closed on her waist lightly, holding to her as if to keep her from leaving him.

"Then I have a wife's needs."

He raised his head, his eyes hot in understanding. "Will you sate them?"

His cock answered with a buck against her before he verbalized it. "Every one."

CHAPTER TWENTY-EIGHT

Matthew glanced at Sira, then back to his work, his thoughts scattered. Having her spend time with him while he worked had seemed like a stellar idea, at the time. The reality was that her proximity made working impossible.

Sira questioned him with nothing more than his spoken name, probably taking note of his inattention to the matters he'd claimed a need to attend to and his fixation on her.

He set his pen aside and pushed his chair back. "Come here."

Surprise and curiosity warred in her expression. She rose smoothly and crossed the room in a sensual glide he was sure she was unaware she possessed, coming to his side without pause.

Matthew drew her across his lap, smiling at her demure shiver. She blushed lightly.

"I have needs, Sira. Goddess but how I need you." He'd avoided admitting that for days, focusing on her needs. Perhaps he'd been afraid that he'd know no control, that he would confuse wants and needs. There was no mistaking that this was a need that had been driving him all day, a need to have her close, a need to touch her.

Sira rose to him, seeking his mouth.

Yes. Goddess, this is wonderful.

There was nothing gentle about this joining, nothing careful. If Sira wanted him without control, there was little question she was going to get what she wanted.

Their mouths meshed, danced, parted, explored only to return and mesh again. Hands roamed, pulling at clothing, speeding them toward something hot and hard.

Matthew shoved his trousers down his hips, then her skirts to her waist. He turned her away, pressing her hands to the desktop, nipping at her neck as he dragged her panties down her thighs.

Sira didn't question what he had in mind. She levered herself up, and he positioned his cock, then thrust into her. Her body sinking over his wrenched a moan from him. He guided her by a hold on her hips, taking what he needed, what he hoped they both needed.

A click brought his head up, and Matthew forced her hips down, locking her to his body. He pushed the chair as far under the desk as he could, taking their last heartbeat to soothe Sira's fear.

The sight of his father striding around the door sent his heart into palpitations. Matthew swallowed down a growl of frustration; the king wasn't someone he could simply order away.

Worse, he'd probably have something to say about the current situation. It wasn't too late for him to disallow the contract between Matthew and Sira. Though his father didn't openly oppose Matthew, he didn't show favoritism either.

"Ah...Matthew. Here you are." The old man hadn't looked up from the file in his hands, and he was distracted.

Sira's little movement of shock sent tremors down his cock that weren't helping his aim to keep this scene as innocent-appearing as possible.

Matthew bit back a groan of pleasure. "Yes, Father?"

Edward ambled to the bar and poured himself a whiskey. "I have to talk to you about...well, about the charges that were brought as a result of the Bride Ball."

Sira sank further into his embrace, and Matthew wrapped his arms around her.

"Is it important?"

His father drained his drink and turned, nodding. His color dipped, and his gaze trailed up and down their bodies.

"Oh, Sirana. I didn't know you were here. Would you excuse us for a moment?"

She stiffened in Matthew's arms. His move to answer was cut off by the bite of her reply.

"If it has to do with that night, I think I should be included."

Edward hemmed and hawed a moment. "If you insist, I suppose."

"Perhaps we should—" Matthew began.

"You have some concern?" the old man inquired.

Yes! Matthew had several concerns, not the least of which was the urge to finish what they'd started. But how to put that one into words? He shook his head.

"If you're sure, Sirana?"

"I am," she replied.

Edward turned back to the fire, seemingly searching for a way to begin. "It's not as neat as I wish it would be," he admitted.

Matthew tensed at that pronouncement, his cock waning. "In what way?"

"Mora supplied the poison, but she fell victim to her own misadventure. In short—"

"She became a victim," Matthew interrupted him. "More victim than assailant."

He poured another whiskey. "Precisely, I'm afraid. She hadn't used a significant amount of the drug in her bid to bed Benjamin. We can't even prove she meant it as more than a prank."

"So...Mora will walk free," Sira guessed.

Edward swallowed the second drink. "I'm afraid anything more than a punitive slap of the law would be seen as a further hardship to her. She was fed more of the poison than you were yourself, Matthew. She had no more control over who she bedded and how than you did."

"If I wasn't responsible, she shouldn't be either?" he guessed.

"That is what the Counselors believe," he confirmed.

"But the others," Sira managed. "Lodi and Nuay and the others? Surely, they have to pay for their crimes. They didn't have to use the Gorus. They had no right to, and the second crime doesn't make right the first."

"Since the Counselors want Mora relieved of responsibility, holding the drinking mob responsible for what happened next, with a poison that seemed to their muddled minds the perfect solution at hand... If anyone is to be held responsible for what happened under the influence of a mind-altering substance, all will. If we excuse one, we excuse all."

Matthew's stomach dropped. "No one will pay for that night," he breathed. "Not a single person will be held responsible."

"If I hold them responsible—"

"Then hold me responsible," he demanded. If it meant punishment for the others, he'd accept that.

"No!" Sira and Edward answered together.

His father continued. "It would do no good, Matthew. The Counselors would be faced with the same choice. Even if you walked into the proceedings, intent on facing punishment you don't deserve, they would set you free and all the others with you."

Fury burned in him. Matthew fumed at the decision that had been handed down.

Edward sighed. "I did my best to sway them. The best I could do was a series of new laws."

"And those are?" Sira managed.

"Aphrodisiacs are now outlawed in Lenvia. They are too dangerous, too easy to abuse or to have go wrong, in the confusion of the moment."

"It's a poor recompense," Matthew noted, forcing his jaw to unlock far enough to form the words.

"It is," his father agreed. "Uncontracted women at sexual events will be escorted by an older woman, one not seeking a contract of her own, preferably already contracted herself. That escort is to remain sober and vigilant and will be responsible for all actions committed by her charges."

Sira nodded. "So, there will never come a time when no one can be held accountable," she summarized.

"Quite. There are other measures under deliberation. I'm certain a few will pass."

"For instance?" Matthew asked wearily.

Edward paused. "Guards on the bowl at drinking events. Only servants of the house may serve food or drink to attendees. Only the guards may carry weapons."

There was a moment of silence.

His father turned toward them, his eyes skating over them without much attention to detail. "Am I welcome to join you for lunch before I go?" he asked. There was a note of something broken in that, as if he felt he wouldn't be welcome, in light of the news he'd carried to them.

"Of course," Matthew assured him.

Sira wiggled, reminding him that they couldn't rise from the desk.

"If you'd give us a moment," he amended. "I think we need one."

* * * *

Sira watched King Edward depart, her heart aching for Matthew. He wanted so desperately to make this right for her. *Desperately enough to submit to a judgment he hasn't earned.*

"This is all the right I need, Matthew," she assured him.

"It's not."

"It's not, for your sense of guilt. It is enough for my peace of mind."

He sighed, as he always did when he wanted to argue something with her but dared not.

She turned on his lap, drawing his mouth down to hers. Matthew didn't argue the move, but he didn't

resume the frantic pace they'd been lost in when they'd
been interrupted.

Sira eased off of his lap and onto the desk, working
the panties off her legs and spreading wide for him.
Matthew stared at her, his eyes dilated and breathing
choppy already.

"What you pursued before was precisely what I
need, Matthew." It was. She wanted him at ease with
the passion between them. She needed that
connection, the raw passion that existed between
them. It was real and tangible.

He lowered his mouth to her, taking a taste that
turned into a feast of sensation. Sira fisted her hand in
his hair, watching him lose himself in the moment, his
cock going hard and pulsing, weeping fluids.

"I need you inside."

Matthew was on his feet in the next heartbeat, his
cock thrusting home, his mouth covering hers. He
released her lips on the second thrust, licking at the
sheen of her fluids on his own.

"You'll have to be quiet, Sira," he breathed against
her cheek. "Can you do that?"

Her answer died in a half-swallowed cry of delight,
as he doubled his pace.

"You'll have to do better. My father is just down the
hall."

She nodded, biting down on her lower lip, riding
the cascade of pleasure foaming and rising in her.

Matthew took her harder, faster, his hands
clamped down tight on her hips. He gasped out her
name, burying his mouth against her temple.

Climax crashed down, and Sira clawed at his back, choking back a scream. He followed her with a moan, working his way down to her mouth, laying his claim.

They parted slowly, breathing in ragged gasps. "This is right, Matthew."

He nodded, pulling her closer to his body as if loath to the very thought of letting her go. It was a sentiment she understood all too well.

CHAPTER TWENTY-NINE

"What did you say?" Matthew asked, certain he'd misheard or dropped off to sleep and dreamed the announcement. *This is a nightmare, not a dream.*

"Lady Mora Ashgrove to see you, Hein Matthew," Prentice repeated.

It was on the tip of his tongue to tell the butler to show the "lady" out, but that would make it seem he was afraid to face her. Though the words stuck in his throat, Matthew forced them out. "Show her in, Prentice."

He retreated with a slight nod and returned a few moments later. "Lady Mora Ashgrove," he announced smartly but in a voice that those who knew him would recognize as laced in distaste Matthew shared.

Matthew made a show of not looking her direction, feigning interest in the work stacked before him. At the appropriate moment to make his snub clear, he focused on her. His assessment of her made it as far as the pregnant swell of her midsection, and his clenched jaw slackened.

"If you're laying odds," she hinted.

"Not a chance in paradise or perdition," he countered.

Mora sauntered to his desk and dropped a sheet of parchment on it...then a second. Matthew didn't pick them up; he kept his fists clenched to avoid using them against her in haste.

"Go on," she invited. "The first proves paternity. The second proves it's your heir I carry. Both were confirmed via amniot draw."

"Achieved with an illegal aphrodisiac you yourself provided."

Still, he reeled. How had she proven paternity without him providing a sample? Had she somehow accessed the samples taken when Wheatstand reported the attack on Sira? Since it was related to that night, chances were she'd been granted it. But without notifying Matthew?

Mora settled in a chair, arranging herself artfully. "And we've all been forgiven our poor judgment."

"Some more than others," he quipped. If the Goddess was just, Mora and the other "ladies" who'd used the Gorus would pay for it in stigma for years to come.

"The child is still your heir." There was no hesitancy in that.

"Only if I claim him, and I have no intentions of tying myself to you to do so."

A sly smile pulled her lips up. "Whyever not? You could have your little mistress to warm your bed. I wouldn't even demand my wifely needs from you."

Mistress? I don't have— Realization left him cold. "Sira is my wife, not my mistress."

"She carries your second son at best. She may not carry an heir, at all."

"She is my wife, Mora. Any son she presents me will be named my heir. This child. The next. Four or five from now, if she and the Goddess grant me so many."

"Will King Edward support that choice?"

Mora affected contemplation, though Matthew didn't believe the line of thinking was new to her. She'd planned this. She'd foreseen his refusal and was raising the stakes at every pass.

"He can't force me to dismiss Sira. He can't force me to marry you." He could highly suggest Matthew secure his heir, however he had to, but he couldn't force that either. "He can't even name the child Hein, if I don't claim him as such."

"All true," she conceded. "But he doesn't have to be happy about the situation. He doesn't have to give his blessing to you killing your true heir."

His heart stuttered at that. "What are you talking about?"

"If you won't claim your heir, it is a hardship for me to carry it." She paused, letting her logic sink into his rebelling mind. "How am I supposed to support it? How am I supposed to make a coveted position with a bastard son in tow and a body ruined by bringing it forth?"

The very idea of terminating a pregnancy for such a reason went against the core of the Goddess's teachings. Termination was for cases where the health and well-being of the mother were in jeopardy. It was for cases of real hardship—emotional or physical.

The fact that Mora was using the babe as a bargaining bit proved she had no emotional ties to be called a hardship. Her family could easily support the child, male or female, so there was no physical hardship to be argued.

Yet she intended to terminate a viable child in this petty game, invoking the very laws she'd called into play by using the aphrodisiac at the Bride Ball to her best advantage.

Part of him argued that Matthew should let her do it. The child wasn't one either of them had set out to create. It was an emotional hardship for himself and Sira, even if it wasn't for Mora. It wouldn't know love from Mora, even if Matthew came to care for it, and—Goddess as witness—Mora would use such an attachment against him, in the end.

Another part recoiled at the idea of it. Long-ago lessons imparted by his own dirt-noble mother demanded he try to save the innocent child, used as a lead piece in the game. It was morally bankrupt to terminate a child he was more than capable of supporting, that he had created, however that was accomplished.

This was something of a test of his faith and fiber. Matthew had taken responsibility for the harm he'd done Sira in his drugged state. Did he have less of a responsibility to right the wrongs he'd done Mora? Granted, the blame didn't rest solely on himself, and Mora bore more than a small share of it personally, but he was likely the only one who would take responsibility, among the many guilty.

He loathed her. Matthew had never made a secret of that fact, but did that excuse him? Was a wrong done an adversary or an enemy less a wrong?

No. Responsibility for one meant responsibility for all.

"Hein Matthew?" she prompted him.

"I will claim him."

Her smile spread into a sickeningly-smug version.

"But not as heir," he qualified.

It vanished as quickly, and a frightening calm took its place. "I'm listening."

"I'll take you as mistress in name. You'll have freedom to discreetly take lovers, no duties to me, money and a small estate to raise the child on." *An estate somewhere Sira need never see her. And Mora will be forbidden to set foot in this house.*

"But I won't have a coveted position."

"Someone's name means more to you than security and freedom?" He would never understand women.

No. That's not true. I understand Sira well enough. But Sira wasn't like other women. She had a moral center that fell more in line with his than the line he'd seen in other women.

"I'll be your wife and my son your heir, or you will be living a lie, a lie I will not condone."

"It won't be a lie. I choose which heirs to claim. You forget your place, Mora." He owed her nothing, certainly not as much as he was offering her for a bastard he'd been drugged into planting.

She laughed harshly, a sneer twisting her face into a mask that more closely matched her inner non-beauty. "You'll claim a second son on a dirt-noble line, instead of a first son on the daughter of a favored lord? What an intriguing choice, Hein Matthew."

"It remains my choice."

"And if Sirana carries a daughter? If she never presents you with a son?"

"Then your son would be Hein, by default...unless Alana presents Benjamin with two heirs, in which case, even I wouldn't be, let alone my heirs."

"And where is the security in that?" she taunted.

"It's all the security I'm offering. Take it or not." He would never turn Sira out or make her a mistress for Mora.

And even if he wished to give either Mora or Sira more security than that, it was the truth of his existence as the son of the king on a mistress, when an heir existed on his contracted queen; he was only in line for the throne, until there were two heirs of the direct line.

Mora rose, sighing deeply. "Unacceptable. You have a week to reconsider. I offer security—the guarantee of an heir. If you insist on Sirana Firloch as your wife, you will do it without that guarantee."

"Then I will." He tried to make it sound inconsequential, but his moral center screamed at the choice he was making. Matthew was openly inviting Mora to terminate his child.

No. The choice is hers. I've offered an alternative. This is her greed. I will not dismiss Sira for this blackmail.

The slam of the door behind Mora sent a chill down his spine.

* * * *

"You accepted it?" Sira managed, though she felt she might choke on the words.

"I have no more palatable choice." It was stated clearly and simply, as if he had no question that he was doing the right thing.

"What if the choice proves unpalatable?"

Matthew's hands closed on her shoulders. "Less palatable than Mora? How could it be?"

Was he shortsighted or dense? "What if I don't carry your heir? What if the Goddess decrees this our only child together?"

"Then Alana's son is the only heir to the throne. It won't be the first time in history that there was only one. It is the rule, rather than the exception."

"And you would make the choice with no idea whether I carry a son or daughter?" He couldn't; his station in life demanded heirs, if he could produce them. If Mora's tests were to be believed, and Matthew said they were sealed appropriately, he was more than capable of producing heirs. The question remained... Was Sira capable of providing them?

"Enough, Sira," he ordered. "I've rendered the decision. You are my wife. Do you want to be something less than that?"

She shook her head, her heart aching that he'd question it.

"Then it's settled." He dipped his head down and laid a gentle kiss against her lips, pausing there, his words misting into her mouth. "You are my wife, Sira. Nothing else matters. Please, believe me. Nothing else but that."

With that, he was striding out the door and down the corridor.

Sira stood for a long moment, watching his retreating back. On one level, she couldn't dispute that the choice was his own. On another, it was a choice he should go into fully-informed.

A blood test had failed to establish the sex of the babe she carried. An amniot draw would do so, without fail...and with little risk, all told, especially this early in pregnancy.

If Matthew knew she carried a son, he could be secure in the choice he'd made. If he knew she carried a daughter...

Would he reconsider? It was his choice, even if it was one she didn't care for. He was Hein, son of a king. His position held duties and obligations she could only dream of.

If Matthew chose to follow this path, Mora would vilify him in it. The best possible defense was an heir he wanted to claim on the way.

It was up to Sira to safeguard him, if he wouldn't safeguard himself.

CHAPTER THIRTY

"Sira?" The smile on Matthew's face dimmed at the empty rooms. He retraced his steps through the household, calling for her. When he'd reached his office again, he stopped to consider it.

"Prentice," he bellowed.

The old man came trotting out, appearing from nowhere. If only Sira would appear so neatly, but something told Matthew she wouldn't.

"Yes, Hein?"

"Where is my wife?"

His brow furrowed. "She left with Pierce this morning," he reported.

Ah...a day in town. "Where to?" He'd like to join her.

"I'm afraid I don't know," he admitted. "Lady Sirana called for a driver. I assumed she'd wanted to stretch the legs."

Matthew forced back a full-blown panic. What was she doing, a day after Mora's announcement? Had he dismissed her concerns too quickly? Should he have taken more time? Put her more at ease?

Sira, what are you doing?

"Hein Matthew?"

"I want to know the minute she returns. Not a moment of delay, Prentice."

"Of course."

"And...send a guard to her parents. Maybe..." He hoped to the Goddess he was right. "Maybe she just wanted to see her family." *Maybe she needs reassurance I can't offer.*

* * * *

Matthew stopped in mid-step, looking out the window at the approaching vehicle. It was Pierce, hopefully returning with Sira. He forced a calming breath and headed for the entryway, waving off Prentice.

All day. She'd been gone for more than eight hours. He was torn between the urge to shout at her and the urge to hold her tight and never let her leave his sight again.

The door opened when he was halfway across the floor to it. Matthew came to a stop, his heart pounding at the sight of her.

Sira wandered in, a sheet of parchment clutched in her hand. Her attention was far away, and her step slow and solemn.

He stared at the parchment, the metallic taste of fear in his mouth. *She didn't.* Scattered prayers, asking that she hadn't terminated a daughter...or blindly terminated tumbled in his mind, mixing, overpowering each other.

She came to him, offering the parchment without comment and without meeting his gaze. His hands shaking, Matthew took it. Opening it took more fortitude than he possessed.

"It's a boy," she whispered. "Either way, you'll have your heir."

Matthew gathered her to his chest, his heart easing that she hadn't taken the choice from him. "What did you do?"

"An amniot draw. It's all I would have done, either way. I wanted... I needed to know you'd made an informed choice. Your father would have demanded that."

She was likely right about that, but his heart skittered at the thought of an amniot draw. "But the risk—"

"A small one. Much less than you abandoning your chance at an heir."

He held her tighter. "I wouldn't have cared. I told you I wouldn't have."

"Today," she conceded. "You're young, Matthew. It would have mattered more, when you were old."

"To my father, perhaps...if Benjamin hasn't given him adequate heirs by then. Not to me."

For a long moment, she was silent. "You mean to let her terminate, then?"

He sighed, letting his eyes drift shut. "The only way I have to stop it is too high a cost. She's made her choice."

"But we all have to live with it."

And her faith would insist Sira stop this, if she could. The teachings he'd been raised with weren't dissimilar in that, but there had to be a line he wouldn't cross, and Mora had crossed it. The Goddess had given Matthew a second chance with Sira, and Mora wouldn't interfere with that.

But Sira deserved an answer. "Then we will. It isn't our choice, Sira. Would you rather have me give in to her demands, outrageous and unpalatable as they are?"

She was silent long enough to make his stomach shimmy. "No. I wouldn't rather see you blackmailed into a wife you loathe." She paused. "And I wouldn't want to lose you to her or anyone else."

"I agree. Then let me call the stakes in full, and let the blame lay on Mora, where it rightfully belongs."

She nodded and held tight to him.

That was what Matthew needed...what he'd needed from the moment he'd laid his sights on her, Sira in his arms, his personal sea angel.

CHAPTER THIRTY-ONE

Knowing the blow was coming didn't lessen the effect when it fell.

At least Matthew had the foresight to have all missives to his wife redirected to himself. As he expected, Mora tried to take a final twist of the knife by having the notice of termination sent to Sira.

He sat with the notice in hand, relieved and heartsick by turns.

The howling emotional side of him wanted to burn the parchment. The rational side sent him to his cabinet to file it with the other two.

A son reduced to three bits of parchment.

Wheatstand was wrong. Mora's poison hadn't left him a week after the Bride Ball. It was with him still, making the life he was building with Sira sick beneath its pall.

I won't let it! That's what she wants, the only possible victory Mora has left to her.

In the next coherent moment, he was halfway up the staircase, intent on his wife and heir.

Matthew strode to her, seeking Sira's lips. Whatever question she meant to ask disappeared into his mouth.

There wasn't a second question. Sira gave her passion as avidly as she took of Matthew's. It was pure, untainted, the single blessing they'd managed to wrest from the maw of poison and lies and no-win choices.

Hands delved beneath clothing, touching, peeling away the unwanted layers onto the floor of the sitting room. Mouths sampled. Bodies joined in a fierce, uncompromising firestorm of need.

In the moments after, Sira lay over him on the sofa. Matthew stroked at her hair, reveling at the sweat drying in the cool room air. He smiled that they hadn't made it to the bed...hadn't even closed the corridor door before surrendering to the heat between them.

There was a stillness in the air, not just of sound and movement but also of the soul.

"I was wrong," Sira murmured against his throat.

"Wrong?" Where had that come from? What did it mean? Matthew couldn't seem to follow her logic in his pleasantly- muddled state.

"When I believed I'd never feel what I felt the night of the Bride Ball again...I was so wrong."

His heart pounded in a dizzying cadence. Horrified apologies died at his lips.

"I think I loved you, even then, Matthew."

Probably not. "Maybe so. I don't know what I felt for you that night, but it held to my mind and drove me mad to see you again. I dreamed of you, fantasized of you, craved you."

She nodded, strangely silent. Matthew opened his mouth to question her, but Sira beat him to the tape.

"She's done it?"

He nodded.

"And you feel what about it?" There was something hesitant about that, something guarded.

Matthew tried to order that into words; she deserved an honest answer, but what that answer was escaped him. "So much that conflicts, I can't find a place to begin. But it's done...and it was never real between Mora and myself." He combed his fingers through her hair. "This is real, and I won't let her destroy it."

Her head came up, and she stared at him, her expression moving from unreadable to joyous.

"What are you thinking?" he asked, stunned by the effect her smile had on him.

"That there is a perfectly serviceable bed in the next room we should be using."

"Our bed," he agreed. "I've never shared that bed with another...and I never will."

THE END

ABOUT THE AUTHOR

Brenna Lyons wears many hats, sometimes all on the same day: former president of EPIC, author of more than 100 published works, owner of Fireborn Publishing, columnist, special needs teacher, wife, mother...and member in good standing of more than 60 writing advocacy groups.

In her first ten years published in novel-length, she's won 3 EPIC e-Book Awards (out of 15 finalists) and finaled for 3 PEARLS (including one Honorable Mention, second to NY Times Bestseller Angela Knight), 2 CAPAS, and a Dream Realm Award. She's also taken Spinetingler's Book of the Year for 2007.

Brenna writes in 26 established worlds plus stand-alones, poetry, articles and essays. She's a bestseller in indie/e fantasy and horror, straight genre and cross-genres thereof. Brenna has been termed "one of the most deviant erotic minds in the publishing world...not for the weak." (Rachelle for Fallen Angels Reviews) Milieu-heavy dark work is practically Brenna's calling card, with or without the erotic content.

She teaches classes in everything from POV studies to advanced editing, networking to marketing. Brenna enjoys hearing from people who read her work and can be reached by e-mail.

Website: http://www.brennalyons.com/

Facebook: http://www.facebook.com/brenna.lyons

Email: brennalyons4168@live.com

ALSO BY THIS AUTHOR

Available from *Fireborn Publishing*

KEIF'S DEN AND PACK
Keif's Pack
Mother of the Keif
Keif's Den (Coming Soon)

PROPHECY
Prophecy: Revelations
Prophecy: Rapture
The Prophet's Mate
Prophecy: Rampage - Meet Gavin
Prophecy: Rampage (Coming Soon)

THE FANTASY CLUB
The Consort

Beyond the Veil
Fairy Wishes (Coming Soon)
Mine for the Night
Once in a Blue Moon
Overtime Pay
Stay With Me
The Fire God's Woman
The Punishment of Phoebus Apollo
Werewolf U

Available from *Phaze Books*

ANGEL-WING SAGA
Sons of Heaven: Beldon
Daughters of Man: Prize Match
Sons of Heaven: Unexpected Mates
Daughters of Man: Claiming a Princess

BRIDE BALL
Bride Ball
Poison, Lies, and No-Win Choices

COLOR OF LOVE
The Color of Love

FIRE AND ICE
Magmon's Hunger
Magmon's Lover

INSTINCT SERIES
Animal Instincts

KEGIN SERIES
Conquest
The Last of Fion's Daughters
Last Chance for Love
Rites of Mating
In Her Ladyship's Service
Matchmaker's Misery

KIELAN SERIES
The Lady's Lowborn Lover
Time Currents
Cubed

NIGHT WARRIORS
Night Warriors
Will of the Stone
Bearing Armen
Hunter's Moon
Maher Men
Choosing a Mate/Starting a War
Raised to Be His Own
Veriel's Tales I: Crossbearer Turned
Veriel's Tales II: Losing Regana
Blutjagdfrau Lost
The Warrior's Man

Damsel in Distress

STAR MAGES
The Master's Lover

XXAN WAR
Daahan Rising
Crossbred Son
Raashh Decisions

Enslaved
All I Want for Christmas is You
Fates Magic
All's Fair…
Black Sail
Mama's Tales
Dream Walk
Unexpected Daddy
Phaze in Verse
We Shall Live Again
May the Best Man Win
Nevermore
Marked
And It Was Good

Available from **Mundania Press**

STAR MAGES
Written in the Stars

Fairy Dreams
Monsters of Myth Anthology

Available from **Under the Moon**

RENEGADES SERIES
TYGERS
Renegade's Run

Max Sec

URBAN GRIMM
Catch Me, If You Can
Three Wishes
Temptation of Eve

With Great Power
Undead in Blue
Evil Overlords Union Issue #1 Anthology
Undead Embrace
"Playing Games" in *Forbidden Love: Bad Boys*
"Marked" in *Forbidden Love: Wicked Women*
"The Master's Lover" in *Forbidden Love: Sacred Bands*

Available from **Logical Lust**

"Mine for the Night" in *The Cougar Book* Anthology

Available from **Coming Together Charity Anthologies**

INSTINCT SERIES
"Foundling" in *Coming Together: Into the Light* Anthology

"Claim Mate" (available separately and as part of the *Coming Together: Against the Odds* Anthology)
"The Fire God's Woman" in *Coming Together: Under Fire* Anthology

Available **self-published**

KEGIN SERIES
Earth-Born Lord
Graham: Training the Earth-Born Lord

NIGHT WARRIORS
Claiming a Lady

Stone Lord
Mother's Son

COLOR OF LOVE
A Safe Heart

Snapshots from a Poet's Life

AWARD-WINNING BOOKS

EPPIE/EPIC eBOOK AWARDS WINNERS
Coming Together: Against the Odds- 2010
Time Currents- 2010
Coming Together: Into the Light- 2011

EPPIE/EPIC eBOOK AWARDS FINALISTS
Fion's Daughter- 2004
Collected Poems: Book One- 2005 (now titled *Snapshots of a Poet's Life*)
Renegade's Run- 2005
Rites of Mating- 2006
All I Want for Christmas- 2006
Phaze in Verse- 2008
"The Fire God's Woman" in Coming Together: Under Fire- 2009
Three Wishes- 2010
Matchmaker's Misery- 2010
The Cougar Book- 2011
The Master's Lover- 2011
Bride Ball- 2011

DREAM REALM AWARDS FINALIST
Last Chance for Love- 2003

PEARL HONORABLE MENTION
Night Warriors- 2004

PEARL FINALISTS
Schente Night- 2003 (now included in *The Last of Fion's Daughters*)
König Cursebreakers- 2004 (now titled *Will of the Stone*)

JOYFULLY REVIEWED BEST BOOKS OF 2010
Written in the Stars- 2010

SPINETINGLER'S BOOK OF THE YEAR 2007
NOBODY: An Anthology of Dark Fiction- 2007 (Brenna's pieces
of the anthology can be found in *Beyond the Veil*)

TRS's CAPA FINALISTS
Ultimate Warriors- 2004 (Brenna's portion is now available as
With Great Power)
Written in the Stars

LOVE ROMANCE AND MORE CAFÉ BOOK OF THE YEAR
RUNNER UP
Last Chance for Love- 2008

ROAD TO ROMANCE REVIEWERS' CHOICE AWARD
Prophecy: Revelations- 2004

LOVE ROMANCES REVIEWERS' CHOICE AWARD
Black Sail- 2003

ROMANCE JUNKIES BOOK CLUB STAFF PICK
TYGERS- 2003

FALLEN ANGELS ROMANCE RECOMMENDED READ
Devon's Price-2005 (now available in *Bearing Armen*)

JOYFULLY RECOMMENDED READ
Fairy Dreams- 2008
The Last of Fion's Daughters- 2009

TREBLE HEART FINALIST
Prophecy: Revelations- 2003

www.ingramcontent.com/pod-product-compliance
Lightning Source LLC
Chambersburg PA
CBHW020904200626
46814CB00001BA/166